B.C. CROW

THE NEPHILIM EFFECT

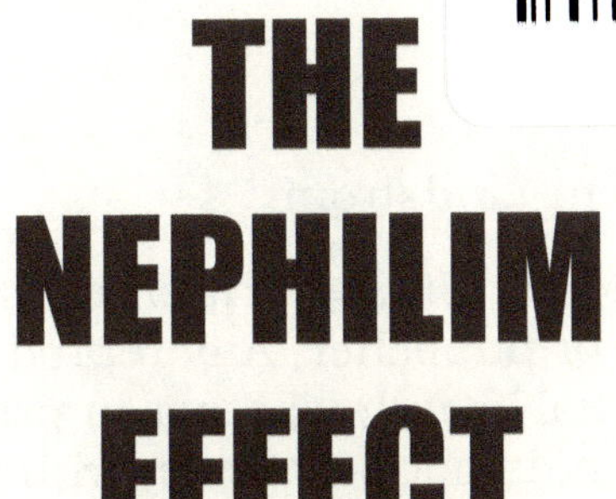

BLUE HOUSE
PUBLISHING

This book is a work of fiction. This book is derived from the imagination of the author. If any parallels to actual people, places, businesses, or institutions is present, it is used fictitiously and or is purely coincidental.

BLUE HOUSE
PUBLISHING
11 N. 500 W.
Springville, UT 84663

Picture of Earth: Courtesy of Nasa

For information regarding bulk purchases, send a request to Blue House Publishing, or email us at BCCrow@BlueHPublishing.com

First print run July 2015 by Blue House Publishing

1 2 3 4 5 6 7 8 9 10

ISBN-10: 1943239029

ISBN-13: 978-1-943239-02-3

Library of Congress Control Number: 2015907719

Books by

B.C. Crow

<u>Nephilim Series</u>

Nephilim Device: Book 1

Nephilim Effect: Book 2

Nephilim Conspiracy: Book 3

To follow B.C. Crow

Visit www.BlueHPublishing.com

To special order bulk shipments for promos, premiums, or fundraisers

Email your requests on the Contacts page of our website.

Special thanks to my parents and siblings. For helping me to polish my books. Not to mention my gratitute for their support. Whether anyone else likes my stories or not, I can always count on positive reinforcement from home.

And as always, thanks to you,
THE READER
For giving a new author a chance.

Chapter 1

1917

Captain's log: Day 1

We concluded preparations for our voyage from Port Said, Egypt, to Naples, Italy then on to Port de Bouc today. The weather is fair, and the tide is with us. The crew finished loading the ship at daybreak. Passengers and cargo arrived all morning. Our guard had been high all morning as rumors were rampant about the conflicts near the waterways. Suez would have been our original departure point, but fighting there has forced us to conduct our business at Port Said. By noon my first mate had blown the horn and announced our departure. Four soldiers from the French Foreign Legion were the last to arrive before casting off. Our ship was full, with only one room left. They all agreed to share the one remaining room, even at full price per man. They seemed to be very anxious to get back to France. But despite this, they do not seem to bring any trouble with them, so I allowed them to come. At exactly 12:15 we began to pull out of port.

Day 6

We arrived in Naples late this afternoon. Tensions between the Germans and the Italians are growing ever more hostile. News of an invasion in Caporetto has stirred the population into anxiety. Amidst this, there is also concern about the allied powers and their arrangements with Italy. Many rumors are circulating, and it does not appear to be safe to stay any longer than is necessary at this destination. I have ordered the crew to stand ready for departure at a moment's notice. I have also informed the harbormaster that we will be shortening our stay to only one day. We may miss out on some late-arriving passengers or cargo, but I do not trust the Italians to keep us safe from the Germans. I fear that even with the Germans fighting on the other side of the country, there may be spies near us. Our guard is heavy, as we are prime targets for the Central Powers.

Day 7

Despite requests to postpone our departure, we have cast off. I will make my recommendations to avoid any stay in Italy for the near future. Whether we are safe there or not, I dare not risk it. The weather is turning, and though the sea is also formidable today, I would rather risk the open waters than the closed harbors.

Day 8

This morning we sounded an alarm. Upon the changing of shifts, it was discovered that the radios had been damaged, and the operator was killed, struck in the back of the head by a heavy blunt object. The crew was called to arms, and small firearms were passed around. The passengers were confined to their rooms while we did a sweep of the entire ship. In less than an hour, we had discovered that one of the lifeboats was missing, and that two of our passengers from Italy were gone. It will be some time before we can repair our communications. Until then we are searching the ship for any indication of sabotage or other threat.

Moments ago our engines shut down. All of the diesel fuel on board has solidified into a stiff rubbery mass. The reason is unclear; however, we assume it was the work of spies from Italy. We are currently drifting without control. If we are unable to regain radio communications, I fear the worst.

Day 9

There is very little progress on the radio situation. We are also unable to re-liquefy the fuel. It won't melt, or even leave your hands oily after handling it. Most unusual. The crew is trying to calm the passengers best as possible, but everyone is growing increasingly frightened.

Day 10

This will be my last entry. I seal it up so that if we are ever found, you may know our fate. Earlier today our radio was fixed, but because of the expended electricity during the night, with no engines to recharge the batteries, we had nothing to power the radio with. It was then that the men from the French Legion confided in me that they may have been the target of the attack. They showed me a plant that they believed would change technology forever. The Germans have learned of this, and will do anything to stop them from arriving in France with the plant. The plant carries an electrical current in its roots, and the Legionnaires demonstrated its natural electricity. The current was weak, but after several hours, we were able to put enough of a charge into a battery to send a quick burst via the radio. Whether we were heard, we do not know; we were not able to receive a responding transmission.

Only minutes ago we spotted lights in the dark night. We rejoiced at first for the arrival of another ship. Only when it got closer did we realize it was not another ship after all, but a German U-boat. I fear there will not be enough lifeboats to accommodate everyone and hope for the safety of those who will make it on board them. Now I seal this log and go down as captains of old, with my ship and remaining passengers and crew. May God have mercy on our souls.

Chapter 2

Ligurian Sea

July 29th, Present Day
(3 days before Flint first encounters Marshal in Egypt)

"If I didn't know any better, I'd say you were trying to hinder me," Lydia Krieger joked. "Is there something down there you don't want me to see?"

"You know that is not true," Grisha replied, his face was a massive wrinkle of concern. His large head was a solid lump of flesh, set against the ever-moving waves behind him. Lydia felt lucky to have such a good and capable team. Grisha, with his dark salt and pepper hair was built like an ox. Still, Lydia thought he might have a softer heart than he usually let on about.

Helping Grisha was the gaunt, but deceptively

powerful British-born man named Sam. He had as blond of features as anybody she'd ever know. One look at him would make you doubt that he led the other half of Lydia's team of ex-militants.

"I think you should send me, or Sam," Grisha continued. "Two thousand five hundred feet is long way down. That would beat world record by almost five hundred feet. There is reason why nobody has dived that deep."

Lydia laughed. "Too bad this won't get reported to the *Guinness World Records*, then. I could have a good five minutes of fame."

"Still, it's very risky," Grisha warned in his thick Russian accent. "Are you sure you won't let one of us go instead?"

"Come on, Grisha, you should know that women are more physically adept in harsh environments like this than men. If something does go wrong, I stand a much better chance of surviving than any of you boys would."

"Perhaps," Grisha consented. "But at that depth, man or woman, I doubt anyone would survive if something went wrong."

Lydia tried to motion for the helmet to be placed on, but her arms were too heavy to lift. This ADS, or atmospheric diving suit, unlike older versions of diving suits made from pliable cloth with frames and heavy helmets, was almost entirely made out of hardened aluminum. Each moving appendage had a series of spherical knuckles, able to pivot along a gasketed rim. When out of the water, the suit was too large and bulky to maneuver. But under the pressures of deep water, the heavily constructed material became manageable.

The helmet was placed on Lydia's head and fastened tight. Lydia was fully aware that she looked more like a shiny robot from some cheap comic book or a black-and-white science fiction movie than a deep-sea diver. Since gloved hands at those extreme depths would crush her bones, or at the very least cut off all blood circulation, the suit instead had a rounded cover that fully enveloped her hands. Replacing her fingers were a few tools such as a drills and clamps that extended beyond the bulk of metal. The cumbersome suit was entirely necessary, since regular scuba diving equipment, even with specialized gas mixes, would only allow a diver to go a few hundred feet below the surface of the water. This suit was like diving in a humanoid-shaped submarine.

With only a few of these suits ever having been made, Lydia had found it necessary to borrow hers from a deep-sea research vessel that happened to be passing through the Mediterranean Sea at that time. Lydia's other mission had been put on hold, as she didn't want to miss this opportunity. The only problem was, because the depth that she wanted to dive was far beyond what the research vessel was comfortable allowing, she had been forced to hijack the ship. Hijacking was not a big deal, since her team was the specialized action branch of the non-government organization that called themselves GRIP. The research vessel was no match for Lydia's trained fighters. Still, even though such drastic measures were sometimes necessary, her team wasn't a heartless band of mercenaries. The researchers were just tied up and kept out of the way until the job at hand was finished.

Officially her team didn't exist. GRIP, or Global Representatives for International Progress, was an organization similar to Greenpeace. They were activists, pushing an agenda. Where Greenpeace strove to improve the environment, GRIP's official goal was to promote the responsible use of technology. Unofficially they were a group of men and women, mostly scientists, who were able to trace their ancestry back to 3000 B.C., when survivors from Mars began to interbreed with the inhabitants of Earth. Since the men of Mars were giants by Earth standards, their offspring were still able to maintain a greater than normal stature. Called Nephilim by their Hebrew neighbors, or in other words, the Fallen Ones, these hybrids were known as men of mighty renown.

Lydia was the shortest member of this little team, being considered short only by the standards of GRIP, as she stood only five feet nine inches tall. The rest of the men on her team were all above six feet tall. Grisha was the tallest, pushing close to seven feet, and was as thick as an ox. The others, who made up the more combative portion of the team, were Sam, Jay, Vincent, and Labeeb. Though all of them had some military experience, these four had specialized training that lent well to their now-often-violent occupation.

"Can you hear me?" Lydia called out from the confines of her helmet, her own voice sounding stronger than she intended.

"Soft but clear," Grisha came back. "Are you ready for this?"

Instead of yelling this time, Lydia clicked a small waterproof keypad inside her cast-aluminum mitten to signify that she was ready. Since Lydia planned to go deeper than the suit generally allowed, she'd had to modify it slightly. Unlike others of its kind, the suit now contained a small scuba regulator that pressed against her mouth. The standard microphones would soon be useless, and she let the regulator slip inside her lips. This regulator installed in the suit allowed the next modification to happen. The suit now had the ability to allow some water to enter in and fill the voids that Lydia's body didn't already take up.

She felt her body lift up from the deck as the ship's crane hoisted her over to the water's edge. It felt more like she was in an elevator than anything else. A chill suddenly ran up and down her spine as she was lowered into the water. She didn't consider it a premonition of any sort, just a hint of nervousness. Every other attempt to locate the whereabouts of the original Martian crash site had been either a dead end or frustrated by GRIP's biggest competitor, a crooked entrepreneur by the name of Shen Mao. If this expedition turned up fruitless, then Lydia knew that finding the wreckage before Mao and his grave robber Marshal Steel did would prove impossible.

As the crane slowly lowered her, the suit began to fill with water. It was still incredibly restricting, but at least she was able to move the joints around her arms and legs. As she was lowered, the pressure of the water became greater. She knew that at depths greater than about 230 feet, oxygen began to turn toxic. As planned, once she reached 200 feet, the suit's umbilical cord halted her descent. She took a minute to key in the command to seal the suit, preventing too much more pressure from developing inside her new diving apparel. Once this was completed, she signaled the boat and they began to lower her again. The depths grew darker and she realized how pointless the lights on her suit were. Though the visibility might have been close to a hundred feet, there was nothing to look at.

After she had been lowered the first five hundred feet, a small aquatic speaker sounded in her helmet, and she could hear Grisha's voice. "How are you doing down there?"

Fumbling with her unseen keypad, like texting in your pocket, Lydia signaled that she was still fine, though she did have an irresistible urge to worry about sea creatures of the deep. It didn't help, either, that the water's current was tugging her on an angle, flipping her around from time to time like a flat fish lure on the end of a fisherman's pole. She didn't believe there were actually any fish or other sea creatures that would consider her a tasty treat, but it didn't stop her from wanting to look over her shoulder for a large sperm whale or giant squid. Every time the current flipped her around, she was greeted by the same dark emptiness as before, which was in some way even less comforting. She wasn't as worried about getting eaten or attacked as she was about something swimming above her, and breaking her lifeline to the boat. Not generally prone to claustrophobia, the confines of her suit in this environment were gnawing at her nerves.

Grisha checked in again at one thousand feet, then fifteen hundred feet. By then the frigid water was beginning to force the temperature of her suit down. The cold served mostly to accent the dark empty tomb that surrounded her. She took in a few deep breaths, trying to relax herself. An annoying bead of nervous sweat—or was it a drop of water that had penetrated her mask?—was making its way across her nose as she tried to look down for any sign of the bottom. She had heard of submarines popping, bending, and groaning under deep-sea pressures, but she hadn't imagined she would experience the same effects in this little suit. Despite its rigid construction, she felt as though it was getting tighter on her body. The creaks and moans of the armor chilled her more than the frigid waters. She almost didn't dare move an arm, lest it break a seal and send the rest of the crushing waters in.

Knowing that if she were to risk any movement, it would be better at this depth than at the full twenty-five hundred feet, so she tried bending the elbow. To her surprise, the pressure had loosened the joints to a point where they moved with much greater freedom. She assumed that this was engineered to be so, and allowed herself to relax a little more.

As she hit two thousand feet, Grisha announced, "You are about to double a world record. How are you holding up?"

Lydia noticed that her air hose, which ascended to the high-powered pump above, was constricting to allow less breathable air into the suit. She fought off a hint of panic, and refocused her mind. With calm, albeit labored, breaths, she signaled for Grisha to continue lowering her.

She almost didn't recognize the sea floor until she was just a few feet away. The cold was causing her legs to cramp up, but she managed to land upright on the ground, though she nearly fell over. Had it not been for the line tethering her to the surface, she would have fallen on her face into the silty pillow below. She ordered Grisha to stop giving her slack as she struggled to maintain her balance. Lydia then engaged the four small water jets that were mounted to her back as she inflated her buoyancy compensator. Once she felt stable, she waited for a minute to let the cloud of silt dissipate. She took a good hard look around her. She felt a depressing current of concern. Her lights were only able to penetrate the darkness for about fifteen or twenty feet in any direction, and in what she could see, there was no wreckage.

Chapter 3

Checking his radar, Grisha noticed he had missed the wreckage by only seventy-five feet, but he was sure Lydia would tell him it was more like a thousand. He talked into the microphone, and guided his partner until she reached the old merchant ship. A small camera mounted on her suit was delivering images of the ship as she labored on and around it. From what he could see, the ship was surprisingly intact, especially considering the length of time that it had been on the sea floor.

Even with the assistance of the suit's fans, Lydia found maneuvering about the hull to be laborious. She had been down for forty-five minutes when she finally found her way to the living quarters. Luckily the ship was designed more for transporting goods than for passengers. There were still several rooms, each of which took a good ten minutes to investigate. As she explored, Grisha had to give Lydia a little extra slack in the umbilical line so she could make her way in and out of the various quarters.

From the record that Labeeb had provided, they were able to narrow their search to a few specific rooms; these were among the quarters that were smallest and least desirable. If someone were to engage in travel, and there were only one or two rooms left, these would be the ones remaining for fare. After Lydia had been down searching for a full hour, Grisha could see that she had found the room. He knew this because, even though she wasn't trying to show it off, he caught the faintest glimpse of some metal that had once belonged to the rifle of a French Legionnaire.

The next half hour was tedious. To attempt bringing anything to the surface would be difficult, and might even compromise the artifacts. Grisha also found it increasingly necessary to guide Lydia around the room, as if telling a small child which toy to pick up and where to put it. He worried that she might be getting nitrogen narcosis from the increase in pressure. That would cause a diver to behave as though they were drunk. Tunnel vision, confusion, impaired judgment, and hysteria were common symptoms. Fortunately, Grisha thought, it could easily be offset by ascending to shallower water—unlike hypothermia, which Lydia might also be experiencing.

At long last they found something worth their effort. Lydia would have missed it had Grisha not brought her attention back to it. Whether one of the Legionnaires had died in his quarters, or he had removed it for some reason, they were able to find his clam-shaped *plaque d'identité*, or dog tags. It wasn't much, but it was the best they had to go with, and perhaps all they would actually require. Lydia gave the camera a good close-up picture, then gripped the corroded metal in her mechanical clamp of a hand.

Grisha was relieved when Lydia made it out into the open ocean again. She was moving much slower now than before, and he found it necessary to send the command via the umbilical cord to release the air from her buoyancy compensator. Without this being released, the ascent would cause the trapped air to expand, propelling her up at an uncontrolled rate. Once this was taken care of, he started the winch and began slowly pulling her to the surface.

As she was coming up, he kept asking her if she was okay. When she refused to answer, he kept talking to her, pleading for her to stay conscious and let him know if she was still listening. At two hundred feet, where he originally planned on start-ing her decompression, a process that would take several hours, she still wasn't responding. He made a quick decision and looked over to Sam, who had been watching the whole time. "Grab Jay and Vin-cent," he ordered. "I don't know what is wrong, but we forgo the decompression stops."

"Won't that give her the bends?" Sam asked, aware that being under two hundred feet or more of pressure for over two hours could not only be pain-ful but fatal.

"I'm leaving the pressure in her suit. But before she is up, we need the ship's hyperbaric chamber ready to go. I will go in with her, so you will be in charge. Get the information on those dog tags to La-beeb."

Sam agreed, and he rushed off to find the other two men. By the time he returned with Jay and Vin-cent, Grisha had pulled the robotic figure of Lydia out of the water, and was easing her onto the deck. They quickly stripped away the propulsion fans, and exerting all of their combined strength, they dragged the metallic body toward the hyperbaric chamber. The suit was designed to keep water pressure out, not in, and Grisha knew he had very little time until the integrity of the suit failed. This and Lydia's unresponsive state added to the urgency of their task.

Once inside the chamber, Grisha disconnected the umbilical cord, and Sam closed the hatch. The pressure inside the chamber was increasing, and Grisha was trying to pop his ears as he worked on unfastening the helmet to Lydia's suit. The pressure inside the chamber soon reached optimal levels, and the helmet came off, splashing ice-cold water all over him. Lydia's regulator was still in her mouth, but her lips were blue, and her head had gone limp. She still had a pulse, so there was still hope. For the next ten minutes, he raced to free his hypothermic partner from the embracing aluminum deathtrap.

The hyperbaric chamber was big in comparison to other such chambers, but it was still cramped, barely able to fit the two of them. Working in this tight space was difficult, but eventually Grisha was able to free Lydia and again check her pulse. It was weak but present, accompanied by shallow breaths. After taking a moment to find the climate controls, he adjusted the temperature for the highest setting. Since the chamber was now warming up, and Lydia was free from the ADS, Grisha pulled out his large sheath knife and began to cut the expensive wetsuit from Lydia's body. He felt no need to remove her two-piece swimsuit that remained, as he had no desire to share the next ten or twelve hours with a humiliated woman. Besides, he was confident in his ability to bring her back from the hypothermic shock, even with the small patches of wet nylon and spandex that remained.

Chapter 4

France

Labeeb's eyes were glazed, blind to everything around him as he listened intently while Sam described their recovery of the French dog tags over the phone. He learned how Lydia had barely made it back alive, but the mission was a success. Sam told him the name, date, and number from the old tags; these were enough to start searching on. Labeeb hung up the phone and started looking up and down at the various filing cabinets that littered the archives of the French Foreign Legion.

"So what are we looking for?" Labeeb's old colleague, François, asked.

Labeeb responded, "Anything and everything that can tell us about this man, or the three others who accompanied him." He showed François a note recapping what Sam had phoned in. "They were traveling back to France in 1917 when they were assassinated. In their possession was something of great importance, and I need to find out where they found it."

"So it's a real treasure hunt, no?" François grinned with that passionate excitement that the French were so adept at expressing. "May I ask what wonder you're looking for—no, that would be too presumptuous. I would be happy to help my fellow Legionnaire, especially one as endearing as you, my good Labeeb."

It was always a pleasure working with François. If Labeeb hadn't been of Indian descent, the two could have almost been brothers. They were both tall. To call either of them skinny would be a mistake. They were lean and quick. They both had impeccable posture, but there was also that tightness about them that suggested they were always ready for anything, like a trap itching to be sprung. The biggest difference in the two men was personality. Labeeb had a somewhat independent streak that often rubbed superior officers the wrong way. François on the other hand was a natural born pleaser, not the stereotypical hard case often associated with Legionnaires. As Labeeb had once done, before resigning and working for GRIP, François was now the man in charge of the archives at the Legion's headquarters. Most documents detailing the exploits of the unique branch of this French army were stored here, usually forgotten entirely save for a few history buffs and occasional reference searches.

As a French-born Indian, Labeeb wanted to immerse himself in the cultures of his two national origins. At the age of twenty-seven, after returning to France from an extended stay in India, he enlisted in the army. He attempted and subsequently failed to join the French Special Forces. It wasn't so much a matter of his qualifying as it was disagreements with his superior officers. He still wanted to put his ambitions and skills into practice, so he had applied for the modern-day French Foreign Legion, hoping this would help improve his abilities, while allowing him to see more of the world. This proved less gratifying than he had anticipated, especially when he was transferred to work in the military offices, and, more importantly, the archive department.

One day while he was archiving various documents, he stumbled across an old unmarked box—the first evidence of something that would consume his imagination, and give his life direction. It was a water-worn ship's log from the days of the old Legionnaires.

Back when Germany was campaigning across Europe in the First World War, a merchant ship had been sunk by one of their U-boats in the Ligurian Sea just off the southern coast of Italy and France. Most of the crew and passengers had died, with only one lifeboat ever making it back to shore. This boat carried the captain's log. Water had damaged it considerably, but the survivors were able to see that its being targeted had something to do with the Legionnaires. It had therefore been boxed up and delivered to the black hole where Labeeb found it hiding.

Since it was long forgotten, Labeeb decided that nobody would care if he took it. He spent several months going through the captain's log, restoring and deciphering the account. He learned two things from it. First, someone friendly to the Germans had created a way of solidifying fuel. Second, there was some form of plant the Germans had learned about, and the French found. The plant was what sparked Labeeb's curiosity the most. He began searching it out, finding few helpful leads. Then one day, after visiting a website that looked somewhat promising, he was contacted by e-mail regarding his search.

In that anonymous person, Labeeb not only found someone who knew what he was talking about, but also offered him a direction to start searching in. The two corresponded by email for a few months, and finally the person told him of an organization called GRIP. Labeeb was informed that GRIP was not all it appeared to be, but if he were to join the group, he might find the answers he was looking for.

Labeeb was excited, but, heeding the warning of his anonymous benefactor, he involved himself in GRIP with caution. He agreed that if he could get into the secretive association he would keep his friend in the loop. With a little coaching, the person behind the emails taught Labeeb what to say and how to act to find acceptance into the exclusive organization.

Once he made it inside, Labeeb found it interesting how everything seemed to tie together. He was looking for a moss that could replace oil as an energy source. This wasn't just another oil rich, bio-diesel producing moss, it was something much more profound. While GRIP was searching for this, they were also trying to stop Shen Mao, who was working at finding the ancient Martian shipwreck to auction off its artifacts. One artifact in particular was a golden journal that GRIP had been trying to secure for the past several years.

Then there was Amos, a German descendant and eco-terrorist. Amos had gotten his hands on the fuel-solidifying substance that had foundered the merchant boat in the Ligurian Sea. The more GRIP learned about Amos, the more they tried to convince the world of his dangerous plot. With only circumstantial evidence, this ended in vain, and GRIP took it upon themselves to save the world from a devastating oil shortage that Amos planned to cause.

Thus Labeeb's team was working to stop Amos. Then if they could find the moss, they would accomplish two things. First would be adding a new source of energy to the world market, lessening the shock Amos was attempting. Second, the moss should be close to the Martian shipwreck, where they would most likely find the golden journal, getting it before Shen Mao.

"I think I've found something," François mentioned after a few minutes of searching.

Labeeb left the files he was digging through to join his old friend. François had indeed found something, although not enough. But like a hobbyist with a metal detector, they had found a ping, and now it was time to go digging.

Chapter 5

The boat ride back to the French harbor felt long and painful. Lydia's body burned in the sweltering decompression chamber where she found herself. Grisha informed her that she had gone into hypothermic shock, and the temperature really wasn't as bad as it felt. Nevertheless, it was an uncomfortable several hours.

By the time the decompression was finished, Sam had already docked the boat at Port de Saint-Laurent-du-Var. This was only minutes away from the Nice-Côte d'Azur Airport, where their private Learjet was waiting for them. Instead of racing straight for the airport, Grisha suggested they move the crew of the research vessel from the room they currently occupied into the hyperbaric chamber. This would give the team just a little more time to clean the ship before getting away. Granted, it wasn't necessary, but it would add one more degree of safety while the team made their escape. With the crew inside, they could control the specific time of the researchers' release. Grisha pressurized it to resemble a dive at two hundred feet below sea level. Though the crew had access to the controls inside the chamber, they were handcuffed in a manner that prevented their hands from reaching the panel. Unless one of them could squeeze their hand or leg out of the shackles, it would be impossible to adjust the pressure setting. Thus, for the next couple of hours, while Lydia's team cleaned the ship of all fingerprints and other evidence, the crew of the research vessel would be building up excess nitrogen in their bodies.

By the time that they were ready to go, Lydia pressed a speaker button for the crammed hyperbaric chamber. It had been very tight in there with just her, Grisha, and the dive suit, so she could only imagine how uncomfortable the four crewmen were. "Thank you for letting us borrow your ship," she told them. "I'm really sorry that we had to do it under these circumstances, but your ship was the only one outfitted with the equipment we needed. You won't have to worry about seeing us again, and I would suggest that you don't try. You've been pressurized to two hundred feet below sea level now for almost two hours. If you want to avoid the bends, I suggest that you give yourselves enough time to fully decompress. The key to your restraints is in your skipper's front right jacket pocket. Good luck to you."

Lydia waited just long enough to see them fumble around until they found the key and unlocked themselves. They would need several hours in the chamber, just as Lydia had needed earlier to decompress. This would keep the researchers indisposed long enough to allow her team to get to the airport. By the time the research crew would be able to emerge and sound any alarm, Lydia and her men would easily find themselves a safe distance from any French authorities.

Waiting on the tarmac was Lydia's modified Leer jet. Having previously been fueled, it was ready for takeoff. Since Lydia's body still had some residual nitrogen in it, she couldn't climb to a very high altitude. This wasn't a problem, though, as she was just flying about eighty miles to the west. Here she landed the jet again at the Marseille Province Airport.

Labeeb only kept them waiting for about an hour and a half before he finally joined them on board. Sam was the first to address him. "What took you so long?"

"Those archives are an artifact in and of themselves," Labeeb replied. "It took hours of digging through folders and files to find what we needed. They really need to digitize that place."

"But you did find what we're looking for?" Lydia asked, feeling a Christmas morning sense of anticipation.

Labeeb spread his notes out across the wing of the jet. A tight-lipped smile betrayed his own excitement. "That tag you retrieved, it belonged to a man who'd been dispatched on special assignment back to France. Just before this, he and three others, most likely the ones who died on the shipwreck with him, were on a patrol. By assessing their assigned patrol, we have about a half-mile to one-mile-wide path to search along. They abandoned their patrol somewhere north of the St. Catherine Mountains in Egypt. By my estimation, I should be able to get us within five miles of where they discovered the moss."

"So let me get this right," Lydia clarified. "You have a five-mile-long, one-mile-wide search area? This should be easy, especially if Marshal Steel is already ahead of us. We find him, we find the shipwreck. We find the shipwreck, and we get the golden journal—and the moss."

"What are we waiting for?" Grisha asked. "Let's go to Egypt."

Just then Lydia's phone rang. She looked down at it; the number didn't show, but she doubted it would. GRIP went to every effort to keep some of their more covert operations secret. This resulted in using secured satellite phones and working in separated cells, much like a terrorist operation. As far as the public knew, GRIP was just another bunch of well-financed hippies.

"Lydia here," she answered.

"Lydia, it's me, Persephone," the voice of her superior introduced. "I have received intel on Amos's whereabouts. He was recently spotted again in Turkey heading north. We believe that he is targeting the Novorossiysk pipelines in Russia."

"Can it wait?" Lydia asked. "We have a strong lead on where Marshal Steel might be. If we go now, we might be able to catch up to him before he finds the records."

The voice on the other end paused for a moment, then asked, "How good are your chances of pinpointing his location?"

"If Marshal is there, then we should be able to find him right away. If not, then we should at least find the crash site within a day or so." Again silence followed Lydia's reply.

When at last Persephone decided, she offered a compromise. "We don't know when Amos plans to make his final move, but Novorossiysk is one of the last major pipelines we haven't secured. He may be about ready. I suggest that you fly over this area you think the crash site may be. If you spot any sign of

Marshal's excavation, then move in on him. If not, then continue on to Russia. Once the pipeline is secured, you can come back and find the ship."

Lydia agreed. If Marshal wasn't already there, then hopefully it was because he hadn't found the site yet, and they would still have time to locate it later. But Amos was a wild card. He was unpredictable, and had a way of changing Lydia's plans at every turn.

As soon as she hung up the phone, she gathered the others around the wing of her aircraft again, and briefed everyone on their orders.

Chapter 6

The conversation had just ended, and Sinclaire stowed his parabolic microphone back into its inconspicuous carrying case. He was nearly three hundred yards away, which was as close as he dared get without risking detection by GRIP's crew. He went back around to the door of his new twin-prop airplane that Shen Mao had bought for him as sort of a down payment on the eventual completion of his mission. GRIP already knew what Sinclaire's other plane looked like, so he had petitioned Mao for early payment. If he was to stop Lydia, he needed to catch her off guard.

Like GRIP's crew, Sinclaire's was just as professional. For hire, his crew of mercenaries had been providing Mao, a rich Chinese man obsessed about the same artifacts that GRIP was searching for. To Mao, Sinclaire's group provided both personal security and more-offensive measures. For some time

GRIP had been the sole focus of their operations. GRIP's group called themselves Nephilim, the Hebrew word for giants in the Old Testament. Translated more directly, it meant the fallen ones. When the sons of God, the true giants, came unto the daughters of men. Their children became mighty men of renown. These *renowned* Martian descendants had gotten too close to stopping Mao by trying to capture his lead anthropologist, Marshal Steel, in the past. Their interference led Sinclaire to search for Lydia's team and, with any luck, eliminate them as a threat to Mao's plan. He would show them what it meant to be called *the fallen ones*. However, he was smart enough not to attempt any such activity at this provincial, albeit busy airport. He now had a good idea of where they would be going next, and with a little stratagem, might find the perfect chance to ambush them.

His plane was slower than their Learjet, but he didn't have any intention or ability to shoot them out of the sky. He simply needed to think a step or two ahead, then intercept them. To his advantage, GRIP didn't know that he had found out about their plans. Looking out his window, he watched as their jet taxied toward the runway. Picking up a special telephone with a state-of-the-art scrambler, he called Mao.

"Do you have something for me?" Mao answered.

Sinclaire knew his phone number would not have registered on Mao's end, since Mao only saved numbers in his head. Despite the few that actually knew how to get ahold of Mao, Sinclaire was always surprised with Mao's uncanny and shrewd tendency to always be anticipating Sinclaire's calls. "A progress report, and a warning," he started. "GRIP has just taken off from France and is heading toward

Egypt. They think they have ascertained the general location of your excavation site. They also have orders to go to Russia on a separate assignment. They plan to fly over your dig first. If they find it and your man Marshal there, they will stop and engage him. Since I would rather kill them without losing any of my own men, I would suggest that Marshal ensure his site is camouflaged well, and that nobody is out in the open for the next twelve hours. If, when GRIP flies over and they don't see anybody, they will continue on to their Russian assignment first."

Mao immediately responded with his crisp staccato accent, "I will inform Mr. Steel to clear out for the day. I believe he is very close to finding what we are looking for, but a few hours delay will not hurt him. What are you going to do about GRIP?"

"One of their crew apparently has a relative at a small Turkish airport. Their plan is to stop there for a night on the way back. They will not be expecting any company, and I see no reason why we couldn't easily dispose of them at that point."

"Very well," Mao approved. "I will ask Mr. Steel to take a few extra precautions at the excavation site as well. If you fail to stop GRIP, I will not want any trail leading back to me."

Sinclaire confirmed, "No problems here. I will also inform my detachment that is with Marshal. They will accommodate him in any way they can."

"It is well enough," Mao stated. "Inform me of any developments."

Mao hung up the phone, and Sinclaire put in a call to Sperl, informing him to accommodate Marshal in cleaning up the excavation site when they were finished. Sperl was a ruthless man, but Sinclaire also recognized a capable man when he saw him. Sperl, unfit anywhere else in the world, had a safe position in Sinclaire's band of mercenaries. After that call, he gathered his own team together and made plans for intercepting GRIP when they landed in Turkey.

Chapter 7

Russia

July 31

The air whipped across her body; Lydia lay flat, her arms and legs outstretched like a four-pointed star. A slight tilt in her ankle or wrist would send her in any direction she pleased. Only now, she closed her eyes and rolled onto her back. When she opened her eyes, she beheld the stars above her. It was one of the most beautiful feelings. The cold pillow of rushing atmosphere, combined with the knowledge that nobody could see or hear her, gave her the only chance for a peaceful clarity. It was the most effective thing she had found for calming her mind, and she loved it.

Closing her eyes again, she tilted her right ankle and wrist; it sent her into a series of controlled barrel rolls. Then with a quick glance at her altimeter, and realizing that she was near the Earth, she did one final backflip for fun before pulling the chord on her parachute.

The chute was packed for low-altitude deployment, and when the force of the sail caught wind and snapped her upright, she was only five hundred feet above the ground. With the expertise of a seasoned paratrooper, she hit the ground and detached the chute. She quickly packed it up and stored it in her modified jumpsuit. By the time she finished tucking in restraint buckles, it looked like an ordinary backpack. She then unzipped a pocket on the side of the pack, and pulled out several small vials, to check on their condition. When satisfied that they were still intact, she put them back away. Undoing a couple of leg straps and pocketing them along the way, her blue suit pants began to flow loosely over her polished khaki shoes. The shoes were made to handle the harshest hikes, but from anyone else's point of view they merely resembled a formal pair of dress shoes. With the jump pack all tucked into itself, she now looked as though she had just stepped out of a corporate jet and was headed to a high-level meeting at a Fortune 500 company.

Pulling out her phone, she checked the time. The night was almost over. Within an hour or two the morning sun would crest the horizon. She used the GPS function to get her bearings and with motivated zeal, she took the first steps on her trek to her first destination. She tried to concentrate on the task at hand; it helped keep her mind off the ever-pressing concerns of her past. One day she hoped to return, but for now she needed to prove her worth. If not, she doubted *he* would ever consider taking her back.

As she hiked along, she soon came to the small

town of Ubinskaya. The sun was just beginning to rise, and the small rural town was already stirring. Within half an hour, she found a small used truck for sale and purchased it for full price. The truck was white with a little wear, and was in working condition. It was perfect. She then visited a hardware store and purchased a bottle of black spray-paint. Then she pulled out two folded pieces of paper from her pocket and laid one out on the driver's door of the truck, peeling back a thin waxy strip from the paper to stick the template on the door. She walked around and repeated this process on the passenger door. After shaking the can of paint, she popped the top off and let it fall to the ground. Three quick passes at each template, and she was finished. She waited for five minutes, and then pulled the stickers off the doors to reveal a logo with the initials "B.N.P." and "безопасность" beneath. This stood for the Baku-Novorossiysk Pipeline Security.

The pipeline was meant to transport crude oil between Novorossiysk, Russia, and Baku, Azerbaijan. Much of the oil coming out of these pipelines would be used all across Europe. While many of the proven oil reserves were known to be located in the Middle Eastern countries, Russia was actually the home to the world's largest known oil deposits. Lydia looked around and found it hard to imagine that several years from now, the mega-rich sheikhs of the Middle East could be replaced by a bunch of mega-rich peasants here. But she maintained her doubts. She suspected that the Russian mobsters and political leaders would more than likely be the ones to reap the bounty from the oil-rich land.

As Lydia bounced along the rough road, she glanced at her GPS again. She was close. She put the device on the seat next to her and began to search the side of the road. She nearly missed her first turnoff. Slamming on the pedal, she could hear the squealing of the old brakes, and knew they were likely wearing down the rotors. At least she would only need the truck for one day. She had five stops to make today, and she found the first one after traveling only one mile up the road. It was the office of one of the smaller drilling companies along the pipeline.

A thick burly man with a push broom for a mustache stepped out of the dilapidated structure. The shack seemed to serve more as a place for sheltering oneself from the wind than a place of business. Lydia stuck the truck in first gear, then killed the engine. She didn't bother to set the brake before she stepped out. There was a good chance the emergency brake wouldn't have worked, anyway.

Though she had jumped from a plane hours earlier, and hiked two miles, she looked as ravishing as ever. She knew it, too. She had planned it this way so she could establish her superiority. The man approached her and took off his hat, then in Russian he commented, "I can't remember the last time I was ever visited by such a beautiful lady."

"Are you Ivan?" Lydia replied in Russian. He nodded his head. "Your wife should be ashamed, then," she continued, but then flashed a teasing smile.

Ivan switched to English and said, "You won't tell, will you?" as he lifted his eyebrows rapidly a few times. "By the way, your Russian is very good."

Lydia stuck out her lower lip then replied, faking a convincing British accent, "Not good enough if you could tell."

"Russian is hard language, but you still speak very well," he tried to convince her.

Lydia noticed that he quickly read the side of her truck as she shut her door. He then asked, "So you are security for the pipeline?"

"Yes," Lydia replied. "I'm afraid that we may have a problem, and I could really use your help."

The man stood up a little taller, obviously pleased that she would come asking for his help. "This is unusual, but what can I help you with?"

"We're keeping this mostly quiet, so can I trust you not to go telling everyone?" Lydia asked.

Ivan took his large finger and made an X across his chest. "I'm Russian, aren't I? Yes, I can keep secrets well enough."

Lydia studied his face for a moment then said, "Yes, I believe you. You see, the fact is that in the last few months we've been gathering information about an imminent terrorist attack on the pipeline."

"You drive all the way out here to tell me this?" Ivan replied, a little disappointment in his voice. "There is often talk of problem or bomb, but it never really happens."

Lydia eyed him. "That's the problem—this time the threat is going to happen. But it's not a bomb."

Ivan studied Lydia carefully. She wondered if he could tell that she wasn't who she was pretending to be. He then asked, "What is threat, then?"

Lydia opened the door to the truck again and pulled out two small glass vials. One had a red cap on it, and the other had a white cap. They were the same vials she had checked just after parachuting in. "Do you have a small sample of oil or diesel around?"

Ivan led her over to a fuel can. "I have a little diesel here."

Lydia smiled and picked up the can. It only contained about one gallon of fuel, which would be more than enough to demonstrate her point. "Last year we discovered an engineered bacteria that we've replicated." She held up the vial with the red cap. "We confiscated it from a man who was a known eco-terrorist. He was just a small player, but he had been making several trips in and out of Russia, smuggling this into the country. After thorough interrogation it was discovered that this pipeline was to be the first major target in a series of sabotages around the country." Though that wasn't entirely accurate, it was still a well-rehearsed story that had worked on previous pipeline personnel, and Lydia felt no reason to adjust it.

"So what does little white powder do?" Ivan asked.

Careful not to use very much, since she needed the rest of it for further demonstrations, Lydia opened the cap and poured a light dusting of the powder into the fuel can. She closed the cap and swished the can around for a second, then slowly poured the diesel out onto the dirt. At first nothing seemed out of the ordinary, and she could sense his frustration at wasting his fuel, but within a few seconds the diesel became thicker, and more gelatinous. By the time the last of it was poured out, it had turned into a mass that was as solid as rubber. Even the portion that had been more liquid before could now be lifted off of the dirt, stuck in the shape of a muddy puddle.

"As you can see," Lydia said as she held the newly formed solid in her hand, "this bacteria feeds on the fuel, and as it does so, it releases a compound that solidifies the diesel. It spreads very quickly, and once it is solidified, we have been unable to re-liquefy it."

Lydia tossed the rubberized fuel to Ivan, who easily caught it. She watched as he squeezed it and examined it carefully. He then commented, "It doesn't even feel oily on my hands."

"If any of this gets into the pipeline, it would spread quickly enough to plug up the entire line in a matter of days," Lydia said casually. "The entire line would have to be replaced." She watched him as he continued to fathom the repercussions of what he'd just been told.

"Why do you show this to me? What is there for me to do?" he asked.

"You have a phone, don't you?" she asked.

He pulled out a cheap cell phone. Lydia nodded in approval, then handed him the vial with the white cap. "We picked out a few pumps along the line that were in a good strategic position to combat the effects of the substance. We are going to be closely monitoring the pipeline for the next few weeks. We have placed sensors all across the line, and when the terrorists strike, we will send you a text message as soon as we notice any irregularity in the flows. When this happens, it is urgent that you immediately empty the entire vial of this powder into the pipeline from your end. It is similar in the way it replicates, except instead of releasing an agent that solidifies the oil, it will release a compound that blocks the terrorist's compound."

"Why not just put it in now?" Ivan asked.

"I wish we could," Lydia replied. "But this bacteria has a short life cycle. It multiplies rapidly, but for some reason it can't survive much more than a week. It needs to be applied as closely to the same time as the terrorists' contamination to have any real effect."

"You can trust on me," Ivan said. "I will not let my phone or this powder out of my sight."

"We knew we could count on you," Lydia said, almost sighing a breath of relief. "And remember, we want to keep this quiet for now. We believe that we may be able to catch these men in the act, but if they suspect that we are ready for them, it may ruin everything.”

He nodded in understanding, and Lydia extended her hand. He shook it and then she turned to go back to her truck. “I’m sorry to drop this on you so suddenly then run, but I have a few more stops that I must get to before the day is over.”

“I understand,” he replied. “Besides, my wife would not like finding out that I spent all day with a beautiful blonde.” He then waved a good-bye to her. As he did so, he dropped his phone onto the ground. Lydia watched as he quickly scrambled to pick it up. He looked at the screen then gave her a large, if not embarrassed, grin and a thumbs-up. She shook her head and shot back a playful scolding. She then fired up the truck and was off again.

Chapter 8

Grisha had just taken off from Greece again as he checked his instruments one last time. He didn't like the idea that Lydia dropped into Russia without him, especially since it had only been about a day and a half since she recovered from hypothermia. She seemed to place too much of the risk on her own shoulders when she could easily delegate it. He had been helping her learn Russian for the last two years, and she was a remarkably quick learner. But she was a better pilot than he was, and being Russian himself, he knew that he would blend in better. This, however, would not stop her. She loved to parachute, and he couldn't understand why anyone would want to jump out of a perfectly good airplane. Besides, there were other ways of getting into a country that didn't require going through customs. For some reason, though, she preferred this way.

He hoped she would be ready for him when he

landed, because if not, he wouldn't have much time before he had to leave her behind. When they had calculated the time it would take to drop off the bacteria to the different drillers along this portion of the pipeline, they hadn't left themselves with a large window for error. She had to deliver all the vials to the designated drillers and be over to the Krymsk airport near Новороссийск (Novorossiysk) by midnight. The airport would be least busy at that time, and they should be able to land long enough for Lydia to sneak back on. If she missed it, though, she would have to rely on her own means to sneak out of the country and rendezvous with him.

Just as he'd done early this morning, he circled the lower end of the Black Sea, not wanting anyone watching the radar to believe that he was intentionally headed for Russia. It had worked the first time when they allowed themselves to drift into Russian airspace. By the time the Russians had hailed the wandering Learjet, Lydia had already left and was falling toward the ground below. Grisha laughed at the gullible air traffic controller. He had told the controller that he was starting off early on a sightseeing tour, flying by visual recognition mainly, and that he'd accidentally veered off course. The controller forgave him since Grisha was quick to apologize, and immediately adjusted his course to take him away from their airspace.

Even though he hoped that the controllers would now be just as gullible, he doubted his ability to convince them again, as it would make much less sense to infringe on their airspace two nights in a row. The operation at hand would likely require a little more finessing this time around, accented by the fact that Grisha would have to actually land on Russian soil without being immediately arrested. Hopefully, if his luck held, the timing would insure that the air traffic controller from last time might be on a different shift.

As if reading his mind, Sam parted the curtain to the cockpit. "I think we're ready. Are you sure we can pull this off? Crossing into Russia for a second time? Seems to me it would raise a few red flags."

"Hey, this is my country," Grisha replied. "You do your part, and you leave the rest to me."

"Just saying, I don't want to end up in some damnable Siberian stink hole because of this," Sam said.

"Go get ready," Grisha said, waving him away. "It won't be long now."

Sam mumbled, "Boss," then ducked back through the curtain.

Grisha felt that he had put on a good face, but inside he was slightly worried. Being from Russia, he knew how strictly the customs soldiers took their jobs. If his story didn't check out one hundred percent, they would try to take the plane, and put him, Sam, and the whole crew in jail. That was the last thing he wanted to happen tonight. The second to last thing that he wanted was to kill his fellow countrymen for trying to do their job if they attempted it. Though he didn't like the idea, he was willing to do even that. Whatever it took, they were close now, and for the good of everyone, he knew they must complete their mission—even if it meant a few innocent men fell along the way.

The next couple of hours crawled by. There wasn't much to do, since the jet all but flew itself. Although it was a small jet, it was large enough to hold up to eight men. It had also been customized with a 50mm gun that retracted up under the nose of the plane. It was rarely used, but Lydia had insisted upon it. This whole jet was her responsibility.

Her skills with aircraft, combined with her combat training, were among the main reasons that she had been recruited to join GRIP, but it wasn't the biggest reason. Grisha had copiloted for her during the last two years, yet every time she left him to fly the plane solo, he felt a nervous sense of responsibility. The jet might belong to GRIP, but unofficially it was Lydia's baby. Despite the fact that he had been part of GRIP long before Lydia, he knew the politics enough to understand that she carried a unique weight with their superiors.

The gun wasn't the only change in the special Learjet. Since they were constantly hopping across the globe, and not always in friendly countries, they needed to make sure it couldn't be tracked. Since radar-absorbent paint would be too conspicuous, they decided to hide their identifying marks instead. Most private airplanes had an N-number on the tail, unique to each aircraft, much like the identifying numbers and letters on a car's license plate. Since the N-numbers were large enough to be seen from far away, Lydia had that section of the tail painted with an advanced form of smart paint. This smart paint was controlled by passing an electrical current under it, which caused the paint molecules to rotate, revealing a different color. By passing this current through in certain spots, the plane could change the painted N-number at any time. Even upon close inspection, nobody would know that it had changed. Any dust that might be stuck to the clear coat of paint on top would not be disturbed.

The other changes were simple hidden compartments within the plane for smuggling their weapons. Some of the hidden compartments were even large enough to fit a person inside, since most countries looked unfavorably at hauling guns, explosives, and wanted men across their borders. Also, since they had to keep large amounts of cash on hand for bribes and other spur-of-the-moment operations, they had built-in compartments to hide those reserves. When everything was locked up safe, nobody would ever be able to tell that the plane was anything more than a small corporate or leisure jet.

Having skirted the southern half of the Black Sea, Grisha began to angle northward. He picked up his mic and announced to the crew, "Attention, this is your tour guide speaking. We are soon to have technical difficulty—which will force us to land in Russia. You have thirty minutes to hope and pray they don't mind our accidental intrusion."

Chapter 9

From the road, Lydia eyed the rusty, post-Soviet styled airport. Though the runway was long enough to handle her Learjet, she knew the strip more often handled lighter, propeller-driven planes. Passing the airport, and moving behind a small commercial building, the brakes squealed as she parked her truck and cut the engine. A flickering light attached to the building gave just enough light to dimly illuminate the white pickup.

With her knife, she cut a strip of the cloth away from the driver's seat. Lydia wiped down the interior and exterior of the truck in every place that a fingerprint might have been left. She doubted the truck would raise any red flags, but she had time and knew it would be foolish to not take the precaution.

Retrieving the rest of the black spray-paint from earlier, Lydia shut the door and sprayed over the logo she had created that morning. As quickly as she got a good wet coating on the logo, she wiped it off with the cloth. The extra coating of black paint acted as a paint thinner, allowing her to erase the morning paint job with ease. She then repeated this process two more times until every hint of black paint was removed from the door of the truck. She then walked around to the other side and repeated the process.

Leaving the keys in the ignition, Lydia abandoned the little white truck, wondering if anybody else might take advantage of the vehicle and make it their own after she was gone. More than likely, she figured, it would sit there for a couple of weeks until it got towed away and forgotten in some impound lot.

A little ways down, Lydia discarded the spray can and the paint-soaked cloth into a waste bin. Another half kilometer to go, and she would be back at the airport. The night was very dark, and easy for her to blend into the shadows. Caution wasn't too terribly important though, there was nobody about. She paused a moment to gauge how much wind there was, and where it was coming from. She turned in a small circle, her wet tongue just barely hanging between her parted lips. She felt the slight coolness react with her mouth. The breeze was very light, so she confidently continued toward the end of the runway. With little to no wind, she knew that Grisha would come in and try to land from the end opposite her. When he eventually comes to a stop, she would be at this end of the runway waiting for him.

There was little cover along the edge of the runway, but near a chain-link fence, a bit of unkempt overgrowth provided ample room to hide. She made her way to it, and crouched down. Unless somebody was looking very hard, they wouldn't be able to see her. Checking her watch, she found the time to be

11:30 sharp. She had timed it perfectly.

Lydia had been able to drop off all five vials to relatively small oil drillers along the pipeline. Only one of them had been hard to track down, and Lydia felt relieved when she found the last three without any delay. Now it was up to Grisha to get in and get her out before any government officials became wise to her presence.

Normally she would have preferred to just enter the country legally; however, her last visit to Russia had met with some difficulties. Despite Grisha's reassurances, attempting entrance now would be far more risky. Hopping from country to country, eluding government officials, and seizing civilian research vessels was not exactly what she considered ideal. When she had accepted the position with GRIP, she was well aware that her job would involve risk. But breaking every law to stop international terrorists was far from what she'd thought she would be getting into when she joined.

Like Labeeb, she also found it amusing that the plant she was looking for was so closely related to the threat that she was now trying to stop. When she'd first met her French-Indian companion, he came to her with the journal of the transport ship she dove to the other day. By that time, Lydia had already fought her first battle with the terrorist Amos. In the account Labeeb brought, there had been some mention of the plant she was looking for, but also mention of all their fuel solidifying before a German U-boat sank them. Since Amos was of German descent, it seemed plausible that he might have the bacteria that could produce such a negative impact on the world's oil supplies. Her hypothesis was that the solidifying agent, though used by the Germans once, had somehow been kept from the government, being passed down until it eventually ended up in the hands of Amos.

Lydia shivered as a light breeze blew over her. The temperature wasn't freezing, but it was still uncomfortably cold. She looked around, debating whether it would be a good idea to take a quick jog around the airstrip to get her blood pumping again, but she decided against it. She couldn't risk being found by anybody. A woman who could barely speak Russian, running around an airport here, that would definitely count as suspicious. Her only hope was that Grisha might arrive a little early, and that he wouldn't run into any problems.

But more than the cold, and deeper than the waiting, what bothered her most was the idle time that allowed her mind to wander. When she had plenty to do, she could push memories to the back of her mind. But now she was flooded by pent-up regret.

The harder she tried to stop it, the more the memory of her turning point invaded her thoughts. It had happened just a few years ago, when she was on her way to the hospital. Her husband was at work when she called. She was pregnant with her first and only child.

After having taken it easy all day, and though the doctor assured her that the baby looked fine, and her body wouldn't likely be ready to go into labor for at least another couple weeks, she found herself fighting through increasingly regular and painful contractions.

Flint, Lydia's husband, told her that he would rush over as quickly as possible. Since at that time he was over an hour away, he suggested she get a ride to the hospital from a neighbor. Lydia consciously knew that her doting husband was right, and perhaps that's where the guilt started. She made the excuse that she didn't know the neighbors well enough to ask them for a hospital trip. Sure, they always offered to help in any way possible, but most good neighbors offered. There were far fewer neighbors that you would actually feel comfortable asking.

Instead, she believed she would have no problem driving herself to the hospital. It was a fifteen-minute drive, and the roads were usually not crowded at that time of day. Why shouldn't she drive? Most labors she'd heard of lasted for several hours before the baby arrived.

Lydia shook her head, trying to dispel that un-forgivable day in her head. She even tried to hum the tune of the first random song that came to her mind. But, inevitably, the more she tried to dispel a thought, the more it found traction in her head. Her chosen song soon made mention of love. "Why does every song have to do with love?" she asked herself.

The memory swept back over her, picking up exactly where it left off.

The roads did appear clear on that fateful day, and she was thankful, because right before she got to a Stop sign, she felt a very sharp contraction. Instead of gently moving her foot to the brake, she slammed her foot down on the accelerator. Only after the engine was revving and she was speeding through the intersection did she realize her predicament. It was her first major warning that she should not be driving.

But like any stubborn fool, she had pressed on, and now lamented, *Why did I do, it? Why didn't I stop and call someone to help me? Why do I keep asking myself the same question every single day?*

She was only a few miles from the hospital when

the event happened that had sent her life spiraling in a completely different direction. The light turned green, and she accelerated the small sedan forward. She didn't even notice the other truck until it flashed into view through the passenger-side window. When it happened, it seemed like a slide show. Or at least that's how she remembered it. She was driving along, and the next second she saw the truck. After that, everything blurred around her as the car was spinning. The windshield came crashing in, and she saw the thin silhouettes of two people reaching for her. One of her rescuers was speaking. ". . . so much blood . . . miss, miss, can you hear me . . . oh my— hey, she's pregnant . . ."

Several days later she awoke in a hospital bed, her husband was dozing on a chair by her side. She'd been hurt but would recover. The worst thing was that she had lost the baby. If only she had listened to her husband, none of this would have happened. Her life would have been changed forever for the better.

Though she didn't mind the continual globe-trotting, it was not what she had wanted for herself. Lydia wanted to hold her son in her arms. She wanted to see Flint come home from work each day and give her one of his warm loving kisses. She wanted her own family. Even if she couldn't have her deceased son, she still longed to have Flint. Countless other women have lost children, and they manage. Their strength just made Lydia feel even more weak and unworthy.

Wiping the tear from her face, she gritted her teeth and wondered why she kept putting herself through this. She tried to think of something different, then she heard the faint coughing of an old military truck firing to life somewhere near the airport. Turning her attention to the runway, and into the sky, she could see the lights of a plane coming down for landing. She was relieved, mostly, because it now gave her something else to think about. The military truck was no doubt en route to question the people on board the plane as soon as they touched down. All Lydia needed to do was find a way onto the plane. She unzipped one of the smaller pockets on the parachute pack, pulling out one last item in preparation.

Chapter 10

"Mayday, Mayday! This is Learjet bravo-hotel-niner-niner-six, requesting emergency landing at Krymsk airport."

"This is Anapa Airport to Learjet, please squawk seven-seven-zero-zero, over."

"Learjet bravo-hotel-niner-niner-six, squawking seven-seven-zero-zero, over."

"Anapa to Learjet, you are drifting into Russian airspace, can you turn to heading 345 degrees and land here at Anapa? Over."

"Learjet to Anapa, we won't make it that far. Requesting temporary authorization to land at Krymsk, over."

"Anapa to Learjet, what is the nature of your emergency? Over."

"Learjet to Anapa, we have lost our engines and are gliding only."

"Anapa to Learjet, you have permission to land at

Krymsk, but be advised, you must remain with the aircraft until you are met by the security personnel, over."

Grisha clicked his mic twice to signify that he understood. "Well, here we go," he said to himself as he throttled back the engines. Once he was sure of his descent, he cut the engines out entirely. With any luck, he would have Lydia and be back in the air before any security officials even arrived. Then by clicking on his mic button again, the lights at the small airport automatically turned on, revealing the old airstrip.

Though he had done it several times, he still didn't feel entirely comfortable landing the jet without any chance of throttling the engines back up if something went wrong last minute. In order to avoid overshooting the runway, he maneuvered the plane into a slip, which helped him reduce his altitude more quickly. He still overshot his landing target, but without engines, he would have to make do. He straightened out the jet and began to pull up on the yoke. Warning buzzers started sounding throughout the cabin, indicating that a stall was imminent. Grisha ignored the buzzing, and the back wheels then screeched in protest as they touched down on the runway. The jet bounced up once, but he didn't ease up on the yoke. They floated back down and the wheels stayed on the runway this time. Then, easing the yoke forward again, he brought the nose of the jet to the pavement. His runway was almost out, and he pushed his toes hard against the brakes. There was no squealing of rubber, only a slow deceleration. He was going to make it.

The edge of the runway was very close now, and he still had a little momentum left. He believed it was for the better, even if it was unintentional. By accidentally overshooting the runway, it placed him in prime position to take off quickly again if he found himself in a bind. As soon as he got as far as he dared, he swerved to the right side of the runway, then slammed on the left brake as hard as he could. The plane groaned and listed in protest, but by using the forward momentum, he was able to swing the jet around so it now faced the open runway from which he had just come.

Sam came up and slapped him on the shoulder. "Hey, good job, you didn't kill us."

Grisha wiped the sweat from his forehead. Then, noticing some approaching lights, he replied, "I did my part, now it's your turn."

Sam looked out the cockpit window in the direction that Grisha had pointed. Then turning around, he yelled back, "Look alive, girls—the game is on!"

Opening the hatch, Grisha extended the foldout steps down to the runway. Then, grabbing a small toolbox, he walked over to the engines and opened one of the storage compartments, and stuck his arms and head in. The truck was parked in no time, with its headlights illuminating Grisha. Two men jumped out. One carried a sidearm attached to his belt, and the other held an old semiautomatic rifle that looked to be a relic from the glory days of the Soviet Union. The first man unlatched the strap on his pistol then ordered in Russian for them to stop.

Like a simple, if not large mechanic, Grisha pulled his head out of the storage compartment. Surprise cascaded down his face. Sam and the other three members of the crew were already outside the jet with their arms raised. Grisha put his hands halfway up, and then stuttered, trying his best to fake a bad Russian impersonation. He gathered by their uniforms that they were simple local police, and though he was Russian, he didn't want these men to know. "нет Russian, no understand."

One of the men then asked, "You know English?"

"Yes, a little," Grisha replied.

"Who are you?" the officer asked. "And why we need come here in middle of night to hold you?"

Grisha tried to dumb down his English a bit. "Engine no work. Bad fuel line. I fix, then I go."

The men were apparently not satisfied with his answer. "Who are you?" they demanded, the second man acting tough as he showed off is antique rifle.

Stifling a nervous laugh, Grisha said. "I fly tours for them." He motioned toward his passengers, who were dressed in ridiculously colorful button-up shirts and shorts. "They visit Greece—want see around Black Sea. So I fly them. Now, I fix jet, very embarrassing, then I leave, okay?"

The first officer then waved his hands in protest. "No, you wait. We check on you first."

Hot blood reddened Grisha's face as his temper heated up to a boil. He'd hoped they wouldn't encounter anybody, and now they had two yahoos trying to show off their power. The airport probably didn't have many foreign planes come down like this, and they might not even know if they should be holding them. His Mayday call must have sparked some red flags. But Grisha was not inclined to wait around for anybody to show up who actually could detain them.

Then the man with the rifle fell to one knee and aimed the rifle into the darkness behind the jet. "Come out, or I shoot!" he declared.

Grisha noticed the surprise on his face when he beheld a beautiful woman, dressed in nice clothes, with a backpack slung over one shoulder. Holding up a small, almost empty roll of toilet paper that she often carried with her, especially for instances when she found herself in Asian countries that didn't use toilet paper, she attempted to use a little of the Russian she knew. Lydia told the guards that she just *had* to take a pee. Only she seemed to forget that the phrase didn't translate clearly. Again Grisha held back a laugh, but the police officers let theirs loose. The first one signaled the woman over and in his heavily accented English, he said, "Don't you mean, you had to leave a pee?" Both police officers began to laugh uncontrollably.

Lydia faked an embarrassed look. Grisha knew now that she was playing them, and with their attention turned toward her, Sam and Jay were able to sneak around the officers. Grisha then slowly reached into his toolbox, and wrapped his hand around a snub-nosed pistol. He still hoped they would be able to make an escape without having to kill these two men, but he wasn't willing to take any chances.

With hands to her face, Lydia tried hiding her shame. One officer came up and reached out to put a hand on her shoulder. She dropped her hands and looked into his eyes; he gave her a big toothy grin, and then she surprised him by lifting his own pistol out of its holster and pointing it into his chest.

His partner realized it too late, and before he could react, Sam brought the butt of his own pistol down on the man's head, while Jay caught the slumping body. Grisha let the snub-nosed pistol fall back into the toolbox. He shut the compartment, and walked over the officer. In perfect Russian he told the officer, "It's not nice to make fun of a lady." He then grabbed the officer around the neck in a sleeper-hold and waited until the struggling man lost consciousness.

Then, resting the man on the runway, he said, "They'll be out for a few minutes—let's get out of here."

Sam rushed past Grisha, slapping him hard on the back. "Good job, big guy," then he paused for a moment and took Lydia's hand, kissing the back of her knuckles. "Madam, would your rescuer be permitted a kiss?"

Grisha laughed when Lydia pulled her hand back and slapped him hard on the cheek. "You forget, Sam, she still hates your guts."

Sam smiled and responded, "Perhaps, but there's a chance that she may still like the rest of me."

"Get in the plane," Lydia ordered, "unless you'd like me to leave your sorry butt behind?"

Sam bowed, and then made a swinging motion with his arm, "Ladies first."

Lydia climbed in, and Grisha followed. Grisha happily surrendered the pilot seat to her as they began to start the engines up again. The familiar slam of the hatch sounded as Sam and his men finished boarding. Then Sam shouted from behind, "This tour sucks, I want my money back!"

Grisha just pulled the cockpit's curtain shut to block out the passenger section. "So, how you like my landing?"

Lydia gave him a half smile, "Did you purposely overshoot and bounce the landing, or was that an accident?"

Grisha faked a hurt expression. "My dear, I only try to make it easier for you to get aboard then take off."

Lydia laughed a little. "Well, you did give me plenty of runway." She then throttled up the engines, and once they were revved to full power, she released the brakes, and the small jet began to accelerate. It was sluggish at first, but in no time they were in the air, and climbing at one hundred and eighteen knots. As soon as they were above the runway, she changed the squawk code on the airplane, so it wouldn't signal an aircraft in distress. She also typed into a small computer a new set of numbers and then pressed the Enter key. Within the next five minutes, the smart paint on the tail of the jet would change the N-number from displaying BH996 to showing JR45. "Next stop, Turkey."

###

In the back of the jet, Sam, Vincent, and Jay were making themselves merry. The operation had gone off smoothly enough. They had a short flight ahead of them until they were in Turkey, and Labeeb decided that there would be no better time than the present for updating his contact. "I need to hit the head for a minute," he told the others as he excused himself and locked himself in the jet's cramped lavatory.

He lowered the seat cover on the toilet and sat down. He typed as quickly as he could on his private satellite phone. The message was short, so that he wouldn't be gone too long and thereby raise any suspicions. He managed to get enough information into the short e-mail message to at least inform his benefactor of the results of their operation in Russia, and to detail the next leg of their journey.

Chapter 11

August 1

"They're all on board with it," Lydia said, referring to the owners of the small oil companies she visited. "And that little stunt we pulled on those police officers should help our story, also."

Grisha looked at his partner. "How can hitting a couple men help us?"

"The way I figure it," she began, "since I told all the drillers about the terrorist plot, a rumor about a foreign jet landing near the pipeline and taking out two police officers could only solidify our case in their minds."

Grisha nodded. "Tell me again, why we doing this, anyway?"

"You know as well as I do, Grisha, nobody actually considers this to be a real threat."

"But if we know, why don't we show them proof?" he asked.

Lydia had wondered the same thing many times over the last few months. From what she understood, GRIP had tried warning everybody, but the whole idea sounded a little far-fetched for them to believe. Governments only seem to recognize new threats after the initial problem is on their doorstep, and it's too late to prevent. Besides, not even GRIP was fully aware of which pipelines would be targeted. They only knew it would most likely be some of the more major lines. For this reason they had spent the last few months traveling around the world seeking out a few small drillers that contributed to the major lines. This stop in Russia was the last in a long six-month campaign of preparation. If they couldn't keep the plot from happening, at least they would be able to prevent it from turning into a major disaster.

Perhaps it shouldn't be GRIP's responsibility to get involved, but if not, then who would? Grisha knew this, so Lydia didn't bother to answer him. Instead she tried to divert the conversation. "So what airport did you say we're going to?"

Grisha pulled out an aviation chart and pointed out a small airplane symbol that was circled in pencil. "It's Erzincan Airport."

"I haven't been in Turkey for a while, are we going to have any problems with customs?" she asked.

Grisha put the coordinates into the GPS unit, then folded the chart back up. "I am not worried about it. My cousin runs most of that airport. It will be no problem."

"Is that cousin on your side or your wife's side of the family?" she asked, only then to realize her mistake.

Grisha stared coldly at her. "My side, of course."

"Sorry about that," she replied. She felt sheepish for taking that small sucker jab at her closest friend.

Funny how humor differs from country to country. A joke in one part of the world, is a strong insult somewhere else. She wanted to tell him that she'd been having a bad night as well, and was struggling with her own sordid past while she was waiting. Like an overstretched guitar string, her nerves were feeling dangerously thin. But she knew he wouldn't really care about her problems right now. It was his past that she'd just dug up.

But as if reading her mind, Grisha replied, "It's okay. We have both been through a lot. Our pasts haunt both of us."

After that, there was silence. Grisha pretended to focus on some navigation charts, and Lydia just stared out the cockpit window. She was always impressed with night flying. The stars were often so much clearer, and the lights of the towns and cities below almost made it look like she was sandwiched between stars on both sides. The silence, however, was not an awkward silence. It was more of a mutual understanding. Lydia didn't like to be reminded of her past just as Grisha didn't like to be reminded of his.

They had exchanged sob stories a few times before, and she knew that Grisha shared as much guilt, and maybe more, from his former life. He used to be a soldier in the Russian army. He had a wife and three children.

Five years before Lydia was recruited into the organization, Grisha had been invited to join. It was what he had always wanted. He had known about the secrets of GRIP's origins for many years. He himself could prove lineage back to the day when giants did roam the Earth. Then when Grisha accepted the privilege of joining GRIP, he became obsessed with it.

His family, however, didn't respect his decision. At first it was harmless enough and only took him away from them for about one week each month. But his wife threatened to expose his organization for what it really was. Whether she really would have, Grisha would never know. In a heated and drunken argument, he'd accidentally set fire to the apartment building where they lived. The smoke from the fire had taken the life of his children, and his wife killed herself the next day. He nearly killed himself out of grief. But then Troy came to him and offered him full-time service in a more action-oriented part of GRIP. To bury his pain, Grisha accepted, devoting his entire life to the cause.

After Lydia joined, she was given command of GRIP's only action group. They called themselves "troubleshooters." They consisted of herself, as team leader, Grisha as her second in command, Sam from England, and his three commandos, Jay, Vincent, and Labeeb.

Jay was from the U.S., a former Green Beret. Vincent was Italian, formerly with the COMSUBIN, or Comando Subacquei ed Incursori, which was their version of the Special Forces. Labeeb, the youngest of their group, was a French-Indian from the French Foreign Legion. Each of them except Sam and Lydia were considered tall, their vertical stature being a genetic remnant of their Martian ancestry. Though they were all under seven feet, only a shadow of their ancestors, who easily achieved a height of nine feet tall, they were still very proud of their pedigree.

Each member of her team brought something valuable to the table, and Lydia though less experienced, was no exception. Before she'd met Flint, she'd gained her own set of skills, though not through the same official channels as the others had. In high school, she joined a college outreach program that enabled her to get her pilot's certificate. By the time she was eighteen, she'd joined with a private military contractor, keeping pace with her male counterparts. Originally she wanted nothing more than to pilot airplanes, but the companies cross-training had proven her to be more than just a pilot and a pretty face. She knew the leadership qualities her employers saw were really just a manifestation of her own mask of insecurity. But the more she accepted their trust, the more she believed in her own façade. Since the private company had no restrictions on gender and combat, only on ability, Lydia found herself piloting and engaging in combat situations. Being one female in a world of males, she'd learned to shrug off the banter that her fellow men in arms so often engaged in.

When she'd met Flint, he was so different from the meatheads in her company. He never seemed intimidated by her military skills, and his conversation did not solely revolve around sex, food, and more sex. In Flint, Lydia found the prospect of a life that she had only dreamed of. While she was good at what she did, her heart yearned for a family. Even now, that dream was still nagging, but further away than ever. Lydia couldn't decide if her decision to run away from Flint was because of her suppressed insecurities, or if it was because of the emotional trauma that losing her son had caused. Now, more than ever, she regretted the decision. Loathing the day that Troy came back into her life, she longed for the chance to make it right again. If she was half the woman she portrayed herself to be, she would have stayed and worked through the pain with Flint.

Ever since Troy convinced GRIP to recruit Lydia, she'd been busy jumping from one country to the next, always on a grand treasure hunt to rediscover the lost mysteries surrounding the history of her Martian ancestors, who crashed on Earth thousands of years ago. It had been exciting, and at times dangerous. There often seemed to be a terrorist or other scavenger searching for the same things, sometimes with the intent to use them for the wrong purpose.

Lydia's biggest discouragement lately, aside from past mistakes, was from a man named Shen Mao. He'd been seeking artifacts for the last couple years and currently sought the one artifact that was most important to GRIP. It was a golden journal that would explain many mysteries about the Martian civilization, and could possibly contain a boon of technological significance. Shen was only interested in financial gain, and if he did find the book, its value to society might be lost forever. He had vast resources and so far had successfully thwarted each attempt by Lydia's group to stop him. It was an embarrassment for her, but she still kept up hope that he would make a mistake one of these days, and she would catch him. Now with most of the major world's pipelines secured, she could return to Egypt and refocus her efforts on finding those remnants of the early Martians.

The Russian mission having gone off without a hitch could not fully ease Lydia's mind over the current terrorist threat. Unable to fully remove the potential disaster from her radar, she let her mind contemplate the menace. Amos was relatively unknown, and she wondered how it was that GRIP had come to learn of him. What she did know was that he was an eco-terrorist. He wanted to significantly disturb the oil pipelines around the globe. If he succeeded, it would have major ramifications on the world's economies. Not only would oil prices skyrocket, but if he was able to hit enough pipelines, he could disable them for months.

Lydia tried to imagine all the products that were oil derived, and not simply fuels. There were plastics, metal refineries that needed to get their energy from somewhere, fertilizers for food, and the machinery to harvest it—practically everything used in today's world was made with or powered by fossil fuels. To significantly disturb a few major pipelines would cause the whole world to fall into economic and social depression.

This urgency had spurred much of the last several months' activities. Lydia felt some relief knowing that she had put in place a means to combat Amos when he decided to strike, even if the various countries around the world refused to accept the threat. Though she didn't agree with Amos's tactics, she did agree that it was silly to rely so much on the unrenewable resource. Now that it was back to a waiting game, she hoped she could spend more time looking for the particular artifact that had piqued her curiosity for some time now.

"So are we back to looking for moss for a while?" Grisha asked.

She jumped slightly, then looked at her partner. "Sorry, I was zoned out, but yeah, I think that sounds like a plan. Besides, if we find it, it may lead us to the original crash site, where we can find the golden record."

"Well, while you were zoned out," he continued, "we nearly arrived at our destination."

A quick glance at the GPS told Lydia how dazed she must have been to have traveled nearly the full length of their trip without noticing. "Thanks for keeping me on track; it's been a long day. I could really use a good night's sleep."

"No problem," Grisha replied. "Just make sure we are on the ground before you decide to doze off."

Lydia faked a laugh, then began preparing for landing. She clicked her mic, waited a moment to remember the new tail number of her jet, then announced, "Learjet juliett-romeo-four-five to Erzincan Airport, requesting landing, over."

A full thirty seconds passed before Lydia repeated her hail. "Grisha, can you check the frequency that we are supposed to be hailing on?"

"I've checked it twice," he responded. "Maybe they are sleeping."

She then called one last time, "Learjet charley-tango-four-five to Erzincan Airport, we are getting no response from you, visual looks clear, so we are coming in for a landing, over."

No response again. Lydia looked back at Grisha, who simply shrugged his shoulders. "All right," she said as she began her descent. She didn't like this at all, and something gnawed at her mind, but she dismissed it. Grisha was probably right. It was a small airport, and at this time of night, anyone monitoring the radios down there could very well have fallen asleep.

Chapter 12

"I don't know about you, but I sure hope they have a nice hotel near this airport," Vincent commented.

Sam looked at his Italian comrade, then back at Labeeb and Jay. Often he wondered how it was that their ragtag group worked so well, despite the varied cultures. While originally from England, Sam had spent most of his earlier years living in other parts of Europe. When combined with Lydia and Grisha, their little team brought many different perspectives and fighting styles to the table.

A breath away from responding to Vincent's comment, Sam held his tongue when Lydia came over the speaker. "We're beginning our descent into Turkey now. It may be nothing, but we're not getting any response from the airport on our radio."

"Right," Sam muttered under his breath. Her trepidation was understood clearly. Lydia didn't want to alarm anyone, but it was rare to not even get radio traffic from other airplanes, let alone from the airport itself. He pulled out his Glock, and chambered a round just in case. Vincent, Labeeb, and Jay followed his cue. They weren't gearing up for war, but they didn't want to be caught off guard, either.

With as long as Sam had been at this business, he didn't take anything for granted. If the radio silence was due to somebody falling asleep at the airport, then it might be reasonable to not hear anything from the ground. But to clear the radio traffic from all planes near the airport would take significantly more effort; even at this hour, there was usually some air traffic about. If somebody did go through that effort, then there really was something to be concerned about.

"I've got a bad feeling about this," Sam told the three men.

"Who could possibly know we are landing in Turkey?" Labeeb offered.

Jay responded, "It wouldn't be the first time one of our enemies caught us flat-footed."

"In any case," Sam continued, "I think it best that we are ready for anything."

The men understood. With their guns ready, they lifted their shirts to strap on some body armor. With these preparations in order, they again slipped into their shirts, hiding the Kevlar vests. Labeeb added a couple of razor sharp throwing rings to his meager arsenal, a kind of trademark weapon of the man. Nobody commented about them, he'd donned the things on almost every mission they'd undertaken, though Sam couldn't recall the man ever throwing any of them.

Nobody bothered buckling themselves into their seats as the jet made its landing. They were all familiar with Lydia's flying. If Grisha had been landing, they might have been a little more cautious, but Lydia was the best pilot Sam had ever known. The landing was smooth as usual, and it only took a few minutes to taxi off the runway.

Grisha then came out of the cockpit as the engines were winding down. "I go now to see if there is anybody to give us fuel. We will stay here one, maybe two, nights, then we go back to looking for Martian moss."

"Be careful," Sam cautioned.

"Hey, don't worry, my cousin, he runs this place. There is no problem," Grisha confirmed as he opened the door and stepped out.

Sam watched for a minute as Grisha walked to one of the main buildings. Small pockets of light from on the buildings created several eerie domes of yellow. The lights only served to ruin one's night vision, and to remind you of just how much couldn't be seen in the shadows. Satisfied that they weren't walking into an ambush, he motioned for his men to get out. They left their big guns inside, but kept their sidearms close and concealed. "Vincent and Jay, see if you can find a place to stay for the night. Labeeb, you are with me. I want to sweep this airport, if only to settle my nerves a little."

Jay slapped Vincent's butt in a playful gesture and said, "Come on, Vincenzo, let's find that hotel of yours. I'm okay with anything as long as the maids are cute enough." He laughed at his own imagination, and then bounded out the door. Sam glared at Jay, not for the things he said, but for the dimmed display of caution in the American's voice. Vincent followed behind Jay, turning only once to give Sam a serious look. Sam simply returned the look of caution with a slight nod. Vincent understood the need to keep an eye out for any trouble. Jay probably did too, but the man's attitude didn't seem to show it.

Lydia then poked her head out the curtain, and Sam put his hand up to stop her. She was his superior, but he wasn't afraid to suggest his own opinion. "I think you better stay with the jet. I doubt there'll be any trouble, but just in case we need to make a quick run for it, I'd rather have our best pilot at the ready."

"I'm glad you sensed my nerves about this place," Lydia replied. "Grisha seems to think there is no problem with it, but I'd rather trust my gut until my gut is proven wrong."

"I'll signal you when it's all clear," he affirmed, and then stepped out the door, his attention at full alert.

Once on the tarmac, Sam and Labeeb silently walked to the end of the airport complex. With tedious discipline, their eyes searched out and tried to penetrate each shadow. Though the tarmac was relatively small, there were several hangars and places where someone could be hiding. They had cleared the first hangar when a truck roared to life. They immediately drew their guns and dove to the edge of a building for cover.

Sam cringed as the tinkle of metal rings threatened to give their position away. Why did Labeeb have to carry those silly razors with him every time they went into a potentially hostile situation? *I'll have to have a talk with him later about that.*

"Look," Labeeb said, pointing at the truck.

Sam risked moving into the open to see what Labeeb was trying to point out. "It's only that bullheaded Russian," Sam sighed in relief. Grisha was standing on the running board under the door of the truck.

"He must have woken up the fuel trucker," Sam speculated as the tanker strained to drive over to the jet as quickly as it could without shifting out of first gear.

"If there will be trouble," Labeeb commented, his Indian accent thick as ever, "at least we will have fuel enough to make a run for it."

Sam put a finger to his ear, pushing the tiny button on a small earpiece. "Vincent, what's your status?"

The voice of his comrade came back through the earpiece with a lot of static interference. "I'm afraid we might want to plan on spending another night on the jet; this airport is mostly isolated. There doesn't seem to be any services for a few kilometers. There is a small residential district next to the airport, but aside from that, we're surrounded by farmland. There may be something in Erzincan proper, but we're walking there if we go, and with as quiet as things are, I doubt we could even get a room at this hour."

Thinking for a minute, Sam replied, "Come on back, I'm on the west side of the airport. I want you to start on the east side and make a sweep of the area. We'll meet in the middle."

"We're on it," Vincent replied.

Sam then concealed his pistol and motioned for Labeeb to do the same. The two stepped out from behind the buildings, careful not to make a sound. They resumed checking every window, door, and garbage can as they went. Even for a small airport, this place seemed too quiet. He began to wonder if he was just letting his nerves get to him when he heard the distinct sound of an aluminum soda can tipping over. This time the sound was too close to be caused by anyone on his team.

Chapter 13

Lydia was growing impatient. There wasn't much she hated more than sitting around, waiting to see if something would happen. Grisha had returned with a fuel truck, and they would be finished shortly. She heard the chatter over her earpiece that suggested they weren't likely to find any lodging nearby. If Grisha wasn't so insistent about this place, she would simply continue on to Egypt.

Sighing, she decided to venture outside to catch a breath of fresh air. Grisha was standing on the wing right next to where it connected to the fuselage, talking to the man fueling them up. With nothing else to do but wait, Lydia decided to do a quick inspection of her jet. She wasn't too concerned about the jet itself, just needing to get out and stretch, to be moving, or doing something. As her attention was focused on looking over the skin of the plane, an alarming sound pierced the night sky that couldn't have emanated from anything but another plane landing at the desolate airport.

Lydia spun around. It wasn't the squeal of the tires that concerned her; it was that she hadn't heard any sound, period, from the approaching plane until that very moment. It had come in with all engines off, and now she could see that it had no lights on, either. Before she even keyed her ear bud radio, she heard the report of gunshots down the field where Sam and Labeeb were. It was a trap.

"Everyone back to the jet, we're under attack!" She ran back to the door. "Grisha, how much longer till we're fueled up?"

Grisha shouted back, "I need five more minutes!"

Ducking inside, Lydia planted her butt firmly in the pilot seat, hands moving with practiced ease as she cycled the engines up. As soon as everyone was aboard, they could take off. She then ran to the back of the cabin and took the assault rifle that Sam had loaded before he left. An airfield was the last place Lydia had ever wanted to stage a battle. There was too much at risk. Your enemy could take cover, and shoot you down as you made your run for the aircraft. Then if they had a grenade launcher, which was possible, they could damage the jet to the point where it would be useless. Lydia ran back outside, grabbing a pair of night-vision goggles on her way. With her naked eye, she could now see multiple flashes and hear the reports of numerous guns. On one side where Sam and his crews had been sweeping, there were multiple bogies, and on the other side, where the runway was, a plane was likely unloading more hostiles.

Believing that Sam and his men could handle themselves, she focused her attention on the plane that had just landed. Kneeling down next to the jet she pulled on her night goggles. The runway lit up in green and black. The plane that had landed was a twin-propeller passenger plane. Six men jumped out, all carrying rifles. She was clearly pinned on both sides; it would take a miracle to escape this one. They had planned it too well. Just then she heard the fuel truck driver talking to Grisha. He was obviously distracted, and he hadn't noticed that Lydia was back out on the tarmac. Grisha tried to calm the man, explaining that it was only a little gunfire.

"Gunfire?" the man exclaimed more than asked, now sounding scared.

"Don't worry, we'll keep an eye on you. You'll be fine," Grisha replied. "I'm sorry we brought you into this, we didn't know it would happen."

"No, I'm sorry," the man countered, his tone changing. "A gift from Amos."

Lydia turned around just in time to see the man pull out a pistol and aim it at Grisha. Lydia knew she didn't have time to take aim at the man, especially with the cumbersome goggles on. Instead she fired a harmless shot into the air. The booming report of the rifle so near caused the man to jump in shock. This second of distraction was all Grisha required to lunge for the man, causing both of them to dive off the wing of the plane together. Lydia turned back around, knowing that Grisha would gain the upper hand now. This was made especially clear as she heard the rubbery crunch of the fuel trucker's bones within his flesh. The driver's smaller body had been used to soften to landing of the six-foot-eight, 260-pound Russian. The man's gun slid away with little protest from its owner, and Grisha delivered three unforgiving blows to the man's head.

Lydia didn't have to look back to know the man was dead; besides, she had already found a more productive way to spend her energies. She yanked the fuel truck's hose from the wing of the plane, where it was still pumping. She then jumped inside the truck and, using her gun to wedge between the gas pedal and the seat, pointed the truck in the direction of the intruder's airplane. Once the truck was moving, she jumped out and ran back to her jet. It would only take about thirty seconds for the truck to reach the enemy plane. Reaching down she grabbed the pistol that Grisha's opponent had dropped. When she looked back at the truck, she could see that the wheels had shifted, and it was going to miss the newcomer's airplane. It was now on course to run right between the plane and the men who had jumped off it.

It would have been preferable if the truck had stayed its course, but it wasn't necessary for her plan. Since the attached hose was still turned on, it was creating a nice trail of fuel. Lydia bounced a few shots off the asphalt near the spilled fuel. Three shots were all it took before the sparks ignited the spilled fuel. A trail of fire leaped up and started toward the truck. She was pleased until she noticed that a trail of fire was also heading back toward her jet. Lydia looked down and realized her mistake. In her haste she had forgotten to account for the fact that the hose had also spilled fuel around her aircraft. With the composite nature of her jet, the fire would significantly weaken the hull of the entire airplane.

She yelled, "Grisha!"

Grisha, who was already at the door of the jet, turned and saw the flames approaching. He ran into the cockpit and, before even sitting down, jammed the throttles forward. Lydia jumped onto the wing then quickly tore off her jacket and began to wipe the spilled fuel from the top of the wing. The engines were whining loudly when she slid off, and though they were at full power, the sleek craft seemed to not be moving at all. After what seemed to be a full minute, though it was only seconds, the engines began to push the jet forward, its momentum picking up as it started to move. The flames reached the airplane, but were far enough away from the wings that they didn't jump up and ignite the fuel that had sloshed over the open tanks. They did lick the side of the fuselage, and then the tail as it lumbered away, but only for a short moment. Once the jet was about twenty feet away, Grisha pulled the throttle back, and stepped on the brakes.

With the plane reasonably safe for a moment, Lydia turned around to see if her plan had worked, the bottom of her shoes ignorantly kicking a metal anchor in the asphalt as she did so. The throbbing of her stubbed toe was immediately forgotten as she watched the flames reach the truck, but it failed to explode as she had hoped for. It simply continued between the other airplane and the killers. Her only consolation was that it had ignited the dry brush that covered the dirt between the tarmac and the runway. If her opposition wanted to get to her, they would have to go around via the paved taxiway that connected the two. It was an accidental bonus, as they would lose their advantage having to come through on the narrow lane.

Unfortunately Lydia's jet was still directly in the middle of them and the other fighters tucked behind the airport's buildings. She touched the button on her earpiece, then turned it a quarter of a turn to enable unhampered communications. "Sam, what's your situation?"

Sam's voice came back, "We were pinned, but found our way around. Are Vincent and Jay back yet?"

"Negative," Lydia replied, then added "Vincent, Jay, where are you?"

But she didn't have to hear them answer as she saw two figures running toward the plane. Instead she barked another order. "Grisha, Vince and Jay are inbound—cover them."

Lydia ran to the door of the jet to find Grisha mounting a mini-gun styled turret to the side where the door would normally latch. He tossed Lydia another rifle, and she ducked back under the plane and took a position to cover their other side. She found her first target and fired, just missing because she jumped as Grisha started to pepper the buildings behind Vincent and Jay with the small turret gun. Her second shot found its target, but the man got back up again. She realized that the men coming from the runway were wearing some military-grade body armor, as her bullets would have penetrated a regular Kevlar vest.

She fired a few more rounds before Jay and Vincent came to relieve her. "I'll take care of this, you should get us ready to fly," Jay suggested. Lydia conceded and ran to the door, being careful to avoid Grisha and his blazing weapon. She then asked, "Sam, we need to take off, where are you?"

"We're skirting around a parking lot at this second," he replied. "I don't know that we can make it back."

"Are there any cars in the lot?" she asked.

"Yeah, there's a few," Sam said, then added, "Wait, don't tell me, I think I can guess."

"The runway is blocked," she said. "Meet me on the south end of the tarmac, it's our only chance."

"I think I know what you're up to," Sam concluded, "and for the record I think you're nuts."

Chapter 14

Amos had listened as Lydia sent her repeated hail to anyone at or near the airport, but ignored her. Unquestionably he was well aware of her team and their capabilities. Though caution was warranted, GRIP's team of *troubleshooters* had been predictable thus far, and this predictability was why his group needed to involve themselves again. If Lydia's team were to be taken out, with the information that they had on him, governments everywhere would likely clue in to his plans. That was the last thing Amos wanted to risk at this stage of his project. His plan would go off well enough as long as he could keep tabs on Lydia. Whether she suspected anything or not, Amos had big plans for her. After all, the enemy you knew was the enemy you could control.

This wasn't the first time he'd had to intervene to save Lydia's crew. Along the way she'd made other enemies than himself. On a previous engagement, he ran into one of these groups while trying to divert Lydia. She wanted to stop him, and he wanted to use her ambition and predictable nature to his advantage. These other men had no respect for the game. They were cold-blooded assassins, hired by a man named Shen Mao, and they meant to destroy Lydia, because she'd already proven to be a thorn in whatever plans Mao might be cooking up.

I am no assassin, thought Amos. *People get hurt all the time in the name of progress, but I would never hurt anybody out of greed.* Though Lydia was a thorn, she made the whole movement fun. Someday, after the world realized the futility of surviving on oil and made the inevitable change to renewable energy, he looked forward to walking up to her and shaking her hand in friendship. He knew of her other objectives, one of which was to discover the plant that would change the face of renewable energy forever. Whether she knew it yet or not, they were in fact kindred spirits. Both were trying to save the environment, only he knew that she lacked the vision or courage to do what was necessary to show the world how badly they needed the change.

"This is Amos," he said into a handheld radio. "GRIP is on the ground, and on the move. Stick to the plan."

Amos shifted in the passenger seat of the small Cessna. It wasn't his, but somebody had left it tied up in an advantageous location. From inside the borrowed airplane, he could see the whole airfield, and direct his men without fear of being discovered.

He was happy to see his newest recruit had pulled off his part well. The Russian named Grisha had woken up the recruit, who pretended to be asleep, and now they were on their way to refuel Lydia's jet. In a way, Amos felt bad for the new guy. He was a good man, who showed some real promise. But it was always hard to send a closer friend unknowingly into a suicide position. The whole trip over, Amos had avoided getting to know the young man any better. Just like his dad once told him when they raised chickens together—never name any of the chickens. Once you named them, it became much more difficult at butchering time. Amos enjoyed the similarity of the two situations. Very different, yet the advice was applicable to both.

The tanker had just begun to fuel up when Amos saw the little dot flash on his tablet computer. When he took the airport two hours earlier, he'd patched into the airport's radar system. The new aircraft was coming in silent. It could only mean one thing. "Look alive, team—Mao's men are inbound."

He pulled up a pair of night-vision goggles and surveyed the four men that Lydia had checking the airfield. She was smart to have guessed something was wrong. The first shot came unexpectedly from the other side of the airport. Someone had made a mistake, and gotten discovered. "Just what I need, surprises," Amos grumbled. Within a minute, gunfire had erupted back and forth between Lydia's men and his own. His men were good, but they weren't professionals, not like Lydia's. It was time to speed things up. He keyed his radio. "Fuel tanker—*now*," he ordered.

He then watched as his man on the airplane attempted to take Grisha out. As expected, Grisha was too quick for him. It only lasted a few seconds, and his man was down. He'd served his purpose, though, as Lydia's team was now entirely in combat mode. Keying his radio again, he announced, "The game is on. Stay back just enough to keep them from getting you. Keep gunfire going, but remember, they are much better trained than you are. After all, we don't want to kill all of them." What he really needed was for the gunfire to mask his own.

As soon as he finished giving his order, he put some earplugs in. He didn't like them, but they would keep him from going deaf in the confined space of his cockpit. His position gave him full view of all the points of battle, but it also could easily expose him if he were to step outside the plane. Thus he decided to stay inside and shoot through the windows. His weapon of choice was a Ruger 270 Winchester with a scope and a large flash guard on the end of the barrel. Not a fancy sniper rifle, but it would be effective for this situation.

Ignoring both Lydia's jet and the battle his men were fighting, he instead focused his attention on the men hired by Shen Mao. Struggling to find a comfortable position in the cramped four-man airplane, he took off his night goggles and aimed carefully through the scope. Originally he feared that darkness would make his job more difficult, but silently he applauded Lydia for her quick thinking. He watched as the strip of land between himself and the runway caught fire. Even through all the smoke, the area was significantly illuminated. Also, it forced Mao's men to approach from the taxi lane. "Easy pickin's," Amos said to himself.

Chapter 15

As if in a dream, and she was tired enough that it could be a dream, events just seemed to roll forward. Her motions all felt mechanical, and her emotions were somewhat dull and unattached. Lydia could still hear gunfire as she throttled the engine up and rolled toward the end of the tarmac. Grisha took a moment away from his mini-gun to grab more ammunition. Inside the jet she felt safe. The truth was just the opposite and she knew it, but for some reason, she felt comfortable, like a child hiding under a blanket.

When she reached the end of the tarmac, Lydia cut the power to one engine, and throttled up on the other. Combined with some left wheel brakes, she was able to pivot the jet 180 degrees. She didn't have to wait long to see a small car, maybe thirty years old, come crashing through the parking lot fence. The little car half carried the chain-link fence with it, or rather the chain-link fence nearly carried the car back with it. With only one headlight, a broken windshield, and some luck, the sedan cleared the barrier and came barreling straight for the jet. Behind it, she could see flashes from the pursuing gunfire.

"Grisha, give them some help," she called out impatiently.

Grisha mumbled something, but she couldn't hear. She jumped slightly as his turret mini-gun roared back to life, raining empty shell casings in a rainbow of brass both inside and out of the jet's doorway. Sitting apprehensively, Lydia watched as the beater car came nearer. Then she snapped back to reality, remembering the fuel cap. "Grisha!"

The man kept firing, and she yelled out again. *"Grisha!"*

He paused. "What now? First you say shoot, then you say stop."

"Did you by chance put the fuel cap back on?"

"No, I thought you did," he replied.

Jay chimed in, "It's pretty hot out there, do you need them on to take off?"

"That or we lose half our fuel during takeoff," she replied.

She stood up to walk back, but Jay raised his hand. "We need you to get us out of here, I'll go up and take care of it."

Fearlessly, or so it seemed, the only American on the team besides Lydia jumped out of the jet and climbed onto the wing, where the fuel cap would be. She could see that Sam and Labeeb were almost there. They were drawing a considerable amount of fire from the enemy, but Grisha made sure that the pursuing gunfire couldn't aim too long or carefully at the two men. She was also surprised by how little fire they were taking in the jet. Occasionally she would hear the thump of a bullet hitting the fuselage, and each time a round pierced the jet, she worried. Oddly enough, the enemy didn't seem to be as concerned about the jet as they were about the people outside of it. She hoped that her team didn't have any surprises waiting for them.

As soon as Sam pulled alongside the jet, Lydia began to throttle up the engines. Grisha emptied his gun one last time, then started unclamping it from the doorframe. Lydia didn't release the brakes as the engines throttled up. Since she couldn't get to the runway, she would have to take off from the tarmac. It would be difficult since the tarmac was considerably shorter than the runway, and she would have to avoid hitting some of the other planes that were tied down on it.

Before long the jet started shaking and sliding forward. The brakes were struggling against the powerful engines. "What's taking Jay so long?" Lydia called out.

Sam ran to the door and poked his head out. "He's not on the wing." As he said this, Sam must have heard Jay's footsteps above the fuselage. Why Jay had climbed onto the top of the jet instead of jumping to the ground, Lydia couldn't even guess. But Jay never really did what was expected of him. Maybe that was why he was good at staying alive. Any snipers out there might have their guns trained to the ground in anticipation, though Lydia thought that Jay's silhouette on top of the jet might make him stand out even more. Within seconds, Jay hollered down, and though Lydia couldn't hear him over the whining of the engines, she could see from the cockpit that Sam was stepping back. She twisted around to watch just as Jay came swinging down from above. His feet barely landed inside the airplane and he struggled for a few seconds to keep from falling backward out of the plane. As soon as he finished windmilling his arms, he smiled. "What are we waiting for? Let's get out of here."

"Close that door!" Lydia barked, as she began to turn back around. But before she did, she saw Jay out of the corner of her eye, suddenly propelled onto the other side of the plane. Lydia knew he had been shot, but instead of going back to check on him, she released her hold on the brakes and let the engines push the jet forward. She knew that Sam or Grisha was by the door and would get it closed soon. Her only focus now was to get them in the air. She would have to worry about Jay later.

Once they were rolling, she could see men coming out from around the buildings, some shooting. Only a few rounds actually thumped into the jet, but of graver consequence were the three men at the end of the taxiway. They were clearly from the airplane that had recently landed, and one of them was kneeling down, lifting a large tubular object up onto his shoulder.

Lydia recognized the rocket launcher, but had no options. With no place to turn, and knowing that to stop would spell imminent destruction, all she could do was keep rolling and hope for a miracle. She tried to call out a warning to her men, but wasn't sure if the words actually escaped her lips.

Chapter 16

Paul Crandall ran his hand along the aluminum railing as he descended from the pilothouse. He had gone up to check his schedule for the next month. It wasn't because he didn't already know it; he was simply trying to find a way to pass the time. He'd gotten precious little sleep, and even now, the morning was too young for the sun to be showing. But how could he sleep. The cleaners were making such a ruckus. They'd shown up last night, intending to work throughout the night. They apparently had a busy schedule, with several other tankers behind his, and all on tighter schedules.

As with all oil tankers, the holds of Crandall's ship needed to be cleaned from time to time. First the crew would run a solution through them that was partially mixed with oil, and then they would spray the holds down. The last part was called mucking. It required men to don protective suits and hand scrub the insides of the tanks. Many people didn't realize how waxy crude oil could be. Thus the tanker crews made sure the waxy residue and caked-on asphaltic remnants of the cargo were eliminated.

None of the crew was required to stay on board while these cleanings took place. They simply hired an outside contractor to complete the process. Only Paul was required to remain, as it was his job as Captain of the ship to inspect the whole procedure. In the end, if anything was done incorrectly or not up to standard, he would ultimately be responsible. Having gone through this many times, he walked over to a storage closet and pulled out a safety suit. It was little more than a plastic rain suit with a respirator, but it would be sufficient for his needs.

Kendal, the foreman of the cleaning company, met him at the first tank. "We're ready for your inspection in the first couple tanks, but the last two still need a few more minutes."

"That's all right, I can't sleep anyways. I might as well start now with these. Maybe when I'm done, you'll be close to ready," he replied.

The foreman pulled on a respirator and followed Paul into the first hold. This cleaning company had been in business for several years, but had been recently bought out by an American enterprise. This was the first cleaning they had done for Paul since the buyout. But from what Paul could tell, moving his flashlight methodically back and forth, the quality of the clean was still as good as ever.

On the way out, he ran his glove across one rougher spot that had been missed. Kendal called out, and within seconds a man was racing down to clean the asphalt deposit. The second hold was similar, though he didn't find any spots that had been missed. But since he had little to do outside, and the next tank wouldn't be finished for a few minutes, he stayed in the hold that he was inspecting.

Walking around, Kendal noticed that Paul was taking longer than before. "Well, does it look satisfactory?" the foreman asked impatiently.

Paul tried to reassure him. "Oh, it looks great." He guessed the foreman believed him to be the type that just needed to find something wrong. Paul wasn't overly picky; he was just bored. So instead he tried to calm the nervous foreman by striking up a more casual conversation. "Your accent seems more American than Arab," he said to the man. "I'm guessing that you didn't grow up around here?"

Kendal tried to smile off his unease. "You are right, I was raised in Eugene, Oregon."

Paul let out a prodding laugh. "So how does a man from the state of tree-hugging hippies come to working on oil tankers in the Middle East?" His goal had been to help the man relax, but he realized that he'd only made Kendal more nervous—as if he had either offended him or the man was hiding something. In either case, he couldn't make sense of the foreman's temperament. Most people wouldn't be offended by his comment, especially if they were in the oil industry. They may not like it, but they should at least be used to the attitude. On the other hand, what could Kendal possibly be hiding? The holding tank had passed inspection, even if Paul was still down in it.

Maybe his best option was to leave, if for no other reason than it might calm the man's nerves just a little. "All right, I'm done here. Why don't you lead the way out?"

"I'm glad, I really do try to do the best on all tankers," Kendal claimed.

Paul just went along with it, especially since the

man was starting to relax. "I think you guys do a great job. Even that small patch you missed in the first tank was so minor, it could have been ignored."

He then waited as the foreman started climbing the ladder. Taking one last look around, he noticed something that seemed out of place on the ceiling to the side of the ladder. It was at arm's length, and looked just like the rest of the ceiling, but something about it seemed a little odd. He decided that it must be nothing, and followed the foreman out.

The bright yellow work lights outside the holds caused him to squint. Pulling off his respirator and setting it down by the opening he'd just emerged from, he asked Kendal, "So how about those other tanks, are they finished yet?" He could see some men coming out of the closest one.

"Let me check on them, I'll be back in a minute." Kendal handed the Captain a Diet Coke.

"Thanks," Paul said. "You read my mind." Though really he didn't care for the drink, he understood that the man wanted him to step aside for a few minutes while he finished his job. Paul complied and walked back toward the pilothouse. Besides, the caffeine might help take away the sluggish drag in his step. He had almost passed the first tank he inspected when he remembered the spot in the second that looked slightly peculiar.

Briefly peering over his shoulder, Paul could see the foreman was already climbing down into the third tank. Curiosity took over; Paul had to know if this first tank had a similar peculiarity on its ceiling. He reached up to pull his respirator down, only to realize that he'd left it back at the second tank. It wasn't a big concern, since in the cleaning process they were required to ensure that all gases were purged, anyway. The masks were more of a safety precaution than a necessity.

Climbing down the ladder, Paul paused so that his head was only a foot below the ceiling. Looking up, he scanned the ceiling where the other spot had been. At first he saw nothing, but then as he was climbing back out, his eye caught a hardly perceptible edge of a metal plate that was slightly uneven with the ceiling. The last thing he needed was for the welds to start popping off on his tank. So he stretched his arm out, just barely able to reach it, and ran his finger across the edge. As he did so, he tried to push against it. To his surprise Paul found that a full square foot of the ceiling shifted. Only now did he realize that this wasn't an ordinary flaw in the tank. Something had been placed on the ceiling, meant to blend in with the rest of the tank. The darkness of the tank had hidden this scab, but now that Paul knew it was there, he needed to understand what it was.

Reaching under his protective suit, he fumbled with his hands until he found his pocketknife. It was a simple knife, often used for whittling when they were on a voyage. Now he flipped the single blade out and pried at the plate. The fake metal tile slid a little until the knife slipped between it and the ceiling. When Paul pulled downward, the object swung down like a trap door, then hinged for a second in protest before falling to the floor with a loud clank, as if he'd just dropped a frying pan on a metal floor.

With less caution than usual, Paul quickly descended the ladder, jumping three rungs before he reached the bottom. He wouldn't have lost much time if he'd just climbed all the way down, and his sore feet told his as much while he bent over and grabbed the object. Even with his flashlight, darkness still seemed to encroach around him in the hold, but when he looked up, he could see clearly enough to understand that the spot where the object fell from looked undamaged. With the fallen tile cradled in front of his chest, he climbed back out into the sunlight. Once out, he took the tile to the mess room and set it on one of the dining tables. Examination showed that the outside was meant to look exactly like the metal container it was attached to; only it had a slight bulge in it. On the backside, he could see that it was lined with several magnets, which had been used to secure it to the ceiling. The center had a small bit of wiring tied to a battery and a small pouch containing a white powder.

The first thought that found hold in Paul's mind, was that it was some form of bomb, though he had never heard of any explosive that was so small. If it was a bomb, he wondered if it was meant to ignite the cargo when fully loaded with oil. Whatever the case might be, it was not supposed to be there. His guess was that it had been put there by the men cleaning, which would explain the foreman's nervous attitude. This was what he'd been hiding.

Paul walked over to the door and looked outside. Kendal, if that really was the foreman's name, was making his way to the mess room. Paul couldn't let the man know he'd found the device so decided to play along for now. *After they leave, I'll recheck the tanks again, and turn the devices over to the authorities.*

Summoning his composure to walk out and meet the foreman or to radio for help, Paul noticed Kendal stop by the first tank. "What are you doing?" he whispered to himself. Then he saw the reason for the pause. The foreman was looking at a small dark outline, the can of Diet Coke, sitting next to the hatch that led down into the tank. Paul scolded himself for his own stupidity. Kendal looked around, and then climbed down into the hold. Paul knew he'd been found out. He raced through his mind, searching for any options that didn't end badly. Being alone on a ship full of hostiles left few good choices.

Paul's ship was currently moored just a little bit away from the main pier. Despite their proximity, there was no gangplank leading directly onto the docks. Besides, the portion of the ship that was closest to the docks was also the portion most heavily patrolled by these men. The lifeboats were out of the question, also; they would take too long to lower. He could, and probably should, run up to the pilothouse and radio in a distress call. He wondered if they could be jamming it, but decided that would be unlikely. He also knew that they would most likely check there first. Again Paul wished that his whole crew wasn't on shore leave. He did have a gun safe in his quarters, but it was only a pistol, and if these men were really terrorists, then they would likely be prepared for such an incident.

With no option seeming good, he poked his head through the doorway again, hoping against all odds that they hadn't noticed the device was missing. But when the foreman practically jumped out of the hold and started shouting at his men, he knew the game was up. Looking down the ship, he could see the cleaning crew racing to their supplies. The first man to start back toward the foreman was carrying an assault rifle.

Knowing there was precious little time to spare, Paul abandoned his other ideas and ran back to the galley table. Without thinking he grabbed the small packet that contained the white powder, and snapped it away from the tile. He stuck it in his shirt pocket and latched the button. The thought occurred to him as he charged through the kitchen that the thing could have detonated and killed him when he pulled it off of the device. He forced the thought away, and tried desperately to plot his escape. Just as he expected, he could hear feet pounding up the metal stairs leading to the pilothouse. Calling for help would not be an option.

Paul skirted around a bolted down table that stood between him and a side door to the galley. Once through the door, the narrow shadow covered walkway split in perpendicular directions. To his left, was the main deck. To the right was the staircase leading to the pilot house. Neither route was a viable option. As he looked directly in front of him at the guard rail, which skirted the edge of the ship, he hesitated, reconsidering. He knew that within minutes the whole cleaning crew would be crawling all over, and would eventually find him. If he didn't want to die, there was really only one option left that he could think of. He doubted whether it would work or not, but he knew that if he didn't try, then these men would surely gun him down anyways.

Chapter 17

Lydia could not believe her luck. She was sure that the man with the rocket launcher was going to end their escape. He was steadying himself and had taken aim when a stray bullet from his companions behind the jet threw him backward. The rocket fired harmlessly into the air.

Peeling her eyes from the battle field for a moment, Lydia checked her speed. Since she was being forced to take off on the tarmac instead of the runway, she knew that she would likely run out of paved area before the jet was ready climb away from the Earth. Her airspeed was just shy of where she felt comfortable, but she was out of options and risked pulling back on the yoke anyway. The nose lifted, and the back tires dragged along the dirt at the end of the tarmac before lifting off the ground. She immediately began to retract the wheels—and not a moment too soon. Had the wheels been any lower when they scraped across the fence surrounding the airport, the metal chain links would almost certainly have netted their flight, slamming them hard into the ground.

Exhaling a sigh of relief, she knew she wasn't safe yet. The small jet strained higher and higher as it pulled itself to altitude, and made a slow turn to the south. Looking down at the airport, she could see the enemy plane begin to move. They clearly intended to follow her, and she wondered if they actually might be able to keep up with and even attack her in the air. She made a quick decision, and hoped that the Turkish military didn't wise up to their situation for a little while longer. She straightened the jet out and tried to put some distance between her and the airport. The timing would have to be just right.

As soon as she felt that she had enough distance and altitude, she made a sharp turn back toward the airport. Grisha then joined her in the copilot's seat. "He's dead," Grisha said softly, but with clear disdain.

Lydia felt a knot form in her throat. Jay was usually pretty fun, though sometimes crude in his humor. But she still liked the guy. The announcement of his death made her next move all the easier. "They're going to pay for it," she said coldly. Then, reaching under her seat, she flipped a hidden switch. Instantly the display on the GPS switched from showing her position and heading to displaying a video of everything directly in front of the aircraft. It had one vertical line bisecting the image, with three more lines at a horizontal position.

She also detected the soft humming that usually signified the landing gear opening. Only instead of a set of tires, a 50mm cannon was being lowered from just under the nose of the aircraft.

The enemy was already halfway down the runway when she lined them up in her sights. She was diving toward them on a forty-five-degree angle. As her airspeed increased for the attack run, she could see the nose of their twin-engine airplane start to lift off the ground. "For Jay," she said as she pushed the triggering button. The gun shook the whole jet each time it fired. At two shots per second, it wasn't as fast as most machine guns, but still effective.

At first she used the targeting device that had once been her GPS. But with every five bullets being a tracer, easily visible in the night sky, she began to rely on the glowing trail that they produced instead. There was little guesswork left. The tracers showed that Lydia was cutting a line directly down the middle of the runway. The enemy plane was just pulling off the ground and wouldn't have the maneuverability to dodge the onslaught, even if they knew what was about to happen. The first couple shots that tore into the front of the enemy's plane seemed to do little to stop it, but after the next dozen bullets ripped through the remainder of it, the plane began to shear apart. First the right wing flew up, tearing violently from the fuselage. Then the plane fell sideways to the Earth. It was only a few feet off of the ground when it started, but Lydia could see it crumple like a tin can. Then, despite having smashed its skin in on itself, a sure enough death for any passenger, the former flying machine proceeded to cartwheel past the runway, shedding parts all along the way.

Lydia pulled back hard on the yoke just as the wreckage was settling, her own jet buzzing over the top at only fifty feet above the wreckage. She was content with the knowledge that anybody on board the plane was likely dead, or at the very least unconscious. If they did manage to stay alive during the acrobatic crash, their fuel would soon ignite, finishing them off for good. This realization did nothing to calm her over losing Jay. Revenge was never a sweet undertaking. Still, her mind was content with the escape and deadly deed as she returned to altitude. Once a course was laid in for Egypt, Lydia engaged the autopilot. Though she knew it was coming, and that it wasn't rational, she prepared herself for the guilt that her conscience was about to pile on for the loss of her friend.

The gun was now retracted, and the GPS screen returned to normal. Lydia reached to unbuckle herself from the seat, only to realize that with all the excitement, she'd neglected to fasten herself in. She shrugged the thought off. *If we had crashed, we'd all likely be dead anyway.* Then she stood up, not only because she wanted to check and see how everyone was, but also for fear of the adrenaline wearing away, causing her to daze off again. After a quick adjustment to the autopilot, Lydia started towards the back to join her friends in mourning.

Grisha grabbed her arm just as she was about to leave the cockpit. "Wait," he said. "You may want to take look at that."

Lydia looked on, and noticed a red light flashing. It wasn't for any of her instruments, though. The jet had been fitted with a miniature rotating satellite dish in the cargo compartment, housed in a small box, it took up about one and a half square feet of space. When outside the box, it looked like a dish that many people had on their homes, only this one was connected to a small motor that turned and tilted the dish to align with any number of communication satellites that were orbiting Earth. It was one of the smallest of its kind, and allowed Lydia to have full access to the Internet while in flight.

Reluctantly, Lydia sat back down. Flipping a

switch next to the light caused the GPS screen to change again and display a note: "Message from command—Call ASAP."

Exchanging looks with each other, Lydia spoke more to herself than to Grisha. "They're not going to give us a break, I believe." She was concerned, wondering how the morale of her group would hold together. They had started getting tired hours ago. Now with the loss of Jay, they were about to receive new orders. She wondered how they would take it if they received a new urgent assignment. But if she dared to be honest with herself, she wondered if she could handle it herself. After all, the blame for Jay's death was beginning to sink in already. She should have remembered the fuel cap when she was on the wing. Though nobody else would accuse her, Lydia's inattention to that detail had cost the life of a man under her command. She had to be quicker, to analyze every detail if she was going to keep putting all their lives at risk under these circumstances. Her gut reeled with the dull pain of disappointment; another death to pile on the hill of guilt.

She didn't realize that she had been blankly staring at the message until Grisha asked, "You want we ignore it for now? Say we had no chance to see it until later?"

"No," Lydia replied. "We'll answer. They know we'll have noticed it by now." She leaned over and pressed her finger on the screen that displayed the message. Immediately a phone symbol started flashing across it. Then the low-resolution video of a woman who could only be Persephone appeared. The pixelated picture was too low-quality to see any real detail, and the image died completely when the computer decided the bandwidth was too low. Instead it chose to focus more on the voice portion of the call.

"Lydia, how was your trip to Russia?" the woman asked.

"Russia was easy, but Turkey was not. We lost Jay." The words were hard to form, and she had to choke down the quiver in her voice.

"What were you doing in Turkey that could have brought this on? I thought this was a simple delivery to Russia and you'd be finished."

Lydia's boss was kind and tried to sound open, but the whole incident was still too fresh in her mind, and she almost felt like she was being accused. Defensively she replied, "Somebody knew where we were landing. They tried to ambush us at the airport."

Persephone calmly replied, "Do you know who was gunning for you?"

"No. I'm guessing it could have been either Amos and his men or Shen Mao's men. I'm leaning more toward Amos, because they were reckless. Mao tends to send professionals, but these men accidentally shot their own men in the crossfire. In fact, if they hadn't, we wouldn't have made it back into the air."

"It could have been either," the lady replied. "Amos is sure to be after you. I'm not sure how much he knows of your activities to stop him, but he does know that you're up to something. Mao, however, could be trying to stop you before you get to him, also. We think he is getting very close to finding the golden journal. Using the information that you sent me on your research, we've tracked down the actual Martian crash site. Mao's men had it camouflaged, which is why you missed it on your flight over. But it appears that his men have been working on an excavation project there for at least several weeks."

"Send me the coordinates, and as soon as we

take care of Jay, we'll head over there."

"I'm sorry, Lydia, but I'm afraid that you'll have to wait to bury your dead."

"Wait a minute," Lydia snapped. "We've been running ourselves ragged for the last several months trying to keep Amos from disrupting the world's pipelines, and at the end of all that we lose one of our men. Now you're telling me we can't afford an extra day or two to lay him to rest? We're all running on frayed nerves. My men need a couple days."

"Lydia," Persephone scolded. "I know that you are all very stressed right now, but we believe that if we fail to act within the next twenty-four hours, the golden record will be in Mao's hands. If he gets possession of it, then it will be lost to us forever. There are things in that record that are of extreme importance. I won't go into detail now, but I guarantee that you and your men will get a nice long vacation after you finish. Please, Lydia—it is very important."

Lydia looked over to Grisha, as if trying to understand his take on the situation. He caught her gaze and sighed. With his head bowed slightly, he gave a subtle nod. "Okay," she replied. "But my men are not going to like this. They sure as hell better receive that vacation time." In the wake of Jay's death, she hated to call it a vacation. Another pang of guilt.

"Thank you. I'll e-mail you the coordinates now. And Lydia—good luck."

The connection ended, and Lydia stood back up out of her seat and walked to the back of the jet. Jay had already been wrapped up in a body bag, one of the few items that she'd hoped never to unpack on the plane. "I have some more bad news," she declared in her most humble voice.

Sam looked up. "Lay it on us. We're in a bad-news kind of mood, anyway."

"We've been ordered to Egypt to collect the golden journal from Shen Mao's men. There won't be time to stop and take care of Jay's body until afterward."

Lydia could see the shock in Sam's face. While Jay was a member of her team, he reported directly to Sam in most cases. Sam would feel the loss more than anyone. Labeeb and Vincent held together pretty well, but she knew they were upset, also. She stood for a minute, waiting for any kind of response or protest, but none came. When she turned to make her way back to the cockpit, Sam asked, "What do we do with his body? Egyptian customs are bound to ask questions if they inspect our plane and find it."

She hated herself for her reply, but it was the only one that made sense. "Store him in one of the weapon lockers." No inspector had ever found the hidden compartments yet. Lydia could tell that Sam was about to argue against this uncomely deed, but he backed off. Maybe it was because he noticed the tears dripping off of Lydia's face, or maybe he just thought better of correcting his commanding officer, which would be a first. In either case she was glad to avoid any further conversation, as she retained little strength to keep from sobbing should she open her mouth again.

Sitting back down in the pilot's seat, she noticed that Grisha had already plotted the new course. "Try and sleep," he ordered her. "You've had long day. You need rest for tomorrow."

Lydia didn't argue. She doubted she would sleep at all, so she just reclined the seat and stared at the ceiling, reliving the day's events. It felt as though her parachuting down into Russia had happened a week ago. However, despite all her grief, within only a few minutes she was fast asleep.

Chapter 18

As he made his way over the rails, the sides of the ship blurred into a massive gripless wall. Paul shivered, even before splashing into the stinking dark water of the harbor. The water temperature was in the low seventies, but it wasn't the temperature of the water, nor the thought of it a moment ago that caused his body to quiver. He knew that any minute the men chasing him would wise up to the idea that he'd tried to swim for it. The Gulf of Suez was usually very busy, but not this early. Plus, the black water still reflected enough light that he dared not swim out in the open. His best bet was to swim under the docks and follow them to shore. If he could make it under them, he had a chance at escaping.

At first Paul slid alongside the tanker to avoid being detected, but the barnacles that formed below the waterline were now several feet higher with the tanker empty. It only took a gash on his arm and a tear in his pants for him to realize that he couldn't crawl along the side of the massive ship. Daring to only swim about two feet away from the side, he switched to doing a gentle sidestroke. He couldn't see the railing on the edge of the ship, but he wasn't so sure that someone couldn't just lean over and see him. As he plowed along, Paul reproved himself for not getting the barnacles scrubbed off earlier. If he got out of this, that would be the next project.

After a minute of swimming, he found himself near the first pillar of the docks. The large wooden poles were covered in tar, and he feared to reach out and grab them. They could very well have the same razor-sharp protrusions that covered the bottom of his ship. Instead he chose to break away from the side of his ship and swim between the pillars. He tried his best to ignore the oily foam and sludge that made its home under the docks, but every stroke seemed to cover his body in more of the harbor mucus.

About halfway through, his foot got caught on something, and he wanted to yell out in frustration. It took a few minutes to untangle his leg from a spool of fishing line that was hovering about a foot under the surface. Without wanting to grab the pillars for support, his head bobbed under the water more than once while trying to free himself. When he finally liberated his leg, his head was temporarily submerged again. Only this time, when he raised it out of the water, he accidentally did so with a large gulp. His body tried to convulse. He couldn't stop the coughing from taking over. At this point he forgot completely about the men on the ship, and could only focus on expelling the polluted seawater.

After swimming the rest of the way to shore, he found himself kneeling on the poorly lit embankment.

Still struggling with a sick feeling in his stomach from the harbor drink, he stood to walk until he was out from under the docks. Not only was his stomach nauseated, but his nerves were shot, and his arm was still bleeding. His whole body seemed to scream out in agonizing distress, so he allowed himself to pause for a moment with hands on knees to steady himself. After a minute of retching, he expelled the sea water from his stomach. Aside from the taste of bile in his throat and nose, he felt much better. Swiping his mouth with his wet shirt sleeve, Paul took in his surroundings. There was little chance of getting to the harbormaster, but Paul was somewhat sure he could hail the official on the radio.

Looking around, he spotted a small tug that was currently empty. The door to the cabin was open and he found his way to the radio. He set the frequency to the harbormaster's radio and called out, "This is Paul Crandall of the oil tanker *Juliana* calling harbormaster, do you copy?"

"This is harbormaster to *Juliana,* please switch to channel twenty-eight."

Paul obeyed. Many harbormasters had a call-in frequency, and then they diverted to another frequency upon hailing in order to keep the main channel open. "Harbormaster, this is Paul Crandall, do you read me?"

"Loud and clear, Paul, what can I do for you?"

"My ship, the *Juliana,* has been taken over by terrorists," he exclaimed. "I narrowly escaped, and I'm transmitting from another tug nearby. They are armed, and are attempting to sabotage my ship."

"Are you sure about this?" the harbormaster asked.

Paul replied, "As soon as they learned that I'd discovered them, they came after me with assault rifles. They are armed and very dangerous, I believe."

"Hang tight and tell me where you are, we'll come and get you," the harbormaster instructed.

"Fine by me," Paul replied. He told the harbormaster the slip number where the tug was tied up, then asked, "What are you going to do about the men on my ship?"

"We'll alert the Egyptian navy, they have a ship nearby."

Paul felt a sense of relief. He knew the Egyptians had the ninth-largest navy in the world, and they were undoubtedly larger than any navy in the region. They would be able to respond quickly and effectively to the intruders aboard his ship. He had done all that he could for now. All that was left was to wait.

Five minutes later, he strained to get a better look at his ship, but from his angle on the tug, he couldn't see onto the deck of his tanker. He thought that he should be able to see some kind of activity near the railings, though. But still, there were no signs of movement. He was just about to go back to the radio when he saw two men in uniform walking along the docks. They would have to be coming for him.

He walked out to meet them. Only when he reached them, he realized that they weren't wearing uniforms at all. Instead they were wearing matching button-up shirts and khaki pants. "Are you the harbormaster?" he called out as they met up.

"Paul, right?" one of them asked. The voice was similar to that of the harbormaster he'd talked to on the radio.

"That's right," Paul replied.

"Well, Paul, I'm sorry, but we are not really with the harbormaster."

Paul didn't understand at first, but then things suddenly became clear. Unfortunately he had no time to react, as his body immediately collapsed to the planking in agony. The Taser that they shot him with crippled his nervous system long enough for the two strangers to approach him and shove a needle into the side of his neck. The convulsing ended quickly, but whatever they injected him with made him weak and sleepy. Paul tried to move, but found his limbs unresponsive. He blinked once, and the world became a little fuzzy; at the second blink, everything went black. The third time he blinked, he found an almost blinding light directly above himself.

"He's coming around," a voice called out. Paul squinted painfully. He knew the man wasn't yelling, but his head ached, and he felt hungover. He closed his eyes for a moment, only to open them and realize that the blinding light was little more than the fluorescent lighting of a small office. He looked around and found his only companion was an Arab man in an old sweat-soaked button-up shirt. Paul tried to stand up, but quickly realized that his wrists were fastened to his chair with plastic zip ties. His legs being free allowed him to get halfway up before the weight of the chair pulled him down again. As the chair hit the floor, Paul fell sideways, smashing his face on the tile floor.

Paul was vaguely aware of the Arab man standing up, but the laughter didn't sound like it was coming from him. He craned his head around to see Kendal again, from the clean-up crew that had worked on his ship.

"You had me worried for a minute," the man said. "I know that you found our little device in the tank. If you tell me what you did with it, I might let you go.”

Since Kendal hadn't found the device, Paul guessed that they hadn't noticed the small package of powder in his shirt pocket. But he also doubted that the foreman would let him live. Closing his eyes, Paul tried to think of his options. At present, only one idea came to mind.

“Would you mind untying me?” Paul asked. “These damp clothes are getting pretty itchy.”

Kendal walked over and helped Paul back into a sitting position. “I'm sorry, but until I get what I need, your comfort is the least of my concerns.”

Paul was nervous. “I can show you, but it's hard to explain.”

Kendal got right in front of Paul's face and warned, “You had better try explaining, because you aren't going anywhere right now.”

“Sorry, but I don't believe you. If I just tell you, I'm a dead man.”

“You'll be a dead man if you don't,” Kendal hissed.

Paul took the gamble. He had to get out of this building. He might not be given a chance to escape if they took him back to the ship, but he would have a better chance than if he stayed here. “It'll be found, and when it is, all shipping traffic will be put on high alert. You won't find it without me, and I won't just tell you where it is.”

Kendal looked upset. He seemed to have a lot on the line. He leaned in, and Paul prepared himself for a verbal assault; however, he wasn't prepared for what really happened. Instead of the foreman shouting something threatening, he gave Paul a good strong push on the chest, which sent him and his chair falling backward. The chair seemed to teeter on its back two legs for a moment, then as if in slow motion the balance of his weight carried Paul down.

His head hit the floor with a loud smack, and he saw for the first time in his life what had been described as stars. It wasn't the stars that circle around your head like the cartoons. But his eyes went blank, and all he could see was bright glittering patches of light in the darkness. It only lasted a few seconds, but he was certain that he'd received a concussion at the very least.

Kendal asked him again to tell him where the device was. Though Paul felt he could talk, he simply let out a little moan. He had to play hurt, which, given the circumstances, wasn't difficult. Besides, it was his only defense at this point.

Having stormed out of the room, the annoyed Kendal paused on the opposite side of the glass wall. Paul could see him talking to someone through the window. The voices were muffled. Then a woman, clearly in a position of authority, and beautiful by any standard, leaned into view from the window. She looked down at Paul for a moment then returned to the foreman. Her voice was muffled also, but Paul could understand her last statement.

"Take him. When you've recovered the detonator, kill him."

Chapter 19

A bump of turbulence woke Lydia up. The morning was just starting to break and Grisha was beginning a descent. "Where are we?" she asked, still groggy. She tried to stretch her neck, which was slightly sore from sleeping in the pilot's seat.

"We are coming down over Mount Sinai right now," Grisha informed. "While you were sleeping, we received a report that there was a large explosion between here and Mount Catherine. They believe it is related to Shen Mao's operations. I've adjusted course slightly to give us a better look at the area."

"How far out are we?" she asked, as her eyes drifted over to check the GPS.

"Not far," he replied. "If you hadn't just woken up, I would wake you now."

Lydia had been in and out of Egypt enough times that she didn't need to consult her charts. Her airport of choice was the Sharm El Sheikh airport on the southernmost tip of the landmass between the Gulf of Suez and the Gulf of Aqaba. One check of her fuel gauges and she immediately knew that she would be tight on fuel. Luckily Grisha had adjusted their course early enough to allow the flyby and still make it to the airport before their tanks ran dry.

They leveled their descent just one thousand feet above ground level, and all eyes were staring out the windows looking for any sign of the earlier explosion, excavation, or anything that would betray Mao's operations. Sam was the first to point out the crater with the charred rock. It took Lydia a moment to find what he was pointing at, since there was little vegetation in the area to start with; the irregularity in the landscape was hard to notice. If it hadn't been for a couple of smoldering embers lighting the ground, she would have missed it completely.

"If they were here, they must have found what they were looking for, and moved on," she observed. However, she still made one circle around the valley before continuing on to the Sharm El Sheikh airport. She began to climb a little, but decided to level off at two thousand feet. "The good news is they weren't here very long ago. Any ideas where they might go?"

Grisha was the first to point out, "There is not enough flat ground for airplane to land on, and it would be difficult for a truck to get to this place. They either travel by camel or by helicopter."

"Chopper sounds more like Mao's style," Sam pitched in. "If our intel is good, then they didn't leave all that long ago, and we may still catch up to them."

"Yeah," Lydia agreed. "But we have no idea which direction they went."

Grisha pulled out an aviation chart of the area. "My guess is that Shen Mao is not here in person. He probably has Marshal working this job. But Marshal will likely go to Shen with the objects if he has found them. So the question is, where do we find Shen?"

"I think he's in the Philippines, but we don't know exactly where," Lydia replied.

"Good," Grisha continued. "Look here, most airports in range of helicopter are small and for tourists. My guess is they will go to Sharm El Sheikh. From there, they fly to Philippines."

Just then Sam, who had silently joined Lydia and Grisha in the cockpit, perked up. He pointed out the window at a small helicopter directly ahead. "What do you think the chances are of us finding ourselves on the same flight path as that chopper?"

Lydia squinted and saw the lighter aircraft. It was early morning, and she saw its lights before recognizing its shape. "I don't think this is a regular tourist route, and I doubt that any tourists would be headed away from the mountain this early in the morning, anyway. I'd say this has got to be our target."

The chopper was about a thousand feet below them when they passed over. "What is the plan?" Grisha asked.

"We're going to force them down," Lydia said coldly.

Grisha understood, and he flipped a small switch on his console. "Jamming their radio now," he reported.

"Let's see how easily they scare," Lydia said with a menacing grin, as she turned the jet around, lining up for a kamikaze course.

"You are crazy," Grisha said, reading her mind.

"I just want to make the air too dangerous for them to be comfortable flying in. We can't let them get to the airport." Lydia aimed right at the chopper, and had the chopper not dived out of the way at the last minute, she might very well have hit it.

Sam, who had been standing in the doorway of the cockpit, gave out a shout, then exclaimed, "I can't handle this. I'm going back here where I can't see how close you're bringing us to death."

Lydia just smiled. Had Sam not been there watching, she might not have made such a close call, but she had a thing for aggravating him. It wasn't that she didn't like the guy, but it was more of a game they played with each other. Other than the now deceased Jay, he was the only one of their team she could really joke with. None of the others understood her sarcasm as well as he did. "Yeah, go stick your head in the sand, Sam. I'll holler if I need you."

"Just don't cut my neck off while it's down there," he shouted back.

Lydia dipped the jet to one side, turning back toward the chopper. The chopper needed some more harassing since it was still pressing on. She flipped the hidden toggle, causing the secret 50mm cannon to lower for the second time in the last twelve hours. Then, with the aid of her former GPS screen, Lydia took careful aim. She didn't want to destroy it outright. Forcing it down would be more practical, as any other action could possibly damage the artifacts they needed to recover.

Lydia placed a few shots into the chopper, hoping to punch holes in the fuel tank. Though she was successful at not ripping the small craft to pieces, she was unsure of the damage inflicted. She decided to buzz the chopper again and see if they were ready to land. She aimed the jet directly at the chopper; and, moments before she hit it, she pulled back on the yoke, splashing the smaller aircraft with a powerful wind vortex.

After putting a little distance between her jet and

the chopper, she turned around to see the damage. The chopper had lost some altitude from her last attack, but she could now see it lurching forward. They were going to make a run for the airport. She knew if Mao's men were to make it there, they stood a better chance of escaping her. Reluctantly Lydia decided to be a little more aggressive in her approach, hoping that she didn't destroy the artifact in the process.

Taking careful aim again, Lydia unleashed a few more rounds into the front of the chopper. The first couple hit, but then the pilot began to swing the chopper side to side to avoid her fire. He was clearly not trained for combat, as his moves were too predictable. She fired again, right as the chopper swung back into her sights. This time the swaying became more erratic, and she knew her bullet had hit something or someone. Discontinuing her fire, she studied her target, watching as it lost altitude. It was a clumsy descent, but they were no doubt trying to land.

Lydia passed them by without trying to buzz them again. She pulled out her aviation charts, allowing herself to pass farther and farther away from them.

"What now?" Grisha asked with tense concern. "Please don't tell me you plan to land on the desert floor."

"No, I just want to be able to mark where they go down. We'll land at Sharm El Sheikh, then drive out to intercept them," she responded as she studied the chart. It didn't take long to figure out where she was. Handing the chart to Grisha, she pointed out their location and instructed, "Keep an eye on their chopper. When it lands, mark it on here so that we can find it easier on the ground."

Grisha took the chart from her and waited as she

turned the jet back around. By now, the chopper was just a dot on the landscape. It had landed, and as Lydia got closer, she could see smoke coming up from the wreckage. At least she wouldn't have to risk destroying the artifact further by blasting apart the chopper. But as she got closer, she found that several men were trying to distance themselves from the crippled chopper. One seemed to be carrying a large bag of some sort. She decided he must be the leader, no doubt trying to escape with the artifacts that they had exhumed earlier.

There was no question in Lydia's mind, Mao's men would undoubtedly be armed. Hoping to avoid an all-out gunfight on the ground, Lydia tried to pick them off with her 50mm. This did little more than scare her targets, since they were so small and quick. Lydia wanted to swing back around for another stab at the men who'd escaped her first volley of shots. She pulled up and was about to bank around when a warning buzzer sounded in the cockpit. A small red light flashed on the fuel gauge; the tank was nearly empty. Understanding that it would take considerable luck just to make it to the airport, she abandoned her plan to attack them again.

"We're going to have to fight them on the ground it seems," Lydia announced.

"Good, I like a fair fight," Grisha replied.

"Sorry," Lydia said to her Russian copilot. "But I need you here to refuel the jet, and be ready if we need to take off in a hurry."

Grisha showed some disappointment, but conceded with a little persuasion from Lydia. "After all, we can't risk both pilots being injured. There is also a possibility of needing to defend the aircraft again from any of Mao's men who might already be at the airport."

The next few minutes were tense, especially when the fuel did give out. But by then they had already settled into their final approach and were on their way down. Lydia was just barely able to keep her momentum enough to get off the runway and onto the tarmac.

"Sam!" she hollered. "Find us a truck, and only take the weapons that we can easily conceal. Customs are slack here, but we can't afford unnecessary risks. We can't stop Mao if we aren't allowed out the gates of this airport."

They all had their instructions, and were shortly making busy with their duties. Grisha was the only one left behind to tend the jet. Lydia didn't like to leave the jet alone when they were on a mission, which was the main reason she wanted to leave Grisha behind. He was good in a fight, but he would be more capable of taking care of any circumstances that could arrive while she was gone. Besides, Sam's team, short one man now, was still the more highly trained part of her crew when it came to combat.

Chapter 20

The car ride back to the harbor was short; however, in the few minutes it took to get there, Paul's headache turned into a migraine. His captor told him clearly that if he tried to escape or call for help, then anybody else around would be slaughtered. He was also told, despite overhearing to the contrary, that if he cooperated, then he would eventually be allowed to go free.

Neither threat of death nor promise of liberation fazed him much. His head was throbbing too badly to think of escape, and in his current state, death sounded quite pleasant. He was aware that he needed to focus, so he asked, "As a token of our new friendship, how about finding me a few pain pills? My head feels like it was just split open."

"I'll give you a painkiller just as soon as you help us find the device that you hid," Kendal replied.

"Yeah, I bet," Paul muttered, knowing full well

what the foreman had in mind for his pain relief. "By the way, I'm allergic to lead bullets—a few ibuprofens will do just fine."

"You just do your part," the foreman snarled. "I'll make sure you're taken good care of."

Paul decided not to push the subject further. He knew that the man was taking too much pleasure in his clichés. Besides, the man had his orders, and Paul was certain that he intended to carry them out, regardless of what Paul might say. Paul had to discipline himself to think beyond the excruciating pain in his skull and find a way to survive the next, and hopefully not last, hour of his life.

The car came to a stop in front of the harbor. The driver allowed Paul, the foreman, and one other man to get out before pulling away from the curb. The foreman gave Paul a shove in the direction of the docks; all the while, Paul's eyes were searching for any possible ways of liberating himself. He found his only chance for help directly in the path they were walking. The Egyptian military and the Egyptian police wore similar uniforms, but as they drew near, he could clearly discern that he was walking up to a police officer.

His captors, however, showed no sign of unease at the possible confrontation, and this worried Paul. If he made a scene, would the police officer be quick enough to respond, or would his captors kill the law enforcer before he had a chance to understand the situation? As they neared, Paul still hadn't thought of a clear plan of action. However, he knew that if he missed this opportunity, then he might lose his only chance altogether.

As they approached the officer, he tensed his shoulders, and decided to shove his captors abruptly and make a run for it. But just as he was about to do so, they made their move instead. Paul found himself completely disarmed and hopeless as Kendal called out, "Sebak, what are you doing around here today, don't you know that there is danger afoot?"

The policeman replied, "Yes, but as the Americans say, keep your friends close, and your enemies closer. What brings you around here today?"

Kendal smiled as he reached into his pocket. "Nothing that should concern you, my old friend."

Sebak laughed "I find that very difficult to believe, as most things you do seem to concern me."

"We're just finishing up a little business with our companion here," the foreman said, slapping Paul on the back with his free hand.

Paul wondered if his other hand was gripping a gun in his pants pocket, and knew it was best to keep quiet and see how this played out. It was obvious to him that the police officer didn't trust the foreman.

"Who is your friend, anyhow?" Sebak probed.

Paul noticed Kendal easing his hand out of his pocket, and got ready to slap a gun or knife from it. Only it wasn't a weapon that Kendal pulled out. Instead it was a nice little roll of bills with a rubber band around them.

"His name is Paul Crandall," his captor stated bluntly, but there was more meaning in his eyes as he handed the officer the roll of Egyptian pounds.

The police officer pocketed the roll quickly, then laughed. "You know, the economy is very difficult sometimes. I feel sorry for men who have a hard time making ends meet in the professions they choose. Sometimes even I feel as though I am underpaid as a policeman."

"I'm sure that as you do your job well, you will continue to find prosperity in your future," Kendal countered.

Sebak smiled and commented, "You know, this has always been something that I like about you. You have a way of making me feel so much better. I will leave you now to your business, and please, try to stay out of too much trouble. Paperwork is a very tiresome thing."

He tipped his hat and strolled away, whistling as he went. Paul felt a pang of despair. He could hardly believe what had just transpired. This group was subsidizing the income of the policemen around here. Even if he did get away, he knew that he couldn't trust the local law enforcement now. And he wasn't sure how far away he would need to go before he could again trust these protectors of the people.

"As you can see, Mr. Crandall, you are alone out here. We are your best friends. You must cooperate fully if you wish to help yourself," Kendal stabbed a finger into Paul's back, prodding him along.

Paul kept silent for a moment as he examined the walkways. The docks were suspended a good twenty feet above the waterline by large concrete posts. There were a few sloped gangways that led to a lower level, usually used for accessing smaller boats. If his group followed the upper a ways before descending to the lower level, they would end up at a small tugboat that would ferry them to the *Juliana*. Paul also knew that if he led them to the device that he'd found in his tanker, they wouldn't be satisfied, since the package containing the white powder would still be missing. If they then searched him, and found it, he knew it would only make them angrier and he might get a nasty beating before they killed him.

Paul took another look down at the water from the higher dock platform and wondered if he stood a chance by diving for the water again. He decided he could reach the water, but there were few places nearby that he could swim to for escape. His captors would easily be able to seize him again. Paul was still important to them, so he didn't think they would kill him flat out for attempting it, but it wouldn't help his overall goal of escaping. Then he got another idea. If they didn't want him dead yet, then he might still try to best them. As long as he remained useful, they would be less likely to make good on their death threats.

Making sure that he had their attention, he chanced his only hope for escape. Breaking away from them, he picked up his feet in a mad dash toward the end of the dock, pulling his shirt off in the process and dropping it behind. He wanted them to see that he intended to dive off into the foamy water below. Allowing his foot to catch on a plank, he stumbled forward. The planned mishap was just enough to slow himself and allow his captors to catch up before he actually had to jump off. In the last second before they reached him, he abruptly stopped at the edge of the dock and spun around, grabbing Kendal by his shirt. Using the foreman's own momentum against him, Paul gave another quick jerk and sent him flying over the edge of the dock.

The other man had just enough time to stop. Paul's head turned before his body, and time seemed to slow. The man looked puzzled, a little unsure of himself. Already close now, he didn't advance or retreat a hair. Paul could tell that he was being sized up. This man wasn't about to get thrown off as easily. Both men's eyes were locked for what felt like ten seconds, though it was less than two when Paul noticed a hand reaching for a concealed gun in the small of his opponent's back. But before he had a chance to grip it, Paul had already completed a full turnabout, and used the momentum from his spin to land a fist hard against the man's face. The man dropped his gun, and as he was stumbling like a drunk about to fall down, he inadvertently kicked the weapon into the waters below. Paul was unable to follow the blow with another, since the impact of the punch had robbed his hand of the necessary rigidity. His sturdy hands now had at least one or two cracked bones.

The man Paul had hit was able to recover more quickly and started his own volley of punches. Paul deflected a few, but the younger man was full of energy and kept them coming. Paul backed up to the edge of the dock, and fell down, his head just hanging over the edge. The man hesitated for a moment, and Paul guessed that he was trying to decide whether or not to send him over the edge.

"Get up!" the man demanded, as his better judgment took over. "I don't want to have to fish you out of the water—stand up!"

Paul sat up, but instead of standing, he let fly a defiant loogie that splashed into the man's face. Overcome by rage the man reached over, only to discover too late that he'd put himself right where Paul wanted him. Grabbing the man by his arm, Paul arched back down and kicked the man over his body. The man tried to grab hold of Paul as he went over, but his fingers found no grip on the bare, sweat-soaked chest of man who had bested him.

Paul crawled onto his knees and looked over the edge right as the man did a back flop onto the water below. He did a quick scan of the area but couldn't see the foreman. He knew that it wouldn't be long before Kendal found a way back to shore. With this sense of urgency, Paul labored to his feet again and ran, hoping to put as much distance between himself and his captors as possible. He stooped down long enough to grab his shirt, which still contained the powder for the trigger device he'd found, and continued running toward the street. He still had a migraine, which was increasing in strength every passing minute. If he couldn't find a place to lie low for a bit until it passed, then his mind would become too cloudy to function at all and he would most likely end up a captive again.

Upon reaching the street, he hailed a taxi and ordered the driver to take him to the El Pustro Bar, where he knew some of his crew from the tanker would likely be. Besides, he had lost his wallet, and knew that he'd need to bum a little cash from his friends there.

Chapter 21

Though Kendal knew it was coming, the shock of hitting the water surprised him. For the moment his mind was focused entirely on crawling his way to the surface. The fall had plunged him nearly ten feet deep in the polluted harbor. Kendal held on to the little amount of air he'd sucked in before hitting the cold, gray abyss. The thought entered his head that he might be swimming down or sideways instead of up.

It only took a few long seconds before his head finally broke the surface of the slimy water again. He gasped for air, and struggled to calm himself down. Before he felt fully at ease, he switched from treading to a cross between the breast stroke and a doggy paddle. Slowly he inched his way toward the lower docks. It was the closest place where he might pull himself back onto dry ground. As he reached the dock, he found a tire mounted to a metal beam. The tire was clearly meant to be used as a bumper for smaller boats, he wrapped his arms around the top and tried to lift his foot into the ring. But while attempting to lift himself, he felt a disturbing pressure on his back.

Kendal stood frozen for a moment, imagining what sort of sea creature was nudging up to him, until he realized that it was his gun working its way out of his belt. Gently, so as not to fully dislodge the gun, he lowered his leg back into the water and tried holding on to the tire with one hand while he shoved the gun back into his belt. This little move might have worked if the arm holding the tire hadn't slipped, causing him to fall backward. When the sensation of his belt loosening reached his brain, he knew that the gun had fallen completely out. He spun around in the water, moving his hands under the surface trying to find it before it sank. One point of the weapon knocked against the back of his hand, but it was sinking fast, and he was unable to grasp it.

Gulping a large lungful of air, he dove under the water. Opening his eyes availed him of nothing. The water was too cloudy to see a thing. After searching as best he could without any luck, he resurfaced. With one last-ditch effort he tried to swim to the sea floor, but the silt-covered terrain below was too deep to reach.

His anger at having lost the gun, and getting bested by Paul, consumed him as he pulled his way up the tire and onto the lower dock. It had made sense at the time that Paul would actually try diving into the water, since that was how he'd escaped the first time. But no excuse would be good enough. Kendal knew that if he lost the sea captain, his boss, Kore, would not forgive him.

Trying to ignore the dripping clothing that had laminated itself to his body, Kendal ran across the dock and toward the ramp. Just before he reached it, he heard another splash from about the same place that he went into the water. He looked over and paused just long enough to see his companion resurface. His subordinate was a wily man, and somewhat reckless. This nature lent Kendal the hope that his companion would have detained Paul, at least long enough for himself to rejoin the two. Now he knew that Paul stood a real chance of escaping. Even if Kendal managed to catch up to Paul before the tanker captain was gone for good, Kendal doubted his own ability to stop the freed prisoner. After all, Kendal was no real soldier. The only thing he had going for him was his gun, which now lay at the bottom of the harbor. Paul had already bested them both once, and now, dripping wet, Kendal knew he stood little chance in a fight against the sailor.

As he sprinted up the ramp to the higher deck, Kendal wished he'd just shot the sea captain in the leg instead of chasing after him. When at last he reached the top, Paul was gone. Undeterred, knowing that Paul couldn't have gotten too far yet, Kendal continued running toward the road they originally came in on; it was the most likely place for Paul to flee to. Whether his soaked clothes slowed him down, or his prisoner had a larger head start than he estimated, Kendal approached the road just in time to see the subject of his pursuit enter into a cab.

Kendal knew he wouldn't make it over in time to stop Paul, so he looked around for an alternative. His own driver was not due back for another thirty minutes, and there was no other cab in sight. His attention instead focused on a young man, perhaps a sailor, who was parking a scooter nearby. Without any hesitation Kendal ran up to the man with a look of distress on his face. The young man looked up, and even gave a questioning look of concern before he was tackled and his head smashed into the asphalt, rendering him unconscious.

With the keys still in the scooter, Kendal immediately throttled the single piston as fast as it would go. There was no difficultly catching up to the cab, but he slowed just enough to keep some distance between them. Paul might be jumpy enough to keep looking over his shoulder. When the cab stopped at a local bar, Kendal parked the scooter on the sidewalk just around the corner. Knowing the situation had escalated too far, he pulled out his cell phone with some hesitation. Kore wouldn't be happy with the call, but to admit his mistake before a remedy became too late would be far better than to face the consequences of covering up the deed and hoping it didn't come back to haunt him. Just as Kendal was about to dial her number, he realized the salty bath he'd just taken, had rendered the phone useless. Kore might need to wait for the update after all. He could go searching for another phone, but instead determined that he might learn more from the captain by trying to eavesdrop.

Knowing that a man walking into a bar dripping wet might attract some attention, Kendal settled on one small detour. While waiting for another unsuspecting man to walk by, he hoped that Paul wouldn't say anything too important in the meantime. It took about ten minutes, but Kendal was able to find his next dry shirt and jeans. The man they'd come off of had been a ragged wino, supposedly on his way to the bar for what couldn't have been his first drink of the day. Kendal had no problem getting the jump on him. Granted, the fresh clothes were less fresh than the foreman would have wanted, but the smelly garments were still an improvement over the wet ones from a minute ago. With the new outfit, he came around the corner and started walking toward the bar entrance right as the doors opened.

Quickly to avoid notice, he leaned up against the building and pulled his dead phone up to his ear as if he was engaged in some conversation. With the phone shielding his face, Paul walked out of the bar, right past him with another man, not even a glance in his direction. Kendal spied as they paid the cab driver, and then reentered the establishment. He was glad that he hadn't tried robbing the cab driver of his clothes instead. That could have turned awkward really fast. Even though the thought had crossed his mind, the cabbie seemed too short for his clothes to fit Kendal's taller frame.

Dropping the phone on the sidewalk, he walked over to the entrance and cautiously let himself in through the front door. Inside was dark and music played loudly. He scanned through the hazy atmosphere, focusing on the various tables until he found where Paul was sitting. The day was still too early for the bar to be packed, but there were still more people than Kendal would have expected. Evidently, Paul had decided to meet up with his fellow crew members from the tanker. It wasn't great, but Kendal knew that he would finally learn what Paul had done with the triggering device.

Finding a table next to Paul was easy. The bar, while not packed, had a good enough crowd that Kendal didn't draw any attention to himself. He sat down with his back to Paul's. With such loud music, it was a strain to hear what was being said, but he was able to glean enough of the conversation to know that he needed to move to the bathroom.

Kendal made it to the bathroom before Paul and two other men stood up from their table. Locking himself in one of the stalls, he listened as the three men entered.

"I'm sorry, but it was too loud out there," Paul said with some agitation. "I've just had the wildest day, and I've been given a mother of a headache."

"You said you had something to tell us," one of his crew prompted.

"Yeah, just give me a second," the captain replied. The sink was then turned on, and a quick peek through the crack in the stall showed that Paul was swallowing a few pills. He must have bummed them from the barkeep.

"We've got a big problem on our hands here," Paul began. He then related the whole incident of finding the triggering device, and his subsequent capture and escape.

When he finished the second man gave a half grunt. "You're not leading us on, are you?"

"I wouldn't joke about something like this," Paul replied. "They didn't check my shirt pocket, and a good thing they didn't, because I've had this bomb, or whatever it is, with me the whole time. What do you make of this?"

The familiar crumple of a plastic bag caused Kendal to wince as it was passed between the men. He silently grumbled to himself for having not found that earlier on the captain. It would have saved a whole lot of time, and he wouldn't have to kill these other crew members now, either. He didn't care if anyone found the triggering device; that might be more easily handled. Without the bag of powder, they would never know its purpose.

"Is it some kind of explosive powder?" one of the

men asked.

"I don't know," Paul returned. "But one thing is for sure, I don't trust the police around here. That foreman paid one of the officers off. He wasn't even shy about telling the officer my name. It was like he was telling him to cover for them when they eventually discover my dead body. I don't know what would happen if I walked into their station with this. I would probably be taken to a back room and turned back over to those terrorists."

"What do you think we should do?" the first man asked.

"I don't know yet, and I'm not sure that I can even think very clearly now, either. For now, I need to borrow a few bucks, and get a motel room. I'll feel much better if I can get a little rest."

"We're here for you, boss," they told him, as they began walking him out of the restroom.

Kendal waited for a minute, then followed them out. He had what he needed to know. All that was left was to find out which motel they would go to, and then find a pay phone to update Kore.

Chapter 22

The new green jeep Sam had found was open topped, and the fresh air was just what they needed. This was especially true for Lydia, as she closed her eyes momentarily to enjoy the wind in her hair. The past couple days were beginning to drag on her; like the end of a spent cigarette, she felt ready to crumble away. If she was able to capture the record Shen Mao's men were trying to smuggle out of Egypt, then she knew things would start settling down for a while. She wondered if she would be able to go to Italy and lose herself for a couple of weeks there. She opened her eyes long enough to see an old diesel truck pass them going the way they had come from. Even one of the passengers of the truck reminded her of Flint. The thought occurred for a moment that when she found the record they were after, she could go home also and see if *he* might be willing to talk to her.

This last thought was just wishful thinking, and even as she thought it, she dismissed the possibility as imprudent. The dream faded as the truck slowed down; they arrived at the section of road where they needed to turn off of to intercept Shen Mao's men. The ground was sandy, but the jeep had a good set of tires on it, and with its four-wheel drive and light-weight construction, they were able to bound across the terrain without too much difficulty.

It didn't take long to find the downed helicopter. Its fuel had ignited and sent up a large plume of black smoke, pinpointing its location. They followed the tracks leading away from the wreckage, only to find themselves back up to the road.

"They could be at the airport by now," Sam exclaimed.

Lydia pulled out her phone and tried calling Grisha. The phone rang three times before he picked up.

"Lydia, you are calling to tell me of your success, yes?" he said with obvious anticipation in his voice.

"Grisha, they gave us the slip. I think they may already be back at the airport by now. Keep your eyes peeled."

"I'm just paying for the fuel now. I'll start searching for them in one . . ." His voice trailed off.

"Grisha," Lydia called into the phone. "Grisha, are you still there?" She knew his phone was still on because she could hear the background noise.

After a moment, she heard, "Our jet, they're taking it! I call you back!" The shortness of his voice, and the increase in his Russian accent, denoted alarm.

With that the line went dead. Lydia thought for a moment, and the realization of what just happened hit her. The very people she was trying to hunt down were stealing her jet!

"Easy there, Lydia," Sam interjected. "You're going to crush your phone."

Looking down at her hands, Lydia was surprised to see her knuckles as white as marshmallows. "Shen Mao's men are trying to steal our jet," she revealed as she put her phone away. "Grisha is trying to stop them by himself as we speak."

"Hey, it's Grisha," Sam tried to soothe. "If anyone can stop them, it would be him."

Labeeb chimed in, "Yes, you will see, for the next several months he'll be talking about how we lost them, and he stopped them all on his own."

Sam chuckled, "Yeah, you're right. I'm sure we'll get back and he'll be waiting to rub it in our faces."

Lydia turned around and began to chew on the edge of her finger. It was a nervous reflex, one that she didn't realize she still did anymore. She thought the habit had been broken years ago. About a minute into it she came aware of what she was doing. Immediately she pulled her hand away from her mouth and tried to imagine her next move if Mao's men succeeded in getting away with her jet. This was one scenario she'd never considered.

Thirty minutes later, after a tense race back to the airport, Lydia found herself running past the terminals to the tarmac where she had parked the jet. There seemed to be a heightened sense of alertness about the security guards, which prevented her from getting through. She didn't have to ask to know that the problem revolved around her property, but she did anyway. "What's going on?" she asked one of the security officers.

Trained to keep the public from panicking, he simply stated, "There was a small disturbance outside. Don't worry. We are just taking a few precautions. There is no danger expected here."

The man then tried to walk away from her, not wanting to go into detail about the situation. Undeterred, Lydia grabbed him by the shoulder and turned him back around. "They didn't by chance just steal my Learjet, did they?"

The security officer's face went very serious. "Are you telling me that you are the owner of that jet?"

Lydia let out a frustrated groan. "So they did get away with it? What happened to my copilot, Grisha?"

"I don't know enough about it, but come with me." The officer motioned then led her to a room that most travelers didn't often see. There she found Grisha with a medic attending to some wounds. He glanced up at her; a look of shame was evident, even though his face had begun to swell up severely.

She rushed over to him. "What happened?"

The medic turned to face her. "Please, this man has a dislocated jaw, and maybe even a cracked rib."

Grisha, however, pushed the medic away as he grumbled, "Ish okhea."

Lydia watched as Grisha reached with two fingers into the back of his mouth, pressing down on the back molars. He then let out a painful moan as he increased the downward pressure. The crack of the jaw resetting itself made Lydia shudder. Grisha tried to force-stop his moaning as he rocked back and forth for a moment, gathering his nerves again.

More freaked out than anyone, the medic jumped up and stared at the Russian, apparently not knowing what to think about this man who'd just popped his own jaw back into place. Grisha, shaking his head and massaging his face, leaned forward and looked at Lydia. "I was paying for fuel when you called. I turn around to see the jet as it taxi toward runway. I jump in, find one man. I almost had him when more boarded behind me. They brought me down before I saw who they were. I woke up only five minutes ago. I'm sorry. I let them get away."

Lydia knew that Grisha would never forgive himself. The proud fighter had never been bested in a fistfight for as long as she had known him. To not only get taken out but also severely beaten was disgraceful to the Russian. Even worse was that Grisha had been armed. Not even Sam dared to poke fun at his mishap. Grisha would be internally punishing himself for some time.

The pensive silence was interrupted as a phone began to audibly vibrate. Lydia pulled it out of her pocket and looked at the name on the screen—Persephone—then answered the phone with, "I'm afraid that I have bad news."

"I already know that you've lost your jet," Persephone said. "I want you to forget about it for now. We're tracking it, and we'll know right where to find it. I'm also suspecting that since you lost the jet, you were unable to recover the golden records?"

"Yes, ma'am," Lydia admitted quietly.

"Never mind that for now," her higher-in-command ordered. "By tracking the jet, we might even discover where Shen Mao is hiding. You must make your way to Cairo, but stop by Suez on your way. Once there you must find a man named Paul Crandall. He captains a large tanker, one that has recently been targeted by Amos's men. We are trying to find out where he is, but we can't trust the police. They are as corrupt as the Devil himself, and Paul will likely be aware of this. Find him. He holds the key to proving that Amos is targeting the world's oil supplies."

Lydia was stunned, "You mean that they're targeting tankers, too? I thought we just needed to worry about the pipelines!"

"Apparently Amos has larger plans and resources than we realized. Find Paul, and take him with you—if not for our sake, then at least for his own protection. Our sources put him at a small motel close to the pier. I'll send you a text with the address. And Lydia, once you have him, don't delay in finding Shen Mao. He already has a head start, and we can't allow him to get away." With that last bit of instruction, the phone went dead.

Lydia mused at the network Persephone had at her disposal. Named after the Greek harvest goddess, she was the head of GRIP. When Lydia's family life had fallen apart, Lydia's brother, Troy, had talked Persephone into recruiting her. She didn't know all about how the organization came to be. What she did know was that for generations, dating back to the time the Martians landed on Earth, there had been a secret organization geared toward preserving Martian history and preventing a similar fate from happening to Earth.

This organization varied in size, but in the last couple decades they seemed to be getting larger. Persephone, the senior member of the group, once told Lydia the organization would continue to grow until it no longer was secret. The world was quickly approaching a point where technology and people's attitudes were nearing that of the Martians before their self-annihilation. GRIP would soon bring the truth to the world, in hopes that people would see the dangers and the consequences that could likely harm the last world in our galaxy capable of supporting life.

Lydia wasn't sure yet, but she believed that this time of going public might occur when GRIP foiled Amos's large-scale attack on oil resources. GRIP would then have a monumental opportunity to usher in a revival of worldwide concern and hopefully spark an outbreak of environmental responsibility.

"We need a chopper," Lydia announced. "I don't know of any airport at Suez, so we'll need something small enough to land without a helipad."

Chapter 23

August 2

Paul was suddenly awakened. It was 3:00 in the morning, and dreams of the previous day haunted him, causing him to sit up abruptly. He'd fallen asleep yesterday afternoon. He could hardly believe that he'd slept so uncharacteristically long, and he was still in his street clothes. A quick glance around the small, cheap motel room revealed two of his crew sitting watch. At some point during the night, though, they had succumbed to either drink or fatigue; and while they were still sitting in their chairs, they were both clearly only keeping guard of some fantasy within their own sleeping minds.

The migraine that bothered him yesterday was just a dull memory of it's former strength now. Paul feared it might come back in full force, but for now it was manageable. Lying back down, he tried to coax himself back to sleep, the morning was still very early. But after ten or twelve hours of rest, sleep would not come again. Twisting and turning, he got up and walked into the bathroom, careful not to wake his two crewmen. After gently shutting the door behind him, he turned the sink on and splashed some water over his face. One glance in the mirror revealed how worn down he'd become. His generally rugged bull-dog face now looked more like a droopy bloodhound. His body felt clammy and itchy, so he decided to take a shower.

For a man who didn't care to stay in a shower very long, Paul found that half an hour had passed from when he first turned on the refreshing water to the time that he stepped back out. Walking back into the room, he grabbed the pair of jeans and the T-shirt that his friends had brought him. Slipping them on, and transferring all the contents of his dirty pockets over, he found a renewed sense of dignity. He was clean, dry, and only shy one thing to feel ready to begin his day. Grabbing the key for the room, he slipped out the front door and crossed the sidewalk to the lobby.

The manager of the run-down motel was already up, and had a pot of coffee on. Paul poured himself some of the steamy beverage, wondering how clean the mug really was. Then, sitting down on one of the outdated sofas, he drew in a heavy breath, letting the aroma of the coffee serenade his senses before bringing the porcelain to his lips. His solitude was soon disturbed when he saw another guest walk in, looking just as tired. She went to a small fridge and pulled out a small bottle of orange juice then took her place right across from Paul. She picked up the previous day's newspaper, and lightly skimmed it before putting it back down.

Paul found the woman to be very attractive, with

long blonde hair and firmly toned arms. Even her obvious fatigue played to her favor. It was a natural beauty that he recognized, one that would be there whether she just made herself up for the day, or just finished a long hard day. Paul wanted to say something to her. He'd always wished that a woman such as this one would walk into his life someday. Even though he was a good twenty or thirty years older, he longed to try. Some might consider him to be too old to fancy thoughts of romance, but he wasn't dead. Even at fifty-one, he didn't consider himself that old. But as often happened to men of his age and station in life, he radiated a certain dignity, mainly noticeable through the eyes of the younger, suggesting that he was beyond this primitive yearning. In this case, his better judgment got to him, as it often did. He had larger problems to worry about today. Until he had those resolved, there would be no time for chasing after pretty women.

He was about to stand up and return to his room when the lady looked him square in the eye and seemed to be pleading for something as she said, "I don't know about you, but it's been a long night, and I fear that it'll be a long day, also."

Paul immediately forgot his better judgment. "I guess that makes two of us, then. I've got terrorists chasing me down, what about you?"

Paul half expected her to be interested in his little comment. Most women he knew would be full of concern or at least suspicion. Instead she looked unimpressed. "They're chasing you, and I'm chasing them."

Paul sat up straight. "What do you mean, you're chasing them?"

"Sorry," the woman replied. "I'm just a little tired, I guess. I've been chasing down a group that's trying to disrupt the oil supplies of the world. I've done all that I can, and I feel like I'm so close, but the trail I've been following has just gone cold. I can't get anything out of the police around here, and nobody seems to have seen anything."

"Are you serious? Why are you telling me this?" Paul asked suspiciously.

"You asked," she replied nonchalantly. "Besides, you are either telling the truth about getting chased by a terrorist, or you're trying to seduce me with a wild story. Either way, I'm at a dead end, and I'm willing to listen. And though I really doubt that you could help in my investigation, I've got nothing better to do except maybe try to get some sleep. So go on, you have my undivided attention."

Paul could hardly believe his ears. "So you're telling me that you are chasing down some terrorists who are trying to disrupt the world's oil supplies?"

The woman didn't say anything; she just looked at him as if to say, *Is there an echo in here?* She then waved her hand with a slight note of impatience.

"Okay," he said. "What if I told you that I am the captain of an oil tanker that was recently rigged with some sort of bomb?"

The woman's eyes immediately lit up. "Can you take me there and show me the bomb?"

Paul couldn't help but smile. "I wish I could, missy, but I'm not sure it's safe. I narrowly escaped with my life yesterday, and I doubt I'd be so lucky if I tried to return. Besides, my guess is that they may take the precaution of pulling all the bombs off of my ship before I get there."

"Please don't 'missy' me, I am very capable of handling myself," she said irritably. Then she paused before continuing, "Sorry, I'm just a little strung out. Can you describe what the bombs looked like?"

Paul fought the urge to dismiss himself. This woman, though pretty, was a little pushy for his taste. She reminded him of a couple feminists that he once knew. While he had nothing against women seeking empowerment, he disdained the attitude that often went with it. But though he found it unusual, she seemed to be telling him the truth. For all he knew, she could be a very pleasant woman, but just on edge this morning.

So, without much hesitation, he began to explain. "The device itself was about the size of a large Frisbee, except square, and it contained a white powder." Paul watched as she leaned in closer. He felt a slight urge to lean in also and put his hand on hers, despite his dimming attraction. But resisting the urge, he reminded himself that she was interested in what he was saying, and not who he was. Besides, she wasn't his type.

She continued to press him. "What was the powder like?"

Paul hesitated, wondering if the terrorist could have tracked him here and planned this as an elaborate way to get information. But throwing the dice and hoping for a turn in luck, he replied, "I can do better than that." He reached into his jeans and produced the small plastic bag of white powder and set it on the table between them.

She picked it up and shoved it back into his hands. "Put that away, I believe you now." She then did a quick nervous glance around her. "Okay, so you were telling the truth. You can help me. Do you want to shut these guys down?"

Now it was Paul's turn to be cynical. "Of course, but how? I don't trust the police here, and I doubt my employer will be any more effective than me when it comes to dealing with terrorists. And even if they know how to deal with terrorists, it may be too late. Besides, how do I know that I can trust you?"

"I don't think I need to coax you to trust me. You're a smart guy; if you didn't think you could trust me, then you wouldn't have just shown me that powder. But this isn't just your ship that we need to be worried about," the woman said, confirming what Paul already suspected. "With your help, we can prove that these terrorists are for real. Up until now, the authorities have been ignoring our warnings, but you have proof. Will you come with me? I can offer you protection, and we can take these guys down for good."

"Wait a minute, you don't work for any government?" Paul retorted. "Who are you, then?"

"My name is Lydia, and I belong to a group called GRIP. It stands for Global Representatives for International Progress," she replied. "We are a non-governmental organization, kind of like Greenpeace, but with a different agenda. The man we believe to be responsible for this terrorist group is named Amos. He is very dangerous, and apparently has a wider reach than we expected. If you come with me, I'll tell you all about it."

Paul looked over his shoulder. Though he couldn't see his motel room from here, his mind was on his crew. "Let me tell my crew where I'm going, first. I don't want to risk them returning to a hostile ship." He got up to go back to his room, then turned back around. "By the way, where are we going?"

Lydia looked up at him; her eyes were remarkably clear for being as exhausted as she claimed. She gave him a small smile that seemed to penetrate any defenses he had left. "Cairo, to start with. From there, I'll let you know as soon as I know."

Chapter 24

The path that led away from the road seemed to be nothing more than a short walking trail, used by drivers who needed to stretch their legs for a few minutes. At the end of the trail, there was a small clearing of matted-down vegetation. The untrained eye wouldn't recognize the camouflaged trap door hidden below the weeds. It was a fairly unsecured opening into the top of the mountain. The door was heavy to lift, but not extremely difficult to access.

The massive steel door beyond it was significantly more forbidding. After traveling down a small staircase, the confident, well-composed man approached the thickened vault, behind which his subterranean base was located. There were no special locks or retina scans for entering. Precautions of that nature were deemed unnecessary. Surveillance cameras and a willing team of security forces ensured that any and all intrusions into the base would be constantly monitored and dealt with if necessary.

A strong hiss sounded as Troy opened the massive steel vault. Inside was a circular staircase that wound down fifteen feet into the mountain. At the bottom of the staircase was another fifteen-foot hallway. At the end of the path, Troy entered a large open cavern. What hadn't been hollowed out by nature had been finished by GRIP. The ceiling had been plated with several inches of lead, which they extended out to camouflage the base. To any government satellite that might be probing subsurface installations, the base would simply appear as a natural deposit of the dense material.

In the center of the room stood a large object that resembled a fictional version of a spaceship, far too bulky-looking to actually move through Earth's atmosphere. By design, the ship wasn't ever meant to travel by conventional means. Troy ascended a ramp and entered one of several laboratories within the structure. Though the ship was completely surrounded by stone, concrete, lead, and iron, he had no doubt that he was close to getting the ship fully functional. He was only missing a couple of parts that would make escaping from the mountain and traveling through space possible.

The first missing part was the most critical. It was the mechanism that would bend all space and matter around the ship. The ship itself was designed for only minor maneuvers in space; all long-distance travel would be done by bending space around the bulbous hull and pushing it through, similar to pushing a marble through a rubber hose.

The second missing part, a main power source, was less important now than before, owing to the skilled help of some of his scientists. While the power source was not so critical anymore, Troy still thought it a good idea to let his sister, Lydia, keep searching for it. She had been leading a special GRIP team in search of both pieces for the last couple of years, and she was finally within reach of finding the part for the engine. The power source, though, continued to elude her. Troy was skeptical that she would ever find a living sample of the electrified moss that once powered the Martian spacecraft. Lydia claimed to have a good idea of the area it should be in, but if it still existed, Troy thought it would have already been discovered. According to his knowledge of the ancient ship, the moss would grow on the interior walls of the spacecraft. The Martians had used it in the original spaceship that came to Earth, because it was uniquely suited for space travel.

The moss supposedly wouldn't absorb light on the same spectrum that most plants on Earth do. Instead it photosynthesized using solar radiation and transmitted electrical current through its roots. When planted on the metallic mesh that covered the interior of the ship, the electricity would be collected and used to power everything. Since it absorbed solar radiation, it was said to create a protective barrier for the spaceship's passengers from the deadly gamma rays.

Sitting down at his desk, Troy powered up his computer. There was a message waiting from Persephone, and another from a man on Troy's team named Bernard Jublain. Troy read the e-mail from Persephone first, then entered a small command function on his keyboard. Within seconds, he found the locator beacon on Lydia's jet. It showed that it was en route to Southeast Asia. Troy scarcely had to question where it would end up. He'd known for some time that Shen Mao was hiding out in the Philippines; however, any attempt to find him had been futile. Though the Philippines was a small country, its infrastructure was significantly lacking, making it an ideal place to hide. If Shen Mao had been Caucasian instead of Chinese, they might have been able to track him down there. But as it was, a large percentage of the Filipino population was of Chinese descent.

The e-mail from Bernard, a gifted hacker, gave Troy even more cause for alarm. With little time to prepare, he shot off a quick reply to Persephone, then grabbed a suitcase and headed for the armory. He knew that Shen Mao's men would significantly outnumber—and outgun—him, but he hoped to get the jump on them. He filled the case with several Glock pistols, and added extra clips. He already had in mind the men he wanted to come with him. While they weren't as experienced as Lydia's team, they still knew how to hold their own in a fight. Troy hoped it wouldn't come down to that, but he needed to get to Marshal Steel before the final delivery to Shen Mao could be completed. If Bernard was not mistaken, and he rarely was, then Troy only had until this evening to accomplish his task.

Wishing desperately to know exactly where Shen Mao was holed up, Troy could only hope to intercept Marshal on his way to deliver the artifacts to the greedy crook. If Mao was allowed to get not only the golden record, but also the propulsion device for the Martian ship, Troy feared that he would lose any opportunity at recovering it. Bernard recently had intercepted an e-mail meant for North Korean officials, describing a demonstration at the residence of Shen Mao. The e-mail was fairly cryptic and partial, so Bernard wasn't sure where exactly the meeting would take place. All he knew was that the demonstration was tonight.

The most devastating reality was by far more dangerous. If the device from the ancient ship was still in working order and Mao tried to use it, it could incinerate Earth's atmosphere. Undoubtedly this would kill all life on the planet, as the Martians had done to their own world. Troy hoped that Mao wasn't foolish enough to attempt it, but anything was possible. Even though GRIP had built a ship of its own, at least they'd had the foresight to bury it within the depths of this mountain. Supposing that GRIP recovered the device, the launch chamber created inside the mountain for the ship was airtight, allowing large pumps to turn the cave into a vacuum chamber. Troy doubted that Mao would find such a vacuum chamber as this in the Philippines.

Despite the looming threat, Troy maintained a nervous hope. All he needed to do was to intercept Mao's courier. He was unsure why Marshal would confiscate GRIP's jet when they had their own. Perhaps they were trying to spit in GRIP's eye, but their mistake was now to GRIP's advantage.

Chapter 25

"Cost is not the issue," came a woman's voice. It sounded more like a whisper to Paul, who was eavesdropping behind Lydia. "We need those records."

"I won't fail you again." Determination peppered her tongue, then Lydia hung up the passenger's seat-back phone. Paul had watched as she'd bribed several men out of their seats on a plane trip to Hong Kong from Cairo. From there they were able to book a flight to the Philippines, with the last leg connecting to the island of Lapu-Lapu.

"That sounded like your boss," Paul commented as he leaned forward in the seat behind Lydia.

"It's a good thing we're able to track our jet," Sam said as he winked at the flight attendant who was replacing the ice on Grisha's head. Paul just sat back and rolled his eyes at the flirt sitting next to him.

"I can't wait to show those guys what I think of my new bruises."

"Please, Grisha," Lydia said. "You're lucky to still be alive."

"We'll get the plates," Grisha replied. Through pursed lips, his Russian accent still showed signs of annoyance at the whole incident. "But I will get the men who hit me."

Paul didn't know much beyond the names of his new companions, but he could already tell this Russian was one tough guy. He wasn't sure who had hurt the man's pride, but if they could do that to this man, he didn't want to meet them. Lydia seemed to be the leader of the group, and he could tell that they all would be good in a fight. His major fear was that Lydia might be too good and too close to her team, blinding her from the danger that he was noticing in Grisha. Having worked on a ship with a lot of tough guys, he had learned of a few characteristics in men that sent up red flags. This Grisha guy seemed to be bundled up in those crimson banners.

While the Russian was clearly tough, he carried a vengeance like few that Paul had ever seen. Whatever had happened to the man was almost a day past, yet he still seemed to have steam hissing out of his nostrils. Like the monomaniac Ahab, sailing to his doom with little care about his crew, so seemed the blindly determined Grisha. This man's white whale might easily compromise whatever mission they were on for the sake of settling a score.

Paul wasn't sure why he was traveling to the Philippines with these people, anyway. Lydia assured him that they were after a terrorist named Amos, but an even larger threat was taking priority for the moment. Paul offered to stay behind until they finished their little mission, but Lydia insisted that he come. She argued that she wouldn't be able to protect him otherwise. Besides, she assured him, the Philippines would be a very short detour, and they would be back within thirty-six hours. Paul just hoped that whatever was higher priority than disrupting the world's oil supplies would not put him in harm's way also.

He then watched from behind as Lydia again reached forward. She swiped a credit card and placed another call on the jet's passenger phone. It rang three times before a man answered.

Paul couldn't make out the voice on the other end very well, but he heard Lydia say, "Troy, it's me, Lydia. How are you?"

The voice mumbled something and she replied, "Not good, I'm afraid they got away with the plates."

Another pause and then she replied with some astonishment, "You mean he's going to auction off the plates?"

Paul leaned in closer to see if he could hear what was being said without drawing any attention from Sam. Luckily, though, Sam was distracted by a flight attendant on the other side of the aisle, who was returning his flirtatious gestures.

"That means he must have something other than just the plates. Who is invited to this party?"

Paul could hear a little better, but the words of this Troy fellow were still muffled. With a quick glance again at Sam, Paul risked leaning in closer still.

Lydia continued, "Why would they invite all those types of people to bid on a plant and some old plates?"

This time he could make out some of the other man's words. "There's more . . . instructions. They . . . contain history and technology designs."

"What kind of technology are we talking about?" Lydia asked.

"Well," the man continued, ". . . suggest that they . . . contain a schematic for the propulsion drive that brought *them* to Earth . . . they could . . . a working replica of the engine."

Paul leaned back suddenly, since Sam began to shift in the seat next to him. He was trying to piece together the conversation that he had just heard. Something was going on, and it didn't make sense to him yet. What was this about "them" coming to Earth? He wondered who his new friends really were, and what they were up to. They seemed to want to help him, and he believed them. But they weren't willing to tell him much about their current diversion, and this made him a little suspicious. He could tell that something big was going on. He wondered if it was his controlling nature as a ship's captain, or something else, but he committed himself to finding out what this was all about.

Paul found it impossible to eavesdrop any further, as Sam struck up a conversation with him. This British flirt smelled of body odor and bad breath; Paul found it difficult to be anything but annoyed with the less than ideally hygienic man. If only he didn't stink so bad, then not only would he be a tolerable man to sit by, but the flight attendant might not have blown him off so quickly. This would have allowed Paul to continue listening in on Lydia's conversation.

The conversation that ensued was completely pointless, and only aggravated Paul even more. Clearly it had been a mistake to come with these people, and he rued the moment he'd succumbed to their will. Considering himself a resourceful man, Paul believed that he could have and should have found a better way to handle his own misfortune. *Why then,* he wondered, *did I allow myself to be seduced into this trip? Was it a pretty woman?* He was even considering the possibility that he'd been duped into another branch of those same terrorists and flown away to silence him. Whatever the case might be, he was becoming more certain every hour that he needed to find a way to get away from these people.

Labeeb watched as everyone else on the plane was distracted. Lydia was talking on the phone to her brother; Grisha couldn't see past the end of his fury; Vincent was asleep; Sam was talking it up with their new friend Paul. The small green light flashing on the side of his phone meant that he had received a message from his secret benefactor. The trip to the Philippines was not something that Labeeb had thought to e-mail about, but somehow his anonymous friend had taken notice to the course change. With everyone distracted, Labeeb slipped into the privacy of the jet's lavatory to read the message.

Labeeb, I have noticed that you left Egypt, and are on a flight bound for the Philippines. I believe the only reason you didn't inform me of this change in plans was because you didn't know yet exactly where you would end up over there. Just so that we're clear, I'm not upset. On the contrary, I'm delighted. I have an associate who is currently residing in that country, and this may provide the best opportunity to get a sample of those two bacterial compounds you have with you. As soon as you arrive at your destination, let me know where you can be found. I will have someone meet you to collect the two compounds.

Labeeb was overcome with a nervous sweat. He was being asked to betray GRIP and smuggle the oil-solidifying compounds and their antidote off of

GRIP's jet. Not only would this be difficult and dangerous, but also, at present, the jet wasn't even in their possession. With a deep breath to help settle his nerves, he began to type a response into his phone. He'd known for some time that his mysterious friend wanted the samples, but this was the first time he'd actually tried to make any arrangement to get them.

Chapter 26

"Hello, Amos, we need to discuss something," Kore ordered as Amos stepped into her office.

"You don't look happy," Amos commented, wondering if he had done something to offend his only financial backer. Kore was a beautiful woman, in much the same way that a cobra is a beautiful snake. So sleek and smooth. Every movement was fluid, almost betraying but also accentuating her venomous nature. "I hope I have not displeased you in some way."

"You have done everything we could have hoped for," she replied. "The problem is not you, but it will affect you."

"I'm listening," Amos countered.

"Yesterday a captain on board one of the oil tankers that we have been cleaning discovered our sabotage. He escaped to a local motel, where he was picked up by GRIP's star commando, Lydia."

"How big of a threat are we looking at?" Amos questioned.

"His name is Paul Crandall, and from what we've learned, he stands a chance of becoming a very large threat. He has in his possession the solidifying agent from the release trigger on the tanker."

"If he's with Lydia already, then it might be too late." A small bubble of unease found its way into his speech.

"It's all right for now," Kore calmed him. "GRIP has Lydia chasing some other case for the moment. But you can be sure that as soon as it's finished, Lydia won't want to hesitate in bringing this to the public eye. My estimate is that we have about two days before she sounds the alarm. How much time do you need to finish all of your preparations?"

"We're there," Amos blurted prematurely. "Well, I mean we're pretty close, just a few finishing touches. Then it's a matter of coordination."

"How long will you need before you can give the signal?" she asked.

Amos thought for a moment, then with a slight quiver in his answer he ventured, "I really need about three days minimum."

Amos shifted in his chair as Kore stared him down coldly. "I might be able to make it in two days, but that will be pushing it."

"I don't care if you and your men don't even sleep one wink in the next couple days—you better be ready in forty-eight hours," Her eyes narrowed, focusing with laser point intensity, leaving no room for argument.

Amos stood up, and gave her a slight bow with his neck. "We'll make it work." He then walked out of the room and whispered too quietly for Kore to hear, "--somehow."

Stupid! Amos scolded himself as he wondered how he might actually accomplish what he'd just promised. The short walk to his office did give him a moment to reflect, and regardless of the pressure, no argument could go against the timeframe Kore put before him. She was right about the urgency. Everything Amos learned about Lydia proved to him that she wouldn't wait long before exposing their plot. And now, for the first time, she had solid evidence and a witness to back her up. Even worse, she was now aware that his plans extended beyond just pipelines. He doubted that she knew about the third phase of his plan. It was the one part that still needed work, and would require considerable effort on the part of a couple of his subordinates.

The United States and several other countries kept a large stockpile of oil in reserve for emergencies. With plans to expand, the U.S. alone had close to seven hundred million barrels of oil stored in deep subterranean caverns. Based on current energy needs in the United States, these sites would contain enough oil to fully supply the country for less than fifty-eight days. Practically though, given the rate it could actually be distributed, it really could supply only about half the country's needs per day, effectively spreading the reserve over approximately 150 days.

Amos knew that he must disrupt these strategic reserves for his plan to succeed. He'd already contrived the scheme for delivery of the bacteria that would solidify the oil; unfortunately, he only had one oil truck to deliver the crude with. The U.S. storage facilities were spread across two states, Louisiana and Texas. The logistics would be difficult, especially since the Department of Energy controlled everything that came in and out of the facility. His plan was to use a small time-triggered release capsule, similar to a medicinal pill, that could be pumped into the caverns with the crude. He was fairly certain that it would work; the biggest hang-up was that his men hadn't begun making their practice runs to the oil reserves yet. Also, they hadn't secured a contract to deliver the oil yet. This meant that not only would they need to improvise when they got there, but they might even have to hijack trucks that were already scheduled to make deposits.

Amos was usually far too reserved to try something without having all his bases covered. But in this instance, he knew he had no choice. They would soon have every government agency searching for him. His only hope was to act now, and then go into hiding. He suspected that his men doing the delivery would surely be discovered and arrested because of the advanced timetable. They might even be killed, but it was a necessary risk. The world needed to know that their reliance on fossil fuels must end. The cost of ignorance would be poisoning the world and only pushing away the inevitable. At least this way the people would start to see how severe their addiction to oil was, and maybe develop new energy and products that were actually sustainable before it became too late for any real action.

He pulled up a customized coding program that attached an e-mail into the image of a YouTube video. The only way to find the code was to have the compliant decoding software to match, and know which video to run through the decoder. In his case, he used a couple of generic humorous house pet videos to embed his message. A link to the video was then sent in a spam e-mail to thousands of unsuspecting people, as well as the few he wanted to find the message.

Once it was sent with his instructions, he began to make preparations for his own hiding. His plan was to disappear in Alaska and enjoy the solitude of the many inlets, bays, and forests. He thought for a moment of whether Lydia would ever want to join him. It was a long shot, but an entertaining thought to him. Maybe down the road when she saw the good that would come of this.

Chapter 27

Before long, the plane touched down in Hong Kong, Lydia's personal phone signaled that she'd gotten another e-mail. Her next flight to the Philippines still had a few minutes before leaving, just enough time to check the digital message.

She was disappointed when opening it revealed only a link to some stupid internet video of two kittens playing with a two-legged puppy. It wasn't the first time she had gotten similar spam messages, and she wondered where the sender could have gotten her e-mail address from. She immediately deleted the message and began to board the plane for Manila. From there the plane would make one final leg down to Lapu-Lapu. Before the attendants asked her to turn her phone off, she tried calling Troy again to see how he was doing. She was disappointed when he didn't answer.

Paul must have seen the disappointment on her

face, because he asked, "Would it be better if I waited here for you to return?"

"That won't be necessary, Paul," she replied. "Troy is very capable, and I doubt he'll need us when we get there."

Paul didn't let it go, though. "So who exactly is this Troy, and what could possibly be more pressing than stopping terrorists from crippling the world's oil supplies?"

Paul had appeared a little snoopy ever since they were ordered on this detour, Lydia noted, though his suspicion was warranted. She would have felt the same way if she were in his position. She, herself, had in fact been annoyed earlier when she was ordered to the Philippines. Had Troy not explained the urgent nature of stopping Shen Mao, she would have been on Paul's side.

While a keen understanding compelled her to accept the diversion, she also was well aware that she would be late in arriving there. Already the sun had begun to sink below the horizon. As the turbines from the connecting jet throttled up, the vibrating cabin was propelled down the runway and thrust into the sky. The only light remaining outside the window was a sliver of sunshine that shone once they had reached altitude. It only lasted a few minutes before that too was swallowed by the far side of the Earth's almost invisible boundary.

Grisha still sat on one side of Lydia for this last flight, but Paul had managed to position himself in the other seat next to her. She guessed that he wanted to be closer in order to pry into her business, and this was an easier location to accomplish that task. They would only be on this jet for another two or three hours, and all of them were eager to get out. So far only Lydia and Grisha were aware of the scope of the danger.

When Paul posed his question about the mission, Lydia thought about how to phrase her reply. Grisha was quicker, and leaned over to scold Paul, "The less you know, the better. Just know this: If we are alive by time we land, all is okay. If not, then whole world is dead also. Now stop pestering."

Lydia wondered if Grisha had given up too much in his statement. But she also wondered if Paul had already figured out some of it. Grisha, however, had clearly not intimidated the sea captain, since he pressed on.

"Whatever we're doing here, it is obviously important, and you've dragged me all the way from Egypt. If you want my help with these other terrorists, you can start by coming clean with me on what all else is going on. You can start with this secret organization of yours, GRIP."

"I've told you what GRIP stands for," Lydia started, but Paul cut her off.

"Yes, you've told me what it stands for, but that seems pretty vague. Why don't you tell me who you really are?"

Lydia was feeling defensive now, but Grisha even more so. He was still mad about losing the jet, and he seemed to get agitated more easily than usual. He reached across Lydia and wrapped his large callused hand around Paul's neck, warning, "One more word, and you sleep for rest of the trip."

Lydia grabbed his arm and pushed it back. "I'm sorry, Paul, but we're all on edge a bit here. I'm not supposed to tell you much about who we are, but trust me, we really are trying to save the world from men who, consciously or not, threaten the lives of everyone on this planet."

"So let me guess, then," Paul started, trying to

piece together things he'd overheard. "We are on our way now to stop someone who is inadvertently going to use something that could harm a lot of people."

"Yes, you could say that," Lydia conceded, not wanting to give any more away.

But Paul continued to surmise, "And this thing he's going to use has to do with a Martian spacecraft?"

This time Lydia was surprised, and even Sam, who was now sitting in the row ahead of them, turned around to proclaim, "Wait, how did you find out about the spaceship?"

Lydia wanted to bury her head in her hands as Paul gave a grim smile before concluding, "So there really is a spaceship from Mars. I'm guessing, then, that your main purpose is somehow linked to this big cover-up. What's so special about the engine part from that craft and the record we're after that warrants distraction from my terrorist problem?"

This time Sam was the most surprised. He looked at Lydia with wide eyes and accused, "You didn't tell me about the engine part they'd taken."

Lydia flushed with anger. Part of her was mad at Paul, but he had an excuse. He must have eavesdropped on her calls to Troy. She also couldn't be mad at Sam, since she really should have told him. "I meant to tell you, Sam, but I was trying to keep it from Paul here, and we didn't have a convenient enough time to chat. Besides, Troy and a few others are already trying to intercept the engine component before Shen Mao gets his hands on it. We are really just showing up to provide backup in case Troy gets caught or pursued after taking the device."

Paul then asked, "What's so special about this engine, anyway?"

"It's not an engine," Labeeb clarified.

But Sam finished the explanation. "It's said to be more of a component that is meant to handle all the calculations and special processes needed for bending space."

Lydia then scolded, "Sam, a little restraint here!"

But Sam countered, "I'm sorry, Lydia, but he's already pieced the important parts together. What could it hurt to let him in? At least he won't be second-guessing your every move anymore. Besides, we've dragged him along this far; seems to me that he's got a right to know."

Lydia hated to admit it, but Sam had a point. She drew in a deep breath, and slowly but audibly let it out. She then glanced around to make sure that nobody else on the jet was eavesdropping. "Okay, but please, Paul, we've held this secret for thousands of years—please respect our desire to keep it this way."

Paul tilted his head, but Lydia wasn't willing to accept the half convincing compliance to her request. She stared him down hard for a good thirty seconds until he gave a more satisfying gesture of acceptance. Without breaking eye contact, she cautiously explained, "A man named Shen Mao has taken two very valuable items from an ancient Martian wreck. The first is a record of the first men from Mars who arrived on Earth. It details their history and technology. The second is a device that, as Sam said, can bend space around a ship. This device was first used when they launched from Mars, only it caused their atmosphere to ignite, destroying all life on the planet. Mars used to be very similar to Earth, and we're afraid that Shen Mao has created something that will demonstrate the space travel capabilities of this device. He is supposed to showcase it to some of the world's top terrorist powers within the next hour."

Paul sat silent for a few minutes to digest what

Lydia just told him. He then asked, "Why have you guys kept this a secret for so long?"

Her reply came easily. "It was at the request of the first generation of men in our secret society. They have been warning us not to let this be known to the world until we were advanced enough to understand the technology and its possible consequences. The only problem is that we kept it such a good secret that eventually the ship's crash site became lost to even us somewhere around the Dark Ages. Shen Mao, shortly after having been let into our organization, betrayed us and has been searching for the ship ever since."

Paul was puzzled. "If this Shen guy was once part of your organization, then wouldn't he know about the dangers of using the device?"

"We hope he's taking the necessary precautions," Lydia answered. "But he is a strange man, and carries with himself an air of indestructibility. Our biggest fear is that he might sell it to a nation that won't be as responsible. If this happens, then our worst nightmare may very well be realized."

"And the oil terrorists?" Paul extended. "What do they have to do with this whole Martian cover-up?"

"Actually they don't have anything to do with it. We just happened across their plot. Since none of the world governments know who we are, they won't trust us. And those terrorists are able to cover their tracks pretty well. We had the means to stop them, so we took it upon ourselves to do so. First we took a sample of their bacteria, which, as we explained earlier, can solidify oil. We then used our own pool of scientists to create similar bacteria that could counter the effects of theirs. For the last year or so, we have been trying to stay ahead of them and plant our version in pipelines to counter theirs. We had no idea their network extended as far as your shipping tankers. GRIP is really trying to do more good than just keeping secrets about our ancestry, and I can assure you, once this immediate threat is stopped, we'll put all of our efforts into stopping Amos from releasing his attack on the world."

Paul appeared to have run out of questions for the meantime, and he sat back in his seat. Lydia was more than happy for the break, and she reclined her seat also. It seemed like they had just taken off when the pilot turned the "Fasten Safety Belts" sign back on, and they began their descent into Manila. Only one more leg, and they would be in Lapu-Lapu. Lydia hoped that Troy wouldn't need her help. With any luck they would meet her brother at the airport and take the jet back.

Troy was definitely not the militant type, but there was something commanding about him. When his will bent him in a certain direction, nothing could dam his flowing ambition. This iron resolution always seemed to give Troy exactly what he was after. Ambition was a powerful tool, especially if one knew how to channel it, but her brother's methods were always a mystery to Lydia. While growing up she'd never expected him to achieve much, but then again, many of the world's greatest innovators didn't exactly fit any predefined mold. But her brother was just that: a brother, not a Beethoven or a Tesla. Troy's nonconforming mentality was the attribute that first took him away from home many years back, searching for a way into elite society. Their father belonged to GRIP, though the organization must have identified itself by a different name, because she'd never heard of GRIP until her own recruitment. Troy always expected that he would follow in his father's footsteps. But when their father died and both Troy and Lydia were denied association into the Martian society, for whatever reason, he ran away.

Only a couple of years ago did Troy show his face again. His reemergence coincided with the loss of Lydia's newborn son. In order to distract her from the terrible loss, he presented her with a unique opportunity. During his sabbatical from the family, Troy had found a way into the organization that he'd always dreamed of. She wondered how he could have finagled it, but now he seemed to have a bit of pull in the organization. Everyone knew and respected him. It was on his recommendation that Lydia had been granted a chance to join.

Lydia looked over at the sea captain sitting next to her. Paul was the antithesis of Troy, about as square and reliable as a man could get. His word was gold and a code of honor shone in his eyes. Granted, she still considered Troy to be a man of honesty and honor, but her emotional brother often displayed more of a prodigal demeanor. While she loved her kin, she couldn't help elevating Paul's character above Troy. Lydia wondered what might become of Paul. Few outsiders ever learned of GRIP's true nature. She wondered what kind of protocol would be followed in his circumstance. Understanding that his pushy nature was the determined leader manifesting itself, Lydia found it impossible not to respect Paul, even if he had managed to pry the secret of the mission from the group.

Of course Paul didn't know everything. Lydia's mind drifted for a moment to the coveted moss. She wondered, if she ever found it, whether it would replace the world's dependence on oil. She couldn't help but agree with Amos on his motivation, but the extremist still had to be stopped. Now with Paul's help, she just might find Amos's base of operation and stop him before he had a chance to carry out his reign of terror. Even more, GRIP might finally convince some governments to help stop the plot.

Her biggest concern now was, should she go to the Egyptian government with Paul's evidence, or the newspapers? The latter had a tendency to spur the other, whereas the government might on its own accord drag the investigation out. Regardless of the route, she had a feeling that Amos would advance his schedule because of Paul's escape, so there was precious little time to waste. For this reason alone, Lydia decided that both options might be too slow. As soon as they were finished here, she would lead her team and anyone else she could recruit in an assault on Amos's base of operations. This hinged on Paul being willing to cooperate and be their guide. Lydia knew that Paul might hesitate for the same reason she did. They were essentially taking the law into their own hands. The fact of the matter was, any other way might cause too much of a delay. Plus, if Amos had friends in the government, like he did with the Egyptian police, they would most likely get tipped off. *No*, Lydia confirmed resolutely. *I will stop Amos, along with this Kore lady he is working with.*

A few minutes later, the plane's tires screeched, and a wave of humidity rushed into the cabin as passengers were transferred at the Manila airport. Lydia and several others remained on the jet, since it would soon take off again to finish it's leg to Lapu-Lapu. From her seat, she could see out the windows. Nothing looked familiar, yet it was all the same. Just another busy airport with random lights, some fixed, some moving. In less than an hour she would be in Lapu-Lapu. There she hoped to find her jet and learn of Troy's progress.

Chapter 28

August 6

It had been a long and restless night. Troy tried to sleep, but it wouldn't come. Part of the restlessness came from an aching bullet wound to his arm, the remainder from the excitement of having just finished raiding Shen Mao at the greedy man's auction. During the night, he was able to get back in touch with Lydia, his phone full of text messages and voice mails expressing his sister's concern. She was now in Lapu-Lapu and had checked into the Shangri-La beach hotel for the night. Troy gave her directions for finding Marshal's base of operations in Cebu. He doubted that she would find anything, but since she was in the neighborhood, he figured she could search the place. Maybe she would find something important.

The loss of the golden record was disturbing. Troy went over every scenario in his mind of who could have taken it, but to no avail. The culprit was gone, along with any trail. Since Flint had destroyed the engine component, all Troy had left was a copy of the translated diagrams for the construction of Mao's tiny ship. It was an extrapolation of the ancient record that Mao had once stolen from Troy. *That double-crossing weasel*, Troy thought when he pondered on Shen Mao. *I hope your last few minutes in this life were hell!*

Ever since Mao had been allowed into GRIP, the Chinese entrepreneur had acted as if he were the most loyal member of the organization. For project failures, he assumed responsibility when none was expected. In success, he pawned the glory off on others. The enthusiasm brought to the table by his shrewd behavior had elevated him to be entrusted with the highest level of confidence.

When the day came that Mao looted GRIP before disappearing, Troy decided that measures needed to be taken to ensure a more faithful structure for GRIP. Since it was within his power, he'd made a rule that anybody joining GRIP had to prove without a doubt that they were of true Martian blood. This rule he bent only once out of necessity, but he'd managed to convince that other man of his glorious, albeit made-up, origin.

Ironic that Mao would find himself betrayed by his own Marshal Steel. The past being unchangeable, Troy's last hope was that in Marshal's betrayal of Mao, he might have made a copy of the golden record and stashed it someplace at his compound in Cebu. If it was there, then Troy could quickly have it interpreted, and re-created. The whole process of making a new propulsion component and adapting it to his ship in Hong Kong would only take about a week with the resources at his disposal.

Troy was pacing back and forth when Flint came up from behind and startled him. "Good morning, but by the look on your face, it might not be a good morning after all."

"Did you have to destroy the artifact in the ship?" Troy accused, only to realize how hostile he sounded.

Flint looked surprised. "I thought the whole idea was to keep it from ever being used!"

"I'm sorry," Troy said as he continued pacing. "I'm just a little upset at having lost the record."

"Come again?" Flint said. "I must have slept through that part of the evening. You didn't catch Marshal?"

"No," Troy said, shaking his head. "I got outside just in time to see him pull out in a car."

Flint thought for a second, then ventured, "So Marshal still has the record you need?"

"No," Troy replied again. "He doesn't have it, either. When I got to where his car had been parked, I found the briefcase he'd taken. It was drenched in mercury. Somebody there was playing him or Mao, or maybe even both of them."

"So what now?" Flint asked.

Troy looked up and gazed across the sea. "I don't know. But I think this is where we part ways. When we get back to the airport, I can take you as far as Hong Kong. But then you're on your own." He paused, realizing that if Flint took him up on the offer, he would need to get a regular plane ticket back to Hong Kong. Troy knew that there was too much at stake here. He couldn't risk letting his sister meet up with Flint at this time. He needed her full attention on the more pressing matters at hand.

Flint was about to reply when Troy added, "That is, as long as you are content with not stealing our jet again."

Flint laughed. "You know what? Saving the world is tough business. I think I'm ready to spend the rest of my vacation not getting shot at."

Troy let out a courtesy chuckle. "So what's your plan?"

"I think as long as I'm here, I'll see a few of the sights," he replied. "Besides, before I get Philip onto a plane, I want to make sure he'll survive the trip."

"The islands can be very beautiful," Dusty, Marshal's former partner, said, as she broke into the conversation. Troy noticed she was clearly affectionate toward his brother-in-law.

It was an interesting coincidence that Flint should be the one he ran into out here. Though the two had never formally met, Troy had seen the wedding pictures of Lydia and her husband. He was relieved that Flint didn't recognize him. When he'd taken Lydia away from Flint, she was a wreck. Now she was independent and following a good course in her life, and he didn't feel any need to change that.

As Troy was reminiscing about these things, he noticed that Dusty's comment invoked a small flutter of excitement in Flint's eyes. "Well, good morning, sunshine," Flint said as he turned around and gave her a sweet kiss on the cheek.

"What do you say we check out the local bakeries?" Troy offered, relieved that he wouldn't have to work at keeping Flint and Lydia from seeing each other. "After all, we should have about an hour before the ticket office opens for the ferry to Cebu."

Flint smiled. "Sounds like a great idea. My stomach feels like my throat has been cut. I think only Monk can relate right now." Monk was Flint's autistic friend, who'd fought and received a nasty tear around his neck in last night's battle. Then remembering a couple of strangers that he'd helped that evening, he asked, "By the way, what happened to that other girl and her friend? The girl he was referring to was named Amelia Zimmerman, one of only two respectable people at Mao's auction. She'd saved everyone from a grenade. Her friend, James Pruitt, the other respectable attendant had been shot in a bad way during the whole commotion. "Did he make it?"

"I think he'll be fine," Dusty said. "He was in tough shape, and had lost a lot of blood by the time we got him to the hospital, but they said he should recover. His lady friend happened to be the same blood type and was able to stay with him and donate."

By this time, Philip Noon, Flint's mentor and father figure, who'd followed him into last night's conflict, had woken up and made his way into the conversation. Troy, on the other hand, purposefully drifted away from it. He had other things on his mind that seemed more important than hospitals and bathrooms.

Dusty and Philip ended up making their own plans to find a pharmacy and told them they would meet Flint and Troy at a bakeshop around the corner.

"I'm sorry that your record got lost," Flint said to Troy as they left.

"It's all right," Troy replied. "From what I understand, it was written in the Martian language. If they try to translate it, they'll pop up on our radar again somewhere." At least he hoped so.

Right after the ferry ride back to Cebu, Flint handed his beat-up backpack to Troy. "I don't think I'll be able to take these with me through airport security. Some of the guns in here are mine and some are from Marshal's men. I hope you won't actually need them, but I can't take them with me."

Troy took the bag, not really wanting to, but understood Flint's position. After all that he'd put Flint through, he decided not to argue about it. Flint then said something that immediately put Troy back on edge. "I think we'll go back to Marshal's compound for a few minutes, gather up Dusty's belongings, then go island hopping for a week."

"Sounds fun," Troy said, mechanically putting his hand out to be shaken—though his concerns were now on Flint running into Lydia again.

Flint shook it, and Troy and his men stepped into a taxi for the airport. "I'll be seeing you around!" he shouted to Flint, hoping for the opposite, as the taxi pulled away.

Flint shouted something back, but Troy didn't hear. He was debating whether or not to go to the airport or to turn around and head for Marshal's compound in an attempt to divert his sister from coming face to face with Flint. As soon as he made up his mind, he picked up his phone and dialed Persephone.

Chapter 29

"Are you sure nobody will still be here guarding the buildings?" Flint asked Dusty as they approached Marshal's complex.

"Relax," Dusty said, with a small pout. "Don't you trust me?"

"Don't forget," Flint reminded. "You did kidnap Philip—one of my best friends. You then earned his trust, only to betray him, and then used that info to try and get me killed. That happened only just yesterday, and then you ignored me when I told you to stay outside of Mao's yard."

Dusty pushed him playfully. "That was before I realized how handsome you are. Now let's go, and stop being such a baby."

Flint smiled as they exited the taxi and walked up to the complex. His nerves were still on alert, despite Dusty's assurance that nobody would be left here. He walked cautiously through the front gate, even as she marched boldly to the building where her belongings were. Convincing himself to follow, he continued to look around for anybody lurking. It took Dusty a good twenty minutes to pack her belongings, because she kept leaping playfully back into Flint's arms. Flint, however, was too high-strung to allow himself to get very romantic. Instead he insisted on packing her bags and getting out of there.

Dusty was disappointed, but she didn't push the matter. Flint suspected she too was a little uncomfortable with the place, even if her playfulness betrayed her anxiety. After all, it had been somewhat of a prison to her for the last several months.

Once Dusty was all packed up, they extended the carry handles on her luggage and then, with one arm around each other, exited the building. Dusty was on his right, and he let her through the door first before rejoining her side. Since he had only one arm free to manage the luggage, he paused briefly to adjust his grip on it. But in that moment, he caught a familiar scent. He recognized it as the same perfume from the jet that he'd previously stolen. It was also the same mild aroma that he would come home to when his wife Lydia was still living with him.

"Do you smell that?" he whispered to Dusty. The smell was very faint, and he wasn't sure if she would notice.

"Smell what, your greasy pits?" she joked, only to quiet down when she saw that his face was deathly serious. "What is it?"

"It's something that doesn't fit here," he whispered. He then turned into the slight breeze, where the smell was coming from. Immediately his reflexes triggered. Flint dropped the luggage and heaved as he dragged Dusty as fast as he could across the yard and through the gate. A single rifle shot rang out, and he could almost feel the bullet as it passed above his head.

Making it through the gate, he ran with Dusty and hid around a small bakeshop. A couple of children watched them with curiosity as Dusty sank to the ground and started to cry. Flint pulled her head up and with a determined look ordered, "Be quiet. It wasn't your fault, and we're okay. Just relax for a minute."

He then popped his head around the corner to see if they were being pursued. He saw no sign of anybody coming. So strange, he thought to himself. He had seen two people, one man with a rifle, and the other a woman with binoculars at her face. It had to be more than mere coincidence. The man with the rifle reminded him of the big Russian he'd met in Egypt when he stole GRIP's jet. He didn't get a good look at the woman with binoculars, yet she bore an uncanny resemblance to Lydia. And there was that fragrance coming from her direction.

He knew it was impossible, and if they were part of Troy's group, then they should be on the same side now. He was just about to duck back around and check on Dusty when he saw the hostile couple step out of the gate. Their rifle seemed to be gone, and they walked over to a waiting taxi. From this angle, he couldn't clearly make out the woman, but he felt compelled to understand what was going on.

"Come on, Dusty," he said to the shaken woman, still kneeling on the ground. Her eyes were red, but she had stopped crying. "We need to follow them."

"Follow them?" She laughed sarcastically. "Are you crazy? They just shot at us!—which I swear, this time, I had nothing to do with!"

"I know," Flint replied as he pulled her to her feet. "But they were the same people who work with

Troy. I'm afraid our friend might have decided to have us killed."

"Why would Troy do that, after we helped him save the whole friggin' world?" she asked as Flint hailed another taxi.

"I don't know," Flint replied. "My only guess is that he doesn't like the idea that we know about his little Martian cult. Plus, if that's the case, I don't want to have to worry about looking over my shoulder the rest of my life, wondering if I'm being followed."

"I don't want to go," Dusty whined.

Flint opened the cab door but paused, looking into the woman's eyes. "I won't make you come, but I need to see about this. Besides, there's something else."

Dusty waited for a minute. It wasn't long, but long enough that the driver turned around impatiently in his seat, wondering if they were going to get in. She then asked, "What is this *something else*?"

"I can't put my finger on it, but there is something strange to me about it, and I need to know."

Flint knew he must sound silly. But Dusty stepped into the cab with him, anyway. "Okay, but once you figure out, whatever it is, that'll be it, right?"

"Of course," Flint promised.

She then reminded, "And then we spend a little time playing?"

Flint laughed. "Don't worry, I look forward to a little relaxation."

The taxi they were supposed to follow had since disappeared, but Flint wasn't worried about that. He knew where they were going, anyway. "Mactan airport, in Lapu-Lapu," he told the driver. The driver took his foot off the brake, and they were off.

Dusty tried to take Flint's hand again, but he had

a hard time accepting it. Dusty was really a great woman, and very beautiful. But the perfume lingering in his memory reminded him too much of Lydia. Now the idea of being flirty with Dusty seemed wrong to him, yet he didn't want to shut her out completely. If the two they were following had nothing to do with Lydia, as Flint knew must be the case, then he didn't want to hurt his chance at a relationship with Dusty. Nothing seemed to make sense, which compelled him to get to the bottom of it all.

Chapter 30

Grisha was beside himself the whole way back to the airport. Lydia had never seen him so touchy. He smelled the blood of his prey, and wanted to sink his teeth into the man who'd stolen the jet from him. Grisha's whole body seemed to shake like a large drum of nitroglycerin, and in the event that he blew, Lydia decided it was best to stay as far away from him in the cab as physically possible.

As she observed her smoldering companion, she began to doubt her earlier actions. When she'd glimpsed the man outside Marshal's compound, her heart had done a backflip. He looked remarkably like the husband she'd left behind. But it couldn't be Flint. He had never been to the Philippines, nor had he ever expressed any desire to do so. As she re-called, Alaska was the only place he'd ever dreamed of going. There was no reason he should be near Marshal's compound. And though he did know how to fly small airplanes, he wasn't the type to beat up a Russian and steal a jet.

Perhaps she should have ignored Persephone's orders and investigated more deeply. After all, this whole trip to the Philippines had turned into a colossal waste of time. First she was commanded to come here, then, just as she arrived at Marshal's compound, Persephone called and countermanded that previous directive, ordering her back to Egypt.

The airport looked nothing like what Lydia remembered from last night. She wished as she entered it that she could stay one more day at the Shangri-La hotel. It would have been nice to sit at a beach resort and rest from everything. Too much time had passed since she'd pampered herself, but she still had two more missions to fulfill before she could think about relaxing. Even after that, she wondered if GRIP would find something else to keep her moving. The first and most important thing was to find and stop Amos.

Inside the airport, the first person Lydia saw was Labeeb. "Were you successful?" he asked, his French-Indian accent giving him an overly cheerful tone.

With a heavy grunt, Grisha just brushed by the thinner man, mumbling something about conceited Frenchmen.

Confused, Labeeb asked, "What is the matter with him?"

Lydia sighed. "I held him back from taking out the man who stole our jet."

Labeeb pursed his lips. "Oh, he will not easily be made happy anytime soon. By the way, Troy is waiting for you. He has been talking with the people here, and is getting permission to take possession of our airplane again. Come, I will take you to him."

With Labeeb leading the way, Lydia had to quicken her pace to keep up. The airport was small, and Troy met them at security. He said something to the men, and they admitted the group to the terminal. From that point, Troy led them to a concourse gate, and in no time they were boarding the jet. Sam, Vincent, and Paul had boarded first. Paul, however, had immediately stepped back out of the jet waving his hand at something invisible, as if shooing a fly away from his face. A look of disgust was on his twisted face, an expression soon copied in varying degrees by Vincent and Sam as they also exited the jet.

"Is something wrong?" Lydia asked as she approached.

"Yeah," Sam muttered. "Those people who stole this jet, they also trashed it. I think they also made off with our slush fund."

"Not to mention the stench," Paul added, looking incredulously as if Sam completely overlooked the most noticeable problem. "It smells like something died in there."

Lydia suddenly remembered Jay. The poor man's body had been locked up in the jet for a few days now. Only Troy and Paul were unaware that there actually was a dead man in the jet. But this gave her a perfect opportunity to dispose of her decomposing comrade.

For show, Lydia had to fake a look of surprise and grief, only because the death of the man had already sunk in. She then raced up into the jet as everyone watched. She came back out, with tears in her eyes. Only the tears were real. She hadn't expected to see Jay in such an awful state inside one of the smuggling compartments. The jet, having stood on the hot runway for the last two days, aided in the decomposition of his body more quickly than she would have guessed.

"Lydia, what is it?" Troy asked as he ran to his little sister. Sam, Vincent, and Labeeb only stared at one another, trying to understand the card that she was playing. Only Grisha ignored them all and climbed on board to start getting ready for takeoff.

"It's Jay," Lydia sobbed. "Whoever stole the jet, they killed Jay, too!"

Paul stepped forward. "Who's Jay? I thought Grisha was the only one on board when they stole your plane."

Lydia wiped a tear away and lied. "I thought he was the only one on board. He was supposed to be out getting supplies. We haven't heard from him, but I didn't think he would have returned to the jet."

"I'll take care of it," Troy soothed. "Just wait here, and don't go back in there till I get back."

Undoubtedly, Troy understood what Lydia was up to. He played his part as he jogged back to the terminal. This would mean a little more paperwork before they could take off, but at least it was a good excuse to unload the body here. It might even step up the airport's security and help motivate them to find the men who stole the jet. If that happened, maybe even Grisha would find his way back here and extend his revenge. As for Lydia, she was mostly just happy to get her jet back.

Turning around, she took another look at her modified Learjet. The joy she expected to find in its recovery was overshadowed by the events at Marshal's compound. Try as she might to forget him, Flint still had the firmest grasp on her heart, and no object would fully replace the void left by the man who'd touched her very soul. Lydia's obsession with her husband even caused her to see him in places that he couldn't possibly be. First in Egypt, then here in the Philippines. This distraction was starting to become a problem. She was wondering what she could do to remedy it when she felt a hand on her shoulder. She knew that it must be Paul's, and though she really didn't need any consoling, she let him take on the role.

"What do you say we get out from under this hot sun, and wait in the terminal?" he softly suggested.

Lydia squeezed one more tear out so Paul could see it run down her face when she looked him in the eye. She sniffed hard and wiped her face dry, then without saying a word she let him guide her back to the terminal. Once inside, she remained alert. Her eyes darted back and forth between the other people. Most of them were Filipino, with the occasional older American, no doubt veterans from World War II, looking to find love in the arms of a young Filipina. She knew them by the more common slang of D.O.M., or dirty old men.

She also noticed one other face. He looked slightly Filipino, but something about him stood out as being different. He was short and bald, and very familiar. He stared back at her, and she wondered if she'd seen his face somewhere in her distant past, or if she just remembered his face from walking to the jet moments earlier. When Paul pulled her aside, she lost sight of the man, letting her curiosity about him slip away.

"Let's sit down here and wait till everything is all cleared up," Paul spoke as he ran his strong hands through her hair. She let him, even though it annoyed her. Normally she would have enjoyed the gesture, but the combination shampoo-soap from the hotel and the tropical humidity didn't give her a clean feeling. She felt as though her hair was still greasy and coarse. By the time the embarrassment

of it took root in her mind, all thoughts of the familiar bald man were gone.

Chapter 31

His flight to Hong Kong didn't leave Lapu-Lapu for another two hours. With no place else to go, and nothing of any significance to do, Monk tried to distract himself by watching a movie in his mind. His autism had endowed him with a rare ability, an eidetic memory that allowed him to remember everything he came in contact with in pure clarity.

While this ability made it a trivial thing to rewatch a movie in his mind, he liked to challenge the memory by replacing the characters with the faces and voices of those around him. At that moment he was beginning the story of *Ben Hur*. He'd already replaced some of the characters successfully, and had begun to look around for the slave girl when he found an interesting group walking past him.

They stood out, being tall Caucasians on an island of small Filipinos, but he also recognized two of the people. One was a man he wasn't surprised to see here, Troy. After all, they had both been working together on stopping Shen Mao and Marshal Steel only fifteen hours earlier. The other was a woman who, along with a man of her own, followed after Troy by two minutes. Monk wouldn't have guessed that she should be here. All the same, his perfect memory immediately recognized her as being his best friend's wife, Lydia.

Monk had only known Flint for twenty-three and a half days when he met Lydia for the first and only time before she ran away. Even then, their acquaintance was a brief eight minutes. Monk remembered that she had treated him with the same awkwardness that people generally treated him when they didn't know how to act. In fact, Flint had been the only person, except for one of the nuns who raised him, who actually treated him like a normal person. The kindness of these two people had influenced Monk more than anyone else. The nun inspired a life devoted to enlightenment. In fact, he was so devoted, that when he spoke, with few exceptions, he almost exclusively quoted religious texts, or what he deemed to be inspiring speeches from notable people in history. Flint on the other hand, inspired a sense of true brotherhood and friendship. Both people gave Monk a deep and binding obligation to honor. Now with Flint's lost love mysteriously showing up in the arms of a strange man, Monk felt compelled to solve Flint's riddle of her disappearance.

At first Monk wondered if she noticed him, but the man with his arm around her quickly distracted her, and she didn't look back at Monk again. Deciding to abandon his replay of *Ben Hur*, he made his way behind the two, and without looking directly at them, focused all his attention on listening to their conversation.

Chapter 32

Sticking his head back out the doorway, Grisha looked to see if Lydia was successful in taking Paul away from the jet. When assured that they were gone, he called for Labeeb and Vincent to help him with the body. Sam was already busy inside, tidying up the place, and stowing away any sign of the weapons they carried. The men who'd stolen the jet had taken all the cash from it, but left most of the weapons on board, though they clearly had been handling them.

Any minute the Filipino custom agents would be crawling all over the jet, and Grisha had only a moment to make the scene look as though Jay had been shot inside the jet much earlier. It wasn't too difficult a task, since Jay had gotten blood on some of the seats and floor that he came in contact with when he'd been shot. The big trick was to pull his decaying body out of the body bag where he was, and place the heavy corpse below the seat where he had been bleeding a couple of days before.

To Grisha this was simply a task that needed doing. For Labeeb and Vincent, he could tell that they were trying hard to hold back from vomiting. Not only were they maneuvering a dead, stinking body, slimy with days of hot decomposition, but also it was their friend. Grisha didn't feel the same sense of desecration. He hadn't been as close to Jay as the others.

As soon as the crime scene was staged, everyone else got off the plane. Grisha, however, went into the cockpit and flipped the power switch on, and began checking gauges. Everything checked out fine with the exception of one. He then picked up the radio and called into the airport's fuel station and ordered a truck to replenish the tanks. Then, flipping the power switch off again, he followed the others out of the jet.

As soon as he finished this, he saw a small crew of Filipinos rushing over, with Troy quickly walking in pursuit. The men rushed past him, and Troy stopped and asked, "How's the plane?"

Grisha quietly replied, "Everything is set."

"Lydia?" Troy said with a raised eyebrow.

"She's in the terminal watching our guest," Grisha explained. "As soon as they get Jay off, and plane has chance to air out, we should be fueled and ready to go."

"Very good," Troy continued. "I want you guys to leave without me; I think I'm going to go back to Marshal's compound. I've got a feeling that he may have made a copy of the golden record before going to Mao's."

"We were just there," Grisha complained. "Why were we called off if you suspected this?"

"I didn't want to compromise Lydia," Troy whispered back. "Between you and me, we know what would happen if she met up with Flint again."

A puzzled look came over Grisha's face. "What does this have to do with Marshal's compound?"

"Her husband, Flint, was likely to be around there today," Troy answered.

Still confused, Grisha looked at Troy for an explanation. He expounded, "The man who stole this jet wasn't Marshal or any of his men. It was Flint." Troy then paused, and allowed Grisha to soak in the information. He must have guessed that this would raise more questions, because he then continued, "Flint thought that he was stealing the jet from Marshal's men, and was in pursuit of them the whole time. We actually just finished a raid on Shen Mao's place together. Don't tell Lydia, though. I don't want her to lose focus, especially as we finish this business with Amos."

Standing in place for a minute, Grisha allowed the new information to sink in. All the pieces were fitting together now. This explained why Lydia had stopped him from shooting Flint earlier at the compound. She must have caught a brief glance at him, but he doubted that she actually believed the man was really her husband or she would have run up to him at the time. Though his pride still demanded revenge on the man, he was seeing the benefit of not actually killing him. If he had, then Lydia would surely have turned into a mess.

"Don't worry," he reassured Troy. "Our mission is more important. I will not say one word to Lydia."

Troy nodded in satisfaction. "Good, you know what to do, then." He turned to walk away, pausing to ask something he'd forgotten. "By the way, Grisha, in your opinion, how close is Lydia to finding that space moss?"

With a shrug of his shoulders Grisha frankly replied, "You ask me, it is wild goose hunt. I think it does not exist anymore."

"Okay," Troy replied, half expecting this. "We'll move forward with our backup plan."

"By the way," Grisha asked, "what if you not find what you are looking for at Marshal's place?"

"Then I guess I'll have to go back to Bohol, and search Shen Mao's compound for anything that we missed before," Troy replied somewhat reluctantly.

Grisha watched as Troy walked away. Then he returned his attention to the jet to accommodate the efforts of the Filipinos with their investigation, but by this time they were already pulling Jay's body out of the jet. Most of the Filipinos carrying the body were skinny little guys, wearing secondhand denim shorts and white polo shirts. Only one man was standing aside, dressed in slacks and a button-up shirt. Grisha went up to him and asked, "Are you in charge here?"

The pudgier-looking fellow puffed his chest out a little and gave Grisha a slightly condescending look. "Are you with the crew of this airplane?"

"Yes, I am copilot," Grisha responded politely, even though he wanted to slap the smirk off the little guy's face.

"What can you tell me about this whole incident?" the Filipino asked in staccato English, each consonant enunciated so precisely that he seemed to have an indignant attitude toward everyone around him.

Grisha shook his head. "I think Troy already explained the issue. I have nothing more to add."

"Then what do you want?" he demanded, briefly propping himself up on his toes to accent his authority.

The urge to thump the top of this cocky little man's head was nearly unbearable. But Grisha had learned it was better to suck up to these types, or they would often make leaving all the more difficult. "You see," he began, forcing a little flattery, "I can see that you are very efficient in this work. I was wondering, we are in big hurry, when do you think we can take off?"

The Filipino thought for a moment, and then tapped the side of his chin for a minute more. Grisha was sure that nothing like this had ever happened here before. He was also certain that this man was oblivious to the protocol for handling such a situation. The man then addressed Grisha, "Give us one-half hour to make sure that nothing is left to be done. Your friend Troy has already given us instruction for how he wants the body handled. We just need to make sure that we have our paperwork in order before we clear you to leave."

With a curt smile, Grisha thanked the man. "You have been very helpful. We will finish cleaning jet. You let us know when we may go?"

"Of course," the man said with a smile that seemed far too small for his fat round head. He then turned away and started following the men who were carrying the body out.

As soon as he was gone, Grisha relaxed his face again, and began to help the fuel truck driver who had just arrived. His anger toward Flint was ebbing, as his anticipation started to focus on the thought of encountering Amos again. After they finished with Amos, this little group would no longer be a necessary part of GRIP's organization. He would then be able to rejoin Troy, and focus more on GRIP's other division. The transition was something he looked forward to. He was a little more worried about Lydia.

She might have a harder time.

###

Labeeb, after having taken leave of the jet, found his way into the airport terminal again. He was about to seek Lydia and update her on the progress when he noticed the time displayed on the wall. He was already five minutes late.

"Excuse me, Vincent," he told his companion, "but I need to use the restroom."

"Ah-ya, good idea. I think I will, too," Vincent replied.

Labeeb didn't like the fact that Vincent would be joining him in the restroom; it made things more risky. While they were on board the jet, taking care of Jay and cleaning up, Labeeb had already risked exposing himself to their judgments when he'd pocketed the two vials of powder, one of the oil-solidifying bacteria, the other the anti-coagulation version. Since they were opening and closing many of the smuggling compartments on the jet, this hadn't been terribly difficult, but still, if anyone had noticed him sneaking the vials, a convincing lie would be hard to imagine in time.

Inside the restroom, Vincent passed three stalls and went to the urinals on the other end of the room. Labeeb lagged behind and looked under the stall doors. The middle of the three stalls was occupied, leaving two others vacant. Taking the stall farthest from the urinals, he locked the door behind him.

The toilets were a typical hover-bowl design. Unlike Western toilets, these lacked a seat for sitting on. Instead there was simply a porcelain bowl, dirtied with the shoe prints of those who would stand on and squat to relieve themselves. The floors were wet, and though they looked clean enough, as if just mopped, Labeeb knew better. The saturated tiles

were almost always in this state of dampness because the Filipinos used cups of water and a hand to
clean their hind end with. To a Westerner this might
seem weird, but it explained why each stall had a
bucket full of water with a cup floating lazily on top.
The provided toilet paper was usually just used for
drying or for the convenience of the few Americans
who did pass through.

Happy that he wasn't here to actually struggle
with the process of purging his body of its waste in
this environment, he gave a gentle rap of his knuckles on the wall of the stall next to him.

Three small but distinct taps in reply notified
him that this was indeed his contact. Tugging the
two vials out of his pocket, he held them below the
formica divider, and the glass containers were immediately snatched away from him. There were no
words exchanged, so Labeeb took the opportunity
to relieve his bladder before flushing the toilet and
stepping out. Vincent joined him at the sink as they
washed their hands. Labeeb watched Vincent for
any sign that that he might have noticed Labeeb's
covert activity. He didn't notice anyone else in the
restroom until Vincent nudged him and pointed into
the mirror.

Behind them, coming from the stall that Labeeb
had passed the vials to, a short, skinny Chinese
woman emerged. She looked to be in her upper for-
ties, and had a metallic briefcase in hand. Stepping
out of the stall, she casually walked out of the restroom.

Labeeb looked at Vincent, and Vincent muffled a
laugh, "Either we are in the wrong room, or that was
really a man."

"That or they really need to write *Men's Room* in
Chinese, also," Labeeb suggested.

Chapter 33

"Did I do something wrong?" Dusty finally asked.

Flint had wondered if this was coming. Ever since the encounter at Marshal's compound, he'd felt awkward snuggling up to Dusty, knowing that he was still technically married. And though he didn't believe in fate or superstition, it seemed there must be a reason that he kept finding similarities in women that compelled him to believe they might be his Lydia. This time, in the light of day, improbable as it seemed, Flint couldn't dismiss the familiarity of the woman from the compound. Of course, the last time he'd chased a pretty face that reminded him of Lydia, he ended up finding Dusty.

This could be another such circumstance. On the other hand, this time things felt different. Lydia's disappearance two years ago had left a lot of unanswered questions, and perhaps it was futile hope that propelled him to seek out the impossible. In any case, he had to know.

"I have something to tell you, Dusty," he began, feeling unsure of how she would accept it. "A few years ago, I lost a son. My wife shouldered all of the blame. No matter what I did, she wouldn't let go of it. Then suddenly she vanished on the day she was scheduled to leave the hospital. She left a suicide note, but her body was never found. While I've generally accepted her as being dead, there's always been a piece of me that refuses to believe it."

Dusty looked at Flint and, with a hurt and slightly confused tremble in her voice, asked, "Why are you telling me this now? The last couple days, you haven't been bothered like this."

"I'm really sorry," Flint confessed sincerely. "But there was something about that last little encounter we just had that I didn't tell you. We should have been dead, but I think the woman stopped her companion from killing us. Even more, I could swear that the woman was my wife, Lydia."

Flint could tell that Dusty was skeptical. Frankly he couldn't blame her, and he hoped that she would understand. To be sure, he added, "Dusty, I really do like you. The last thing I want to do is hurt you. But you need to understand, I just have to know. What if that really was my wife, after all this time?"

Whether she understood or not, Dusty's eyes had become slightly bloodshot. He hadn't noticed this before, so it couldn't just be a side effect of the last couple days of stress. Then again, he wasn't sure if he'd actually paid that much attention to her eyes before now. They really were beautiful, with a sad puppy-dog longing. Maybe they were red from all the stress, but he guessed that it had more to do with this new revelation. A dummy could tell she was on the verge of getting emotional. Gratefully he watched as she composed herself and stated, "The first man I fall in love with in years, and he has a wife, and issues. Just my luck."

Flint suddenly felt like a jerk, though he hadn't actually intended any hurt. So he tried putting his arm around her, thinking it might help comfort her. Instead she pulled away and said, "Please, I don't want to be a fallback girl."

Why is she taking this so hard? It wasn't like they'd known each other for very long. "Dusty, please, I didn't want to hurt you. In fact, I really do want to get to know you better. My wife left me. I'm all alone, too. I only want to see her to understand why she left. If she's alive, I don't believe that I'll get her back or anything. After all, she's never tried to get in touch since the day she left. It's just that she left a big hole in my life, and I need to understand why." He then took Dusty's hand and kissed it. "Believe me, I don't want to lose you from my life, either. Let me see this through, keeping in mind, as I said before, that I don't want to lose what we've started together."

Dusty still appeared upset, but squeezed his hand before letting go. "Okay, but if it still works out that we keep spending more time with each other, I want it to go a little more slowly."

"I think that would be best," Flint agreed.

The taxi then came to a halt and Flint paid the driver. Turning back to Dusty he asked, "Are you coming with me, or do you want to wait this one out?"

She thought for a moment, then gave a half smirk, "Well, I've come this far already, I'll see it through. Besides, you seem to attract adventure, and I might lose you for good if I don't keep a close eye on you."

"Don't worry." Flint smiled. "I'm sure this one will

be purely diplomatic. I'm not really the adventure magnet you might think."

"Just the same," she skeptically replied, "I think I'd like to come along."

They exited the car and walked to the main doors of the airport. Dusty was holding one small bag, the only one they managed to avoid losing earlier. Even though they didn't plan on actually flying out, Dusty kept the luggage close, since there was nowhere else to put it for the time being. Flint, having also abandoned his entire luggage to Troy, opted to use the large wad of bills that he'd kept from the airplane to replace his missing clothing when the opportunity presented itself.

Once inside the airport, Flint decided the best course of action was to find Troy. If the Learjet was still where he'd left it, that shouldn't be a hard task. If he could find Troy, then maybe they could both work out the answers to questions raised by the incident at Marshal's compound. Besides, if it was at all possible that the woman really was Lydia, Flint couldn't think of a better and safer place to confront her and the deadly Russian she was with.

"You have a ticket?" the airport security guard asked.

"No, we have a private plane waiting," Flint half lied.

The security guard informed them that he needed to perform a random baggage check. He and one other guard began going through Dusty's bag, and so thorough was their search through the small piece of carry-on luggage that, in no time at all, a few other interested guards slowly joined in. Flint started getting nervous as he noticed them looking at his face almost as much as they were looking in Dusty's bags.

"Which plane you go to?" one of the guards asked.

Flint wondered if they suspected him of something, so paranoid was their demeanor. "I'm just going out to the little Learjet that I flew in on the other day."

The guards, satisfied with the luggage, closed it up and set it aside. A new face suddenly appeared, clearly having some status among the guards, as they flanked him on each side. "Sir, will you come with us for just a few minutes?" he demanded, more than asked.

Not wishing to draw any suspicion or unwanted attention, Flint saw little choice but to follow. He hoped that whatever their intentions, the matter would soon be cleared up. Flint didn't want to lose his opportunity to see if Lydia was in fact here.

The little round Filipino led the way past the security screeners and toward the terminal. However, right before they got to the waiting area, he detoured them to a side room. He opened the door and went inside; the security guards motioned for Flint and Dusty to follow. Inside the room, there was a single rectangular table and two chairs. The man ushered them to sit down. Flint realized that something was terribly wrong. Rooms like this were reserved for those who failed airport screenings.

"I think there may have been a mistake," Flint began to protest. However, the last guard entering the room shoved Flint toward the center table, almost causing him to lose balance and fall over.

Looking toward the door, he heard it click shut, and presumably locked. He knew he was unlikely to escape. "Oh great," he mumbled under his breath. Well, it was time to see how bad the accusations were going to be. The Filipino in command of the situation pulled out a digital camera and plugged it into a laptop. He worked it for a moment, then turned it around and waited to see Flint's reaction.

Dusty was first to react, flinching in disgust. Flint, however, understood what was going on and realized he was in much deeper trouble than he originally suspected. "I think that I'd like to speak to somebody from the United States Embassy," he said with a tremble. The image on the laptop reminded him of the dead body he'd found on the jet during his flight over. Only the picture that he was now seeing showed the body in a significantly greater state of decay.

"There will be time for that later," the man informed. "For now, I must place you both under arrest for murder."

"I didn't kill anyone, and this woman is innocent," Flint declared. He began to realize how foolish it had been to return to the airport. "I just met her here, and I can explain everything!"

"Yes," the man assured. "You will get that chance. But this is not the time or place for it." He motioned for the guards. They pulled out handcuffs and grabbed Flint's and Dusty's hands. But they were distracted as a loud thud sounded outside the door.

The security director walked over to the door and peered out a small window. Without any further warning, the door swung open, smashing against the director's face. The guards holding Dusty and Flint were debating what they should do, but before they had a chance to react, the small bald figure of Monk appeared in the doorway. In tow, Monk was dragging the unconscious body of the guard who had been posted on the other side of the door. Dropping the limp figure halfway into the doorway, blocking the self-locking door from shutting, Monk then charged the remaining guards near Flint.

Flint did a quick jab with his elbow, hitting the closest guard behind him in the ribs. The one behind Dusty came to his aid, but Monk, with a flick of his open hand, sent the guard coughing and gasping as he held his crushed Adam's apple. Monk then wrapped his short leg around the leg of the guard that Flint was struggling with, and did a quick pivot maneuver that sprawled the guard on his back. Leaning over, Monk gave a quick but effective open-handed punch. The guard hit his head hard on the concrete floor and fell unconscious.

The whole assault took less than five seconds, and Dusty still stood stunned. Flint shook his head and gave Monk a grateful bear hug. Monk, with his usual autistic ignorance of emotional expression, just stood there in his embrace, unsure how to react. "Monk, you are the last person I expected to come through those doors," said Flint, "but I thank you for saving us yet again." Flint released his friend Monk, whose fighting skills were as exceptional as anyone Flint had ever met. His deep friendship with the unusual man, plus his skill were the reasons Flint invited him to the Philippines. After the fight at Mao's place though, Flint didn't expect to need Monk again.

"'And the servant said unto him, Peradventure the woman will not be willing to follow me unto this land: must I needs bring thy son again unto the land from whence thou camest?' Genesis 24:5."

Flint had to ponder Monk's statement for a moment, since he hadn't prepared his mind for Monk's cryptic style of speaking.

Dusty shook her head in annoyance, and Flint knew she couldn't figure out why Monk always chose to speak in quotations. But she still ventured a guess. "Are you saying that we need to go back to

Bohol?"

"Genesis 13:1. 'And Abram went up out of *Egypt*, he, and his *wife*, and all that he had, and Lot with him, into the south,'" Monk said.

Suddenly it clicked, and Flint understood. "Lydia was here then—I knew it! But how do we follow them back to Egypt? They think I killed a man."

"1 Peter 4:15. 'But let none of you suffer as a murderer, or as a thief, or as an evildoer, or as a busybody in other men's matters.' 'Let us therefore come boldly unto the throne of grace, that we may obtain mercy, and find grace to help in time of need.' Hebrews 4:16."

"All right, Monk," Flint replied. "But I hope you know what you're doing."

Monk then asked for a little money by quoting the Great Master, "'Render therefore unto Caesar the things which are Caesar's.' Matthew 22:21."

Flint had heard him use this expression many times, and reacted as if his friend hadn't spoken incognito by pulling out a few bills and handing them over. Monk counted them, then held out his hand again. Flint peeled a few more over before Monk walked out, content. A little fear still lingered with Flint, but the arrival of his Hispanic savior greatly improved his outlook. With one eye glued to the small glass window of the interrogation room, he watched as Monk bypassed the security desk again and headed over to the ticket counter. Since Flint was already beyond the security checkpoint, he didn't have to worry about being checked again, and decided to make the most of his time while he waited for Monk to return.

Taking the keys and handcuffs from the guards, he cuffed all the unconscious men together before they began stirring. Then, for good measure, he removed their socks and tore some strips off their shirts. With a little effort, he got the socks shoved into their mouths, held in by the ribbon of cloth that was then tied firmly around their heads. The whole time Dusty held the door slightly open to prevent it from locking and waited for Monk's return. When their chauffer finally returned, the trio left the room, letting the door lock behind them. Flint hoped that it would be awhile before the security detail was discovered. The room looked soundproof, but it was still fairly cheap in construction.

By the time they reached the gate, their plane was about to take off for Manila. Upon checking their tickets, the flight attendant admitted them without any question. Flint was able to disguise his nerves, but Dusty was clearly upset. Once they sat down in their cramped seats on the airline, she turned to Flint. "What did you say earlier about not attracting adventure?"

"You mean, you call this 'adventure'?" Flint jested.

Then with a sudden recollection, Dusty's eyes popped wide open and she exclaimed, "My luggage! We lost my luggage!"

"Ugh, I'm sorry." Flint's muscles tightened, pulling his cheeks back to accent his show of guilt. "I don't think we can go back for it. I also don't think it would be wise to file a missing baggage claim." The last thing he needed was for Dusty to demand what could only be construed as unreasonable.

"You know this is your fault, right?" She scowled.

Flint looked over to Monk for some support, but Monk just shrugged and quoted the Bible again. "'If the Lord do not help thee, whence shall I help thee?' 2 Kings 6:27."

"Thanks a lot, Monk," he jeered. "Well, Dusty, for

what it's worth, I'm sorry. I hope you'll find it in your heart someday to forgive me."

Dusty just blew him off and whispered sarcastically to herself, "This deal just keeps getting better and better."

They were mostly silent for the rest of the flight to Manila. From there Monk was able to get them tickets to Egypt. Fortunately for them all, word had not yet arrived from Lapu-Lapu of Flint's run-in with security. Now that they were finally on the next leg of the journey, he doubted they would catch up with him.

With that worry out of the way, Flint occupied the next couple of hours planning around Monk's description of what Lydia and her friend Paul had talked about. Monk's perfect memory provided the next best thing to an audio recording of their conversations. Though Lydia and her people had left Lapu-Lapu a few minutes before Flint arrived at the airport, he estimated that he would still arrive in Egypt before them. Sure, they had their own jet, but Flint doubted that they would make any better time than his commercial flight, especially since he only had one very short layover. All in all, he figured it to be close. Regardless of who landed first, the trick would be to find them when they landed.

While much of the silence on the trip was due to Flint struggling to form a plan, the rest of the silence could be attributed to his bewilderment. He had seen Lydia. Everything that happened from the moment he'd first decided to follow Dusty in Egypt had led him to cross paths with his missing wife. He struggled with the overwhelming questions to which he could find no answers: *I don't believe in fate, but how can this be coincidence? If Lydia is alive, why hasn't she talked to me? And why is she running around with GRIP? How many people has she killed? What will I say to her?* Excitement, fear, and thoughts of betrayal all played heavily on Flint's mind. For the last two years, he'd wanted nothing more than to at least talk with her again, and to find out why she left, and why she wanted everyone to believe she was dead. So the other thoughts of hesitation surprised him just as much as knowing that she lived and was globe-trotting with a bunch of Martian descendants. *Does that mean she's part Martian too?*

There was one other possible problem. In his recitations, Monk had also mentioned something else about Lydia's conversation. Flint wasn't sure what it meant, but it almost appeared as though Lydia and her friend were caught up in something dangerous. Dusty may have been right when she had mentioned another dangerous adventure. Whatever awaited, Flint was sure glad that Monk had found him and decided to tag along again.

Chapter 34

The rustling of the driver in the back seat was beginning to irritate Bilal as they continued along the trucker's route. Xavier looked at his companion and suggested, "Why don't we just ditch him somewhere?"

Bilal, being less inclined to spontaneity, just shook his head no. But this didn't satisfy his high-strung partner. "They're likely to check on us when we arrive. What happens when they find this man tied up in the back?" Xavier argued.

Bilal understood that it was risky to keep the truck's original driver with them. Not only were they clearly Arab-looking, but also they were making unscheduled stops at the strategic oil reserve sites for maintenance. The man they had tied up in the backseat was one of the subcontracted technicians that the Department of Energy employed to maintain the pumps at two of the facilities. They now had his truck, but they still needed to convince the security at the facilities that they also worked for the same company.

"Let me worry about him," Bilal ordered. "You worry about getting us in."

"Okay, I'll get us in, but you need to do something about the driver. We still have more deposits to make. Sooner or later, someone will notice him."

Bilal knew he was right. Even if they were only hitting one installation, this would be risky, but they had been ordered to hit every reserve the U.S. maintained.

Already their time to prepare was seriously diminished. They hadn't received enough advance notice to finish making the timers for the mechanism that would release the substance into the oil. Their plan now, was to get inside, do a small inspection of the pipes leading down to the crude, and quickly deposit some raw powder into the system. This needed to be done quickly and without drawing any attention to themselves. Since they didn't have any time-release detonators, the solidification would begin immediately. They only had a short window of opportunity to hit every site before their actions got discovered.

Bilal knew this procedure was taking place at some of the other large oil reserves around the whole of the Western world. Some might deposit their powder through the main facility pumps, like he was. Others might drill directly into pipes outside the facilities that fed certain reserves. In any case, his responsibility was to take care of the U.S. reserves, and he didn't want to be the only one who failed.

There was some confusion in his mind as to which organization he was helping. At first he thought it was al-Qaeda, but he'd also received some instruction from men who clearly seemed to be infidels. Regardless, he knew that his current employers were powerful, and about to deal a significant blow the Western world. Even if he were caught and killed, he knew this was his mission in life. To die in the service of Allah would be the greatest way to die. If he didn't, then he would be satisfied to live and watch the fruits of his labor unfold.

Soon they were only fifteen minutes away from their first destination. The landscape at this point was fairly deserted, and Bilal brought the truck to a halt. Xavier looked up and smiled, but to Bilal this was simply a matter of business. He helped the truck's original driver out of the cab and walked with him several hundred feet off the side of the road.

"I'm sorry to leave you out here," Bilal said. "But I must tie you up out here so you can't warn anybody of our actions. If you cooperate with me, I won't hurt you."

The man followed with some hesitation. He, however, seemed relieved that Bilal had given him the hope of being unharmed. As soon as Bilal judged them to be far enough away from the road to not be seen, he asked the man to sit down. With his hands tied, the man struggled first to his knees, then fell sideways. With a little effort, the former driver worked his way into a sitting position. When he again brought his gaze up to his captor, he discovered that Bilal had drawn a large blade. The unlucky driver had no time to react before the knife was plunged between his shoulder bone and the top of his ribcage. The knife was long enough to pierce his heart.

Whether real or imagined, he wasn't sure if Bilal saw a look of confused betrayal in the man, as if a close friend had done this to him. Try as he might,

Bilal couldn't turn away from the accusing face as the life drained from the driver's eyes. This was Bilal's first kill, and though he knew it must be done, he couldn't bring himself to lay a hand back on the hilt of the weapon. So he let the knife remain in the man and stood erect, checking himself to make sure he hadn't gotten any blood on his hands. He then turned around as the body slumped to the ground. Allah would justify him, but that didn't make the act any easier for the inexperienced killer's conscience as he jogged back to the truck.

"You did the right thing," Xavier commented.

But Bilal remained silent as he shifted the truck back into gear and pulled onto the road again.

Chapter 35

The only car the GRIP tactical team was able to rent on short notice was a small sedan, barely large enough to carry all six passengers, let alone a few small rifles. It was perhaps better this way, thought Labeeb. A few small arms might go unnoticed, but a large arsenal could get the troop in major trouble if discovered. Though six fully-grown adults packed into such a small car were also a little suspicious, there weren't many options at the moment. With their slush fund depleted, they had just enough money to pay for fuel on the flight back to Egypt, and to rent the small car.

Immediately after leaving the Cairo airport, they started toward Suez on the Cairo–Sweis road. Being approximately eighty miles away, and having already been going for about forty-five minutes, Labeeb estimated that they still had another forty-five minutes to an hour before they arrived.

Having spent a lot of time in France and India, and under varying circumstances, Labeeb was no stranger to cramped spaces. The body odor, on the other hand, was becoming an issue. Adding to that, almost nobody was in a social mood. Naturally the annoying smell caused the drive to be tense and quiet. During this time Labeeb pushed aside any thoughts of discomfort, and pondered the progression of his personal motives. This was what he had joined GRIP for. Though he wasn't around Troy and the rest of the scientists, he felt that he would be of most use here with Lydia's group. She was, after all, the one closest to finding that piece of the puzzle he craved.

Lydia was quiet for the whole trip. Labeeb suspected that her past life was still haunting her, maybe even more so since they left the Philippines, though he couldn't understand why. Grisha seemed colder than ever. Even though the Russian's accommodating humor suggested a return of his good nature, lately Labeeb had noticed a chilling side to the man. He assumed that it was mostly due to the defeat suffered in Egypt, but even before that, the team's second in command had seemed a little too edgy at times. Sam was Sam; a typical Englishman with typical dry humor. It was hard not to like the Brit, even though he could be a little annoying at times. Then there was Vincent. He seemed to be the one hit hardest by Jay's death. The two had been close, and now Vincent seemed the most anxious to confront Amos about his friend's death.

When Labeeb had joined GRIP, his anonymous benefactor had warned him not to become too attached to the group. To do so might spell disaster for Labeeb, but also may invoke repercussions from his anonymous friend as well. Labeeb understood that this benefactor didn't fully trust GRIP; so, with the warning at heart, Labeeb had involved himself with caution. He agreed that if he could gain access to the secretive association, he would keep his friend in the loop with their pursuits.

His adventures thus far hadn't violated his personal integrity. Everything he had been involved with appeared to be for the greater good of the world. Only a month ago, Labeeb had e-mailed his friend with an argument that GRIP was not as bad as he made it out to be. But his friend still insisted that there was more that Labeeb didn't know yet, and insisted that Labeeb not get too comfortable with the apparent do-gooders. For Labeeb it was difficult to believe, but he had developed a profound respect for his nameless and faceless e-mail buddy. Thus he attempted to preserve an unbiased view of the group.

For the time being, Labeeb would do whatever he could to help GRIP and his benefactor without betraying either. Aside from covertly e-mailing his friend about GRIP's activities and stealing the vials of bacteria, he'd managed to serve the two masters fairly well. Labeeb justified these minor offenses incurred against GRIP as nothing too severe.

Now that they were close to wrapping up Amos's terror plot, they might be able to focus their efforts on the prize piece of the puzzle that Labeeb wanted most. He could care less about this oil-solidifying bacteria, though it was interesting. Labeeb's aim was strictly on acquiring the plant that the Legionnaires of World War I had been smuggling to France when their ship was sabotaged. Whatever Labeeb's benefactor had against GRIP was none of his concern, so long as he found the plant he was looking for. Now that he knew this plant was from an ancient Martian civilization, the thought of eventually finding it was even more exciting.

Labeeb hoped that GRIP would share the plant with the world if they were to find it, but his friend suggested that GRIP would rather profit from it, instead. Labeeb cared little what happened to it, as long as he was involved in bringing it to the world. *But if GRIP wants to keep it a secret*, Labeeb thought, *my minor treacheries will take on a deeper resolve. I will find a way to share the plant with the public.*

While he sat contemplating, Labeeb also wondered if he should have reported to his benefactor on the pending attack against Amos. Ever since he'd stepped out of the airplane, he hadn't found a chance to update his shady mentor. Labeeb knew that his secret friend wanted to know every detail of GRIP's assault on Amos's organization, but this would be impossible to accomplish in the heavily packed sedan. His friend would just have to learn about the engagement afterword.

As soon as they were within five minutes of their destination, Labeeb reached between his legs, where he rested a small carry pack. Carefully placing his hands inside the faded-leather bag, Labeeb removed several rings. Though he considered France to be his homeland, during his years in India, he took to practicing with the chakram, an ancient weapon used by Indian Sikhs, which had become his trademark weapon in the group. It was basically a metal ring about five to eight inches in diameter with a sharpened edge all around. With the capability of severing human limbs, or even decapitating when thrown, it was a formidable weapon in the hands of a skilled fighter. Granted the French-Indian rarely found the weapon to be practical in a gunfight, but when stealth was required, the hollow razor disc came in handy.

Placing eight of these around his left wrist as though they were bracelets, and one larger chakram around his neck, Labeeb stole a glance in the rear-view mirror of the car. To the average man, his deadly jewelry looked uncommon, but people rarely said anything about it. The others on the team assured him that the rings gave him the appearance of a rich eccentric, not a dangerous commando. So with little or no objections, Labeeb almost always went into battle with his tinkling ornaments.

Clearing his head, Labeeb began to meditate on the looming attack. He tried to remember his previous encounters with the terror group, and wondered how badly his own group would be outnumbered. He figured at least three to one, maybe worse. There was also the likelihood that Amos might be expecting GRIP. Amos did seem to have a remarkable ability to follow the team's movements. Vigilance would be required, even before reaching the building that Paul described as their headquarters. For all he knew, Amos could even have eyes on them that very moment.

Apparently Lydia had been thinking similarly, because she had Grisha pull over and stop. Addressing everybody, she said, "If we're to stop Amos, it's better if we don't go together. We can't risk all getting taken out in the same car. Grisha and I are going to find and scout Amos's headquarters. Sam, take the others with you; we'll meet up at this address. Try to blend in." She then handed Sam a torn-off piece of paper with the approximate address of the building on it. "Don't forget extra pistols. When you get to Paul's ship, see if he can grab a few of his crew for the raid. Heaven knows we could use the help. Grisha and I will head straight over to the building and try to survey it. We'll meet up with you all in two hours."

Labeeb waited while Sam and Vincent got out of the cramped car before he exited. They walked back to the trunk and each pulled out a small duffel bag with their rifles and other gear. Vincent grabbed the heaviest and Paul, with nothing to carry, slammed the trunk shut. They watched as Lydia and Grisha drove away.

"We'll stick together until we get to your ship," Sam said to Paul. "Then while you and Vincent are assembling any extra men, we'll keep an eye out for any of Amos's goons around the shore."

Chapter 36

Dusk was falling, and many people were going home from work. With her mind not completely on the road, Lydia found herself slamming on the brakes to avoid hitting the car in front of her. Grisha grunted against the strain of his seat belt. Luckily Sam wasn't here. He would have had some witty remark for sure. But in her defense, the road shouldn't have suddenly became this congested. This seemed like an unusual time and place for the traffic disturbance, but since they couldn't continue driving, they parked the car to continue on foot. The whole time, they were acutely aware that the accident ahead might have been deliberately planned. Amos was not only smart, but he had good connections. He might very well know that she was coming for him.

"If they are on to us, maybe it's better if we not give them easy trail to follow," Grisha suggested.

Lydia hesitated. They had already split up from

the others. To split up again from Grisha might expose them to more risk than she was comfortable with. After some hesitation, she went against her better judgment and agreed. "Don't forget where we are meeting up, and be careful."

Stepping out of the car, Grisha heaved his own small duffle of combat gear, then walked around to the other side of the street. Before long he was turning down another street, and Lydia found herself alone. She exited the car, a hot breeze licked the loose fitting clothes. Each glint of sun off of a building's window was like a heat wave filling in where the breeze slackened. She was wearing cream colored slacks with a button up business casual shirt. Despite the light colored and breathable garb, her skin immediately felt sticky with sweat. Grabbing the last duffle from the trunk, she too began to pack her combat gear down the road. For another ten minutes, though it seemed like an hour, she couldn't shake the feeling that she was being watched. It was the spine-tingling feeling that people got when they knew something was wrong but couldn't say what exactly. She kept looking over her shoulder, trying to hide her nervousness. After all, it could just be her general discomfort playing tricks on her mind.

Early in her relationship with Grisha, he had once talked about how to find a tail, and elude the person tracking her. She tried to remember what he had mentioned, but the years had dimmed her recollection. All she knew was that it would take a long time to get where she was going, because it would require a series of backtracking and weaving around. Instead she tried to improvise, memorizing each face that she passed, and then, with a series of smaller switchbacks, she zigzagged her way through the town, constantly checking for any familiar faces.

Thus far, she could find no sign of a suspicious person, but her nerves were still frayed.

When she stepped into a quiet intersection, she found herself face to face with somebody she did recognize. The other woman seemed to be scrutinizing her also, maybe even comparing Lydia to a picture on a cell phone. Though Lydia had forgotten where she had seen the face, it was too much of a coincidence that any familiar person should cross paths here, of all places. Not wanting to expose herself to undue attention by firing a gun, she bent over to place her duffel bag with her guns on the ground. Then, in one smooth motion, she pulled out a five-inch hunting knife that was sheathed in a side pocket of the duffle.

The other woman took immediate notice of the knife and scanned her surroundings, only to find nothing for a weapon. But this did not discourage her. She unbuckled her small leather belt and, with lightning speed, dislodged it from the loops of her khaki slacks. The belt obviously wasn't needed to hold her pants up. She stood her ground, waiting for Lydia to make a move.

Lydia stared down her opponent. The woman was clearly fit, and showed no signs of fear. Her brown hair was smooth and lightly sun-bleached. Her skin suggested a great deal of time spent outside, since it was tan but not olive and covered in freckles. "Who are you, and what are you doing here?" Lydia asked coldly.

The woman tightened her grip on the belt, her only weapon, and replied, "My name is Dusty, and you're the reason I'm here."

Lydia noticed a little contempt in Dusty's voice, and decided that she must work for Amos. She also believed that Amos wouldn't send just one assassin, so there had to be more. For this reason, she decided not to wait for Dusty's backup to show, and didn't hesitate in charging the woman.

Lydia noticed surprise on the woman's face, but it was quickly replaced with determination, and then the belt came flying over like a bullwhip. Even though Lydia was expecting the whip, it still caught her blade with enough force to rip it from out of her hands. She realized it would have been a better idea to simply pull out one of her guns. But now as she plowed into the woman, the moment was too late, and she would just have to learn how good this Dusty girl was at hand-to-hand combat.

Chapter 37

After walking out of Lydia's sight, Grisha stopped into a small shop and bought a cup of coffee. The car ride had been claustrophobic for the large Russian, and it had given him a headache. He hoped that the caffeine would settle his nerves. Lydia had wanted to meet near the northwest corner of the office building that Paul had described. She seemed to be paranoid, but Grisha doubted that they would actually run into any trouble.

As he approached an intersection, he found an even more delightful surprise. He did one quick sweep with his eyes to make sure that Lydia was nowhere to be seen, then he quietly walked behind the man he'd found. He didn't know how or why the man happened to be in the same place as him again, but he relished the idea of confronting him without anyone to stop him. With a forceful grip, he sank his fingers into the back of the man's shirt and threw him up against a building wall.

"So we meet again," he said, allowing his Russian accent to come out stronger than normal. "But this time, you not be so lucky."

The man struggled to turn around, and Grisha leaned in harder, pinning the man's back against the building. From deep in Grisha's throat, he grunted with amused satisfaction, delighting in the astonishment on Flint's face at seeing him again. But Flint caught him off guard, as he realized too late that he was still holding his cup of hot coffee in the other hand. Flint grabbed the arm that was holding him against the wall while simultaneously slapping the other hand with the coffee. The scalding beverage splashed into Grisha's face, shocking him into letting go of this inferior yet annoying man.

Flint kept his grip on the Russian's thick forearm and did a quick twist, pulling his arm around into a pinching point. The adrenaline was now causing Grisha to forget his burn as his anger roared with all the ferocity of his pent-up rage. Ignoring the pain in his arm, Grisha turned around and let loose a powerful punch as his own shoulder let out a muffled pop.

Flint fell onto his back, and Grisha took the agonizing steps toward resetting his dislocated shoulder. Once it snapped back into place, he let out his Russian version of a rebel yell as he flung himself at Flint who was back on his feet. Grisha was surprised at how quickly Flint was able to react, and his first volley of punches missed as Lydia's estranged husband ducked and dodged. Flint even managed a couple of weak punches on him. This, however, didn't faze Grisha. He became more intoxicated with the idea of a good boxing fight with this man who had made him look like a fool.

I don't care if you are Lydia's husband, Grisha tried to convince himself. If Lydia ever found out that he'd killed her significant other--no she wouldn't, and he shouldn't. But his anger had already clouded his judgment, and the fight was already under way. *This is beyond my control now*, he thought, but couldn't admit that he himself had lost control as they began to exchange a few good hits. Grisha loved to box. He was a big guy, and often surprised his opponents with an agility unusual for his size. For every hit that Flint landed, Grisha got in two even stronger punches.

At one point Grisha decided to taunt the spry little guy. Giving the younger man a big yellow grin, he allowed a few free punches to land square in the face. As Grisha maintained his intimidating smile, forcing himself to look unfazed by the volley of attacks, he could see that Flint was becoming a little more than worried. Grisha knew that many people who got into a fight believed the outcome depended entirely on skill. However, he also knew that psychology played a key role in determining the winner. Right now he was doing a number on Flint, and it appeared to be working.

From this point Grisha knew of two ways the fight would go. In the first, his opponent might realize the futility of his position and try to abandon the fight. With nobody to witness his cowardice, Grisha wondered if this man was capable of admitting defeat so easily. If that happened, then Grisha would gladly trip the man and finish him off quickly and quietly. The second way was the opponent taking a desperate risk. This usually played to Grisha's advantage, because the opponent was often weakened and unsure of his attack. That would provide Grisha a great opportunity to prolong Flint's suffering to fully satisfy Grisha's need for revenge.

GRIP had hired Grisha for his ability to fight, and do whatever was necessary for the success of the team. He was also there to help train Lydia, the rising star in GRIP's leadership. Despite his abilities, Grisha didn't feel like just being another combatant like Sam, Vincent, or Labeeb. He preferred to see himself as a professional with a little sportsmanship. This played a large part in Grisha's disdain for Flint. The way Flint had beat him while stealing the jet was completely void of honor. Grisha was no sadist, but he still wanted Flint to feel every last painful sensation that was due him.

From what he understood of Flint as an adventure seeker, running away was the unlikely choice. Flint had already stuck his nose into affairs that shouldn't have concerned him. No, Flint would try a bold but unfruitful move instead. But how would it come?

Grisha flung a heavy fist, and landed it square into Flint's chest. He could tell that Flint had been severely winded, but he was still quick enough to escape a follow-up blow that might have ended the fight.

Grisha allowed Flint a moment to catch his breath. After all, the longer the fight, the more punishment he could deal out. Then it happened: Flint began his last, desperate effort. Grisha half laughed inside as the smaller man began to charge. *This is it,* he thought. *And you're leaving your head wide open for attack. Well, good-bye, Flint!*

Chapter 38

Not knowing exactly where Lydia would be, Monk had suggested in his own unique way that they split up to look for her. Flint and Dusty decided to patrol around the buildings. Most resembled business offices, as per Paul's description. Monk, on the other hand, went to look for the oil tanker to see if this Paul guy had led Lydia there instead.

He discovered several tankers, any one of which could have been Paul's. Unsure of which one to scout, he went in search of the harbormaster. Monk found him inside a small shack, watching an old black-and-white rerun of *Get Smart* on a small color TV. The harbormaster noticed Monk walk in, but only turned the volume down for a minute as he finished listening to Maxwell Smart quote, "The old Professor Peter Peckinpah all-purpose anti-personnel Peckinpah pocket pistol under the toupee trick."

The husky harbormaster then lumbered his soggy form over to the counter where Monk was, chuckling at the wit of the old American sitcom as he moved. Then he silenced up and waited. Sometimes Monk imagined what people would be if they were animals, and he imagined this oaf as some form of mutant sloth and walrus hybrid. He even seemed to have one tusk-like tooth protruding from the corner of his lips.

Monk stared with interest at the man for a moment before he was asked something in Arabic.

Monk wasn't familiar enough with the language to understand, but by the man's tone, he knew he was being asked what was wanted, as well as to make it snappy so that the sloth-walrus could return to his TV show.

Since the harbormaster was watching an American show in English, Monk didn't doubt the man's ability to speak English. After all, English and French were often used in Egypt as the languages of business. Monk thought for a moment on how to address the man and decided it best to piece small parts of the Quran and Bible together. Taking from 18:17 of the Quran, Monk began with a questioning tone, "'So they set out until, when they embarked in a boat...'"—then flawlessly skipped to Genesis 28:18 of the Bible—"'...And Jacob rose up early in the morning, and took the stone that he had put for his pillows, and set it up for a pillar, and poured oil upon the top of it.'"

The harbormaster puzzled for a minute, then asked, "I'm afraid English isn't your strong point. *Parlez-vous français?*" The whole time he spoke, his bottom tooth flipped at his lip.

Monk tried to ignore the rotting ivory and simply repeated, though in fewer words, "When they embarked in a *boat,* and poured *oil* upon the top of it?"

This time he made sure to emphasize *boat* and *oil* so the simpleton could understand.

The man thought again then asked, "Do you want a boat oiled?"

Monk shook his head, then noticed a large whiteboard that covered one wall showing a list of ships and dates. He stepped behind the counter, aware that he was probably violating the harbormaster's wishes, but the sea blubber made no move to stop him. Monk then began to scan the board, unsure of what he was looking for.

The harbormaster asked, pointing to the board, "Can't find your boat? These are the merchant ships, these are the large oil tankers, these are—"

Monk held up his hand, and stopped him after oil tankers. There were a few listed in that particular section, and it didn't take long for Monk to find the ones that had been there the longest. He knew that if Paul had been delayed for a couple extra days, then the ship was also likely to be delayed. Narrowing his search down to two ships, he asked another question, this time quoting a fraction from Jeremiah 51:57, "'. . . her captains, and her rulers'?"

"This one here is captained by a man named Pyke, and this one by a woman, Sharma or something like that," the man informed. Neither of these interested Monk.

He stared at the board for a minute more, then noticed a spot where the name of the ship had been erased, but the dates still remained. He pointed to the spot and looked back at the man.

"Whoops, that must have been rubbed off," he said casually. "It's been there for several days." He then pointed out the window at the ship. "It just got cleaned a couple days ago, and I don't know why they're still here. Actually I should check with their captain on that. What was his name, Crowlen—no, Cragen—"

"Crandall?" Monk interjected.

"Yes, that's it, Captain Paul Crandall," he said as he turned around to check in one of his ledger books. "Was that who you're looking for?"

By the time he finished asking his question, Monk was already on his way out the door. He had already wasted enough time talking to this half man, half beast. He often wondered why it was so difficult for people to understand him. Sure, he had made a commitment to only quote great teaching from the scriptures and other inspired people, but his friend Flint had always been able to keep up. And Flint never gave him weird looks.

Monk decided not to walk to the edge of the pier just yet. He could sufficiently study the tanker from where he was standing. If it had ever been moored at the dock, it was not anymore. It was now anchored a good hundred meters or so from the pier, so he wondered what his next step should be. He could borrow a boat to reach the ship, but that might get him into trouble, even though he would return it immediately afterward. Besides, then he would have to calculate the exact amount of fuel that he used, so as to reimburse its owner. Since he doubted there was any spec sheets on most of the smaller boats around here, that would be difficult.

He might be able to swim out there, but how would he get on the ship once he arrived? The anchor chain would be his best bet, but the water might make his hands too slippery to climb it. *Perhaps I'm going about this all wrong*, he thought, at the same time thinking of two scriptures and a quote by Winston Churchill that might convey the thought. This wasn't unusual for him, since quotable sentiments were the only language he now used aloud. The quotes didn't distract him from the main point of focus, which was getting to the tanker.

Monk calculated the time it would take for Lydia and Paul to arrive via their Learjet. Again, he didn't have enough information to accurately estimate their speed. With the limited and imperfect information that Monk was using, he estimated that Paul and Lydia were still on their way here. He then pondered the words of Robert Heinlein, who once wrote: "Progress isn't made by early risers. It's made by lazy men trying to find easier ways to do something." With this in mind, Monk decided to wait, but he must find a spot that would give him the greatest advantage.

Without looking around again, since he could clearly picture everything he'd already seen, he began walking toward a small grassy hill, which overlooked the most traveled sidewalk. Though he would immediately be able to notice anybody he saw, no matter how inconspicuous he tried to appear, he also understood that he himself wasn't like most everybody. Monk imagined himself looking dubious as he spied on the sidewalk traffic.

Wanting to blend in with the scenery, Monk reached into a nearby waste bin, pulling out a used newspaper. The cliché disguise was the first act of concealment that entered his head. In any movie he'd seen, people often disguised themselves in public by pretending to read a newspaper. '*When in Rome, do as the Romans do,*' he quoted to himself as he stood erect on the top of the hill, and lifted the paper vertically, to a height just below the bridge of his nose.

Only after looking over the top of the periodical for a minute did he decide to quickly scan the newspaper. He had to raise the paper up a little higher to actually see it. Looking at it turned out to be a good thing, because at first he thought it was written in some weird language, only now realizing it was just upside down. Correcting his error, he brought the top of the paper back to its place in front of his lips. When he looked back toward the sidewalk, he noticed a small group of men walking along. They were staring at him, which wasn't that unusual. People often stared at him. While he didn't recognize everybody in the group, he did recognize the man he'd previously seen named Paul. *But where is Lydia?* he wondered. Only one way to find out.

Walking off the hill toward the group, Monk placed the paper back in the wastebasket on his way. Passing a few small trees in the landscaping, Monk confronted the group that was still watching him. When he came to a stop, he quoted the Quran 27:23, since it fit the circumstance best at this point, "'I found a woman ruling over them, and she has been given of everything and she has a mighty throne.'" Then to finish the question, he added from Genesis 3:9, "'And the Lord God called unto Adam, and said unto him, Where art thou?'"

One of the men tried to push him aside and continue on, but Monk pushed the man back into the group and repeated, "'I found a woman ruling over them . . . Where art thou?'"

"He's must be crazy," one of the men stated with an Italian accent. "Let's go around him."

Monk, however, didn't like the idea and quoted Winston Churchill: "'Here is the answer which I will give to President Roosevelt . . . We shall not fail or falter; we shall not weaken or tire. Neither the sudden shock of battle nor the long-drawn trials of vigilance and exertion will wear us down.'"

Paul stepped forward and asked, "Sir, will you please let us go on our way? We are in a very big hurry."

"Psalms 16:4. 'Their sorrows shall be multiplied that hasten after another god,'" Monk replied.

"Please," Paul urged. "These men can be violent, I don't want them to get angry and hurt you. Believe me, they are more than capable."

At this comment, the Italian gave Monk a peek at a pistol that was tucked into his waistband. Monk had already guessed the group was packing heat because of the way their shirts bulged in the spots a gun might be concealed. It didn't frighten Monk, and he simply stated, "'Nonviolence is the answer to the crucial political and moral questions of our time—the need for mankind to overcome oppression and violence without resorting to violence and oppression. . . . man must evolve for all human conflict a method which rejects revenge, aggression and retaliation. The foundation of such a method is love.' Martin Luther King Jr."

The Italian took a step forward, as the one who looked as though he were from India choked out a small laugh. Monk wasn't sure why, since he hadn't meant to be funny. The Italian looked at the Indian for only a second before continuing his advance. He grabbed Monk by the front of his collar, and threatened, "Step aside, *retardato!*"

"'If we desire to avoid insult, we must be able to repel it; if we desire to secure peace, one of the most powerful instruments of our rising prosperity, it must be known, that we are at all times ready for War.' George Washington," Monk retorted, still holding his ground.

In Monk's understanding, the situation was clearly starting to escalate, even though he originally meant no harm. He also wondered if there was a way to avoid the almost imminent conflict. But the Italian raised his fist, and Monk decided that he would rather not get punched. More by instinct than by conscious thought, he spread his arms out like a cross, brought them quickly in with a slight bend to his elbow, and slammed his two palms into the arm that was holding him. The Italian's elbow was forced to bend the wrong way and came unhinged with a sinewy crack. The Italian's mouth gaped open as if to scream in pain, but so intense was the pain that no audible sound escaped his lips. His fist immediately dropped to nurse the broken arm, and Monk took advantage, grabbing it and twisting it behind the aggressor's back. This time a yell followed as the Italian was forced around, becoming a human shield, in case the others decided to pull out their own guns.

With his free hand, Monk took the pistol out of the Italian's waistband and threw it onto the grass. It all happened so quickly that the other three men didn't have time to react. They stood there, looking surprised, then one with a British accent stood forward and advised, "I'm sorry, we didn't mean to get into an argument. Just tell us what you want, and we'll all be on our way."

Monk eyed the men cautiously, then replied, "Lydia."

The Brit stepped back, his face hardening. "So that's it—you're with Amos, aren't you?"

This brought Luke 3:25 to Monk's mind and he began to recite, "'Which was the son of Mattathias, which was the son of Amos, which was the son of Naum, which was the son of Esli, which was the son of Nagge—'"

"Enough of this!" the Englishman blurted. He

reached into a bag and pulled out a compact military-style rifle. "You guys aren't going to get away with this."

Monk wasn't sure what this man was talking about. He also wondered who this Amos character was. But he had stepped beyond the point of settling anything with reason, so he launched the Italian at the man carrying the rifle, then used the moment to wrangle the gun from the Brit and flung it away. Paul didn't seem to want anything to do with the fight, and backed away. The Indian, however, began to twirl a couple of thin metal rings on his fingers.

From the looks of it, they were some sort of throwing weapon. The edges, Monk guessed, must be very sharp, and he wondered if this was a common weapon in this part of the world. But like every weapon, it had a weakness. Monk dove behind a two-inch thick tree, grabbing and bending the trunk just in time to block the first razor-sharp ring as it came whistling through the air.

To call Monk's emotion surprise would have been going too far. A little curious wonderment did pique his mind as the ring sliced right through the tree. He hadn't expected this weapon to cut so deeply. Luckily it lost enough momentum to only cause a small scratch on his arm. Monk grabbed the ring and, lifting the severed portion of the tree that was still in his other hand, he swung the trunk in front of himself, just in time to block another ring as it stuck into the end of the freshly chopped wood.

Having witnessed and subsequently memorized the way Indian threw the ring, Monk duplicated the action and sent the first ring whizzing back at the man. The Indian was able to dodge, since Monk hadn't thrown the ring completely as he meant. With one practice throw out of the way, he confidently believed the second ring, which he pulled from the tree, would find its mark. The only thing that stopped him was deciding it would be more productive to not kill these friends of Paul. If he was to find Lydia, he needed to form a truce instead.

So he threw the circular razor at a billboard twenty-one feet away, splitting the head of a person on one of the posters. This display was meant to prove to the Indian that Monk had mastered the ring, and that he was in fact sparing them. The relief the Italian's eyes communicated was enough to assure Monk that the message was well received.

The Englishman missed the gesture of peace and had recovered his rifle. He brought it to bear on Monk but the Indian shouted, "Sam, wait!"

"He almost killed you, Labeeb," Sam reminded. Now Monk only had the Italian's name to learn.

"Yeah, he almost did, but then he stopped," Labeeb argued.

"You saw what he did to Vincent," Sam said, not taking Monk out of his sights.

"Wouldn't you have done the same thing?" Labeeb replied.

Sam addressed Monk. "Okay, little guy, come clean. Do you or do you not work for Amos?"

"Proverbs 18:6–7. 'A fool's lips enter into contention, and his mouth calleth for strokes. A fool's mouth is his destruction, and his lips are the snare of his soul,'" Monk ignored the question, and continued his attempt at peace by adding, "'A man that hath friends must shew himself friendly: and there is a friend that sticketh closer than a brother.' Proverbs 18:24."

"This is rubbish," Sam proclaimed, unsure what to do next.

"No, wait." Labeeb stood up. "This guy speaks in

riddles. I think he wants to be friendly." Addressing Monk he asked, "Why do you look for Lydia?"

To which Monk replied, content that he was finally getting somewhere, "Numbers 5:11–15. 'And the Lord spake unto Moses saying, Speak unto the children of Israel, and say unto them, If any man's wife go aside, and commit a trespass against him . . . And the spirit of jealousy come upon him, and he be jealous of his wife, and she be defiled: or if the spirit of jealousy come upon him, and he be jealous of his wife, and she be not defiled: Then shall the man bring his wife unto the priest.'"

"Argh, see what I mean?" Sam said. "It's a bunch of nonsense."

"Hold on, I think I have an idea," Labeeb said. "Are you saying that you are with Lydia's husband?"

Monk sighed resolutely. "Blessed be the Lord God of Israel, that made heaven and earth, who hath given to David the king a wise son, endued with prudence and understanding.' 2 Chronicles 2:12."

Monk could see that Sam was starting to understand, as he began to lower his weapon. He said with a little caution, "Lydia is with a man named Grisha. They are scouting out a terrorist named Amos. Have you heard of him before?"

Monk shook his head in denial.

"I wish you would have just made that clear earlier," Sam grumbled. "If you are here with her old husband, you'll both have to wait until we stop Amos before we can help you."

Monk refuted with a verse from Acts 28:14. "'Where we found brethren, and were desired to tarry with them seven days: and so we went toward Rome.'"

"I don't like it," Sam muttered.

Vincent was still cradling his arm when Labeeb

suggested, "Why not bring this guy with us? He can obviously fight, and isn't that what we're doing, recruiting a little extra help?"

"If he's coming, he's your responsibility," Sam informed Labeeb.

Labeeb was somewhat irritated, but accepted the mantle. "By the way," he noticed, "where did Paul go?"

Chapter 39

Lydia's challenger was quick on her feet, but useless in hand-to-hand fighting. The belt Dusty used as a weapon was rendered pointless as a whip up close. She did attempt to use it as a means of restraint, but Lydia was easily able to counter the move. It seemed a little weird to her that Amos would send an assassin so inept at fighting. But she determined that it must be because he was desperate or meant to use this woman as a lookout.

If Amos truly was desperate, then it could only mean that Lydia was close, and about to completely foil his plans. This gave her a renewed sense of strength and vigor as she put Dusty into a headlock. She was tempted to break the woman's neck, but hesitated. Amos had sent a woman who clearly couldn't defend herself. The fearless girl she had faced only moments ago was now as helpless as a kitten. To kill this woman, who was probably more of a secretary than a fighter, would simply be murder.

Lydia compassionately let the woman go long enough to retrieve her knife. She purposely turned her back on Dusty, while still remaining vigilant. When she turned back around with the blade in hand, Dusty was long gone. It was as she had hoped. With any luck, the frightened girl might have had her fill of danger, opting out of returning to Amos with any report. It was a long shot, of course, and Lydia knew it was foolish to let the girl run away, but obviously Amos was already anticipating their arrival. Whatever the girl chose to do, Lydia was confident they would never personally meet again. Lydia had made it clear that Dusty didn't belong in a combat situation, and she believed that Dusty agreed.

Having dispelled the current threat, Lydia decided that if this was the lot that Amos was resorting to, then she should have no problem pairing back up with Grisha. Looking around, she tried to imagine where the Russian might be by now. Because of her little distraction, she decided that he would already be near Amos, and that she might as well meet up with him there as planned. She also wondered if Amos kept a group of fighters closer to him. Most likely he did. Then there was the other matter of the woman Paul had mentioned, this Kore. Who was she, and was she someone to be worried much about?

Of course I should be careful of the woman, Lydia concluded. Paul had made it clear that Kore was giving orders at the time of his capture. *But how is it that I knew of Amos and not this lady?* Perhaps the day still had a surprise or two left in store. *Anyhow, no time to waste*, she thought as she quickened her pace. Grisha should be close to their rendezvous by now, and Sam would be along in less than half an hour, hopefully with reinforcements.

Chapter 40

His adrenaline was wearing thin, and the heavy blows from the Russian were significantly weakening him. But Flint had a plan, which regrettably involved receiving a little more pain. If he didn't time it perfectly, then he knew that the Russian would kill him in a very unpleasant manner. Leaving his upper body exposed, he got in close and allowed the Russian to place a heavy fist across his chest. Since Flint was so close, though, the punch didn't hurt badly. Well it did, but not as bad as it would have. Backing up, Flint half feigned gasping as though the wind had been knocked out of him.

Encouraging someone so dangerous to punch yourself might be construed as foolish, but Flint wanted the fighter to hit him for two reasons. First was to test the assumption that the Russian would indeed punch the most exposed part of him, allowing Flint to hopefully gain an accurate prediction of the Russian's future behavior. Second was to give the Russian a good sense of confidence. Both of these were important, as his next move would end the fight. He needed to control the Russian's next blow, while at the same time needing the boxer to have his guard down just a little. If not, then this end would be in the Russian's favor. A hint of fear chilled through him, but he quickly dismissed it. Flint couldn't afford to think such thoughts at this time. Fear would only limit his actions. Fear would cause him to fail and die.

Crouching for a moment, he watching the Russian, feeling somewhat satisfied that the Russian had given him a small break. It was the action of an overconfident opponent that Flint had been hoping for. Then, tightening his fists once really hard before unclenching them, he tried to visualize how this charge would happen. *It's now or never*, he thought as he ran toward the boxer, purposely exposing his head.

Flint was sure he could see a smile cross the Russian's face as reared shoulders prepared for a defeating blow. The heavy fist came flying at Flint's face, just as he anticipated. At the same second, Flint shifted his charge and dove at the oncoming fist, arms snapping in front to meet the opponent's. He wrapped his arm around the man's more powerful outstretched limb, losing a bit of confidence as he noticed how hard the muscular appendage felt. But following though, he used the man's momentum and strength to swing himself upside down behind the boxer, like a gymnast on a monkey bar. When Flint's legs were up in the air behind the Russian, he curled them around the powerful boxer's neck.

The Russian lurched forward after his failed punch and tried to catch his balance. Flint was hanging upside down, his leg securely looped around the man's neck. Without a second of hesitation, Flint pulled his core into a more elevated position then swung his body back down again, flexing his muscles again for all they were worth. This caused the Russian to flip backward. The heavier man's arching body just missed landing on Flint. As he'd hoped for, the Russian's head absorbed the full momentum of the fall as it made contact with the pavement. Flint quickly struggled up and looked at the dazed man as he tried to collect himself. But knowing he wouldn't get this chance again, Flint let loose a swift kick into the man's skull, sending his already dazed mind into temporary darkness.

Flint bent his body low to the ground and grabbed his knees, trying to collect his breath and senses. After a moment or two, his eyes never leaving the Russian for fear of a recovery, he determined that he was at least in the right location. Why his Lydia would keep company with this man was a mystery to him. But if he was here, and Lydia truly was with him, then she too must be close by. Flint made up his mind that the best way to find her would be to stalk this man. Risking a few minutes of inattention to the unconscious Russian, Flint went around the corner and found a little shop selling cheap articles of clothing. Without paying any attention to the style or size, he purchased a long-sleeved shirt to cover his own ragged clothes and a scarf to hide his face. Quickly leaving the store, he pulled the shirt over his own, and wrapped his head and crouched down. Checking himself in the faint reflection of the store window, he was satisfied, hoping that nobody with give him a second glance. Hunching his back and trying to look as much like an old man as possible, he left the store.

He hobbled back around the corner to where the Russian was, and found him being helped to his feet by a couple of pedestrians. The tall, prideful man was noticeably annoyed at needing help, and tried to refuse their goodwill. This only caused him to stagger back, almost falling over again. It took him a moment before he could stand on his own, but then he started down the street, leaving behind a few confused onlookers.

Flint followed from about a half block away, wondering how long it would be before the angry man met up with Lydia again. If and when that time came, he wondered how to approach her. She had left him without ever trying to get in touch, and her friend here was obviously not going to like meeting him again. But Flint had never believed in running away from a challenge, even if he knew it might hurt.

Chapter 41

The little bout with that Kung Fu nut had provided Paul with the opportune moment he'd been looking for to escape from Lydia's goons. He'd spent enough time with them now to get a rough understanding of them. They had dragged him to and back from the Philippines. *A big, stupid, waste of time.* Sure, they seemed intent on stopping this terrorist threat, but the secret nature of their business concerned him. Also, the fact that they believed in some Martian plane crash helped to discredit their sanity. *Just a bunch of obsessed conspiracy nuts.* If they were indeed concerned about stopping the terrorists, then they wouldn't need his assistance. He had already imparted everything he knew and couldn't see how they would benefit from his companionship going forward. He now intended to do what should have been done in the first place, and that was to take the issue to the proper authorities, and hope that they weren't all corrupt.

With the small brawl ensuing, Paul took a step back and used the distraction to quietly tuck away. Once out of sight, he made his way to where he might see his tanker. At first he was a little appalled at not finding it in at its last position. But a quick glance around revealed the distinct figure of the ship he would have known anywhere. Since leaving it the other day, it had been moved several hundred yards and moored at a different location. Paul figured his first mate had authorized the adjustment in preparation for filling the tanks with another load of crude. He hoped this meant that they had removed the devices in the other tanks aboard the ship. More than likely though, the terrorists would have taken back all their bombs, if bombs are what you'd call them, to avoid a serious investigation.

With no way of getting back to his ship for the time being, he decided to pay a visit to the harbormaster. From there he should be able to alert any government agency that might be concerned with this threat. His memory of trying to hail the harbormaster over the radio last time was still fresh in his memory. Somehow Kore's men had intercepted that radio communication, but the worry of finding them inside the harbormaster's office still ate at Paul a little. No telling how well connected these people were. But that didn't matter now, his mind was made up. In the worst case scenario, he could just put up a loud fight until Sam's men noticed and came to the rescue. It didn't take long to find the office, but he had to carefully slip in without detection, since his former companions were still within eyesight of the long weather-worn shack. Besides, even if there were no terrorists in the office, they still might be floating around somewhere nearby. His couldn't be the only ship they were trying to sabotage. Happily, Paul found only one person in the office.

By appearance the man behind the counter was an old sea dog, seeming physically more neglected than the messy radio house he stewed in. Paul recognized him from passing, though he'd never put two and two together. The harbormaster was clearly out of shape, and perhaps only well suited for handling the radios in this office. *Maybe not even that,* Paul thought, again recalling the last time he had tried to hail this guy. Whether negligent or under some pressure from the bad guys, this man had failed to answer his radio when he had first run into trouble with the terrorists.

Laughing at something on a small television, the harbormaster stood up. "What do you need?" he called out to Paul in English, recognizing him as being American.

"Sorry to bother you. My name is Captain Paul Crandall, I am responsible for—"

"Ah yes, I was just talking to some other guy about you," the man interrupted. "I'm a little surprised to still see your ship hanging around. I wanted to talk to you about your departure plans."

"I think that discussion can wait for a little bit." Paul regained control of the conversation. "You see, I have a matter to bring to you, and it not only concerns your harbor here, but it stretches into national and international security."

The harbormaster, despite being overweight and sloppy, displayed an almost nimble agility as he quickly moved over to Paul concerning the serious prelude. "Please, Captain, you have my undivided attention."

Paul was surprised at the man's urgency, but at the same time, he was familiar with the proximity to terror that the harbormaster was undoubtedly accustomed to working with. "Well . . ." Paul began as he started to elaborate on his experience of the past couple days.

Chapter 42

Moshe's task was simple: keep an eye out for Lydia's team. It was not a question of if they would show up, but when. There were a few other lookouts posted throughout the city, each hoping to be the first to call and update Kore concerning GRIP's whereabouts. The first man to find and report had been promised a five-thousand-dollar bonus.

Even though one of the men on Lydia's team was supposed to tip Kore off about their location and activity, it had not happened yet. Since Kore was much shrewder than Amos, she left nothing to chance. Preferring to back up her best-laid plans with extra redundancy, she didn't dare place her full trust on human error. Her spy within Lydia's team might, after all, run into any number of circumstances where he would be unable to update her on their position. Everyone walked carefully around Kore. Even Amos was nervous about crossing the true driver of his schemes.

Moshe nearly missed his opportunity to collect on the bounty. If it hadn't been for Grisha's addiction to coffee, then GRIP would have evaded Moshe all together. As Moshe himself was ordering a hot beverage from the local coffee shop, the Russian member of Lydia's team happened to step in line right behind him.

Ignoring the man, Moshe casually completed his order and took a seat at a small table where he could inconspicuously watch the tall brawny man. Grisha seemed in no mood to sit down and enjoy his drink, but instead chose to exit the facility. Moshe waited for about thirty seconds before following. He already had his phone out, ready to call Kore, but when he stepped outside he found his mark had disappeared. His heart skipped a beat, fearing that he might have given Grisha too large a head start. Trying to calm himself down, Moshe jogged to the nearest intersection, where Grisha most undoubtedly would have ventured. To his relief, he found the Russian, but that was not all he found.

The large man was now in the beginning stages of a fight with a smaller yet ruggedly good-looking man. Granted, that man wasn't really small, only when compared to the near-giant Grisha. When Moshe had been briefed about each member of Lydia's team, he was told that Grisha had a bit of a temper; but to just start a fight with a random pedestrian seemed a stretch. Even if Grisha didn't have something more pressing to keep in mind, Moshe doubted that he would waste his time like this.

Not knowing what to make of it, Moshe decided to simply take a picture of both men on his smartphone. He then typed a quick message into it, and sent it off to Kore. He didn't know where the other members of Lydia's team were, but he hoped this was enough to secure him that five thousand dollars.

While maintaining his distance, he watched as the fight continued. Grisha was obviously the more experienced fighter, yet there was something calculated in the smaller man's actions. Right about the time that Moshe expected the fight to end with Grisha coming out on top, the smaller man made a quick turnaround. With a rash, almost acrobatic move, he brought the giant down hard on the asphalt road. By the time he was done with Grisha, the Russian was out cold.

At this same time, a reply came back to Moshe in the form of a text message. Kore's instructions were to capture the smaller man after Grisha had finished with him. Apparently Kore's confidence was ill placed in the GRIP militant, but that didn't change things much. She would still expect Moshe to return with this other man, regardless of who won the fight.

Once the smaller man regained his composure, he ducked into a local clothing shop. By then a few people were taking notice of the sprawled out Russian in the street, and circled around to gawk or give aid. Moshe, instead, followed the smaller man into the store. Moshe knew that to apprehend this person now would only draw attention to himself, so he waited for a more opportune moment.

The man covered himself and did a decent job of making himself look like an old man. He then began to follow Grisha, who was now back on his feet. Had Moshe not witnessed the transformation, he wouldn't have recognized the smaller man. As they walked down the street, a few chances presented themselves where Moshe could have easily captured his target. But as it was, the man was following Grisha in the general direction of where Moshe would have taken him, anyway. Because of this, there was no real hurry to confront the man. *Let him walk there on his own*, Moshe thought. *Then there will be less chance of his escape when I finally catch him.*

He was justified in this assumption. Once they were about two blocks away from Kore and Amos's headquarters, Grisha found his way under the awning of a small dining patio, where he was met by Lydia. The man Moshe was to seize spied on the meeting from several buildings away. *It's time to make my move*, Moshe determined as he stepped up to the man.

"Excuse me," Moshe pretended, "do you have any money? I'm very poor, and need help."

The man said nothing, but tried to shoo Moshe away.

"Please," Moshe begged, "I have a wife and five little children, and times are so hard."

The man let out a sigh, and for the sake of getting rid of Moshe, he pulled out a few dollar bills. As he was handing them over, Moshe instead grabbed the man's arm and pressed a dagger hard against his side. He made sure that the pressure against the dagger was enough to cause pain, but just shy of piercing flesh. He remembered the surprising way that Grisha had been taken down earlier, and didn't want any chance of this man pulling a stunt like that on him.

"Sorry, mister. I don't know what your involvement is with these people here, but I have somebody that wants to speak with you. So if you will kindly accompany me down the street a little more, I won't be forced to put a hole into your side."

"Who are you?" the man questioned.

"I am not important," Moshe replied. "But my

employer is. Come with me now, and don't make a
scene."

Chapter 43

"What news do you have for me?" Kore demanded.

Amos sighed. "Everything is on track in the European and Asian reserves. The reserves in the Arabic nations will be compromised when our pipelines there are hit."

Kore's sharp mind continued to drill, "That is all good, but what about the U.S. reserves?"

Amos was nervous about reporting this part, and for good reason. "Three of the reserves are taken care of, but I don't know about the fourth."

"What are you telling me?" Kore almost hissed. "Are you saying that it hasn't been hit yet, or that it won't be, or do you just not know?"

Amos didn't like the harshness of her scrutiny. She always scared him a little, but she had provided him with funding, and therefore, he was a slave to her oversight. "On the third facility, they were discovered," he said with some hesitation. But he was quick to add, "They weren't caught, but last I heard one of them was shot up pretty bad and they were racing toward the last reserve facility. I don't know if they'll make it or not, but even if they don't, I think that one single reserve will not be enough to worry about."

Kore stepped over to the desk Amos was sitting at, leaned forward, and planted her palms on the glass top of the cheap office workstation. Her shoulder blades popped up, like a shark's fin, silently rippling toward its prey. Then, crouching her head lower, she breathed with a low threating rasp, "Just one reserve left. You've had years to prepare, and you might miss one of only four reserves?"

The hair on Amos's neck stood on end. Her threatening pose, combined with her wispy voice, made for an almost comical scene. If he hadn't known her, Amos would have laughed in her face. Only this shark had teeth. "It's still too early to know. I have faith in my men's ability to finish the job. All I was saying was that the government wouldn't be able to pump enough oil from that last reserve fast enough to make a real dent in our desired outcome."

Kore stared at him for a full minute, accenting the tension in the room. He even considered pulling the gun out from a mount that he had attached to the bottom of his desktop. Suddenly, though, she stood erect and her countenance softened. She still held a glimmer of danger, but thankfully the intimidation was stepping aside for the business at hand.

"You may be right." She smiled. "You might also like to know that Lydia and her men have arrived. I've been informed that they are scouting out our building and forming a plan of attack."

Relieved to have Kore's temper calmed slightly,

Amos replied, "I've been waiting for her. My men have been briefed; I'll have them move into position. Are you planning on staying to watch my brilliant plan come to its finale?"

"No, Amos, I don't want to stick around any longer than I have to. There is business to attend to in Hong Kong. I would like to get there before the global panic inhibits my ability to do so. But if you finish with Lydia before I lift off, you can hitch a ride out of here with me. Otherwise, you're on your own. Either way there is one other thing you might find useful." She smiled again as she motioned to somebody down the hall. "We received a tip that Lydia's husband came looking for her. Apparently she is still quite attached to him. We found him dressed up and stalking one of her men."

One of Kore's guards then entered, pushing a handcuffed man in front of him. "May I introduce you to Flint Krieger," she announced, then added, "just in case you need an ace up your sleeve?"

Jealousy and spite raced through Amos. He was jealous that Lydia had feelings for another man, and spiteful for the simple reason that Kore was going to make Amos punish Lydia with her estranged husband. If Amos was ever to get on Lydia's good side after all of this, hiding behind Flint would not be the way.

This caused pride to follow up the last two thoughts. Did Kore seriously think he needed the extra insurance? Was her confidence that poor, after all he'd done, to doubt his ability to fend off this small tactical team? But, reluctantly, he couldn't dismiss the benefit of having so valuable a hostage.

"Mr. Flint," he addressed, as Kore left. "Your wife is a remarkable woman, one who could potentially save the world. But any doubts I may have had before are gone. You have now cemented the success of my plan. Thank you."

Though he couldn't possibly understand the meaning of anything that was happening yet, Flint still gave him a murderous look. Amos wasn't fazed. He already knew what a true threat looked like, thanks to working with Kore for so long. He only regretted the repercussions that threatened ever being on good terms with Lydia in the future. Amos wondered if he could play this safely without putting Flint on the table. Even if he did use Flint, Amos tried to convince himself, slim as the hope was, that she would understand and respect his actions. Perhaps he was simply enchanted by her simple beauty, but that was still enough to dream on. Besides, living in exile might prove to be very lonely. If only he'd put as much effort into her as he did in the oil scheme, surely he could have found a way to win the woman's heart as well. If only Paul hadn't messed with his schedule. There might have been enough time to consider handling Lydia better.

Chapter 44

Lydia carefully circled around the exterior of the building, which she suspected to be Amos's base of operations. It was one of the taller office-like buildings in the district and didn't appear menacing to any degree. But Lydia had learned never to trust a facade.

Moving about casually, she tried to appear like an uninterested pedestrian. She found it almost odd that her presence had not yet been detected. Surely they must know she was near, but no attempts to stop her had been made, with the exception of the encounter she had a mile back with that poorly trained woman.

After assessing the building as best she could from the outside, she retreated to a nearby café, where, standing outside, Grisha was waiting for her. This was a mistake, in her mind. How long had Grisha just been standing here in plain view? She was about to usher him into the café when she noticed her second in command appeared angrier than usual. She also couldn't avoid seeing a few dark marks on his face and the dark patch of drying blood matting down the hair on the back of his scalp.

"I think I'm glad that I only encountered the assassin that chased me," Lydia said to Grisha, hoping to cool the proud Russian down a little. "Had I gone against the person that did this to you, I'm sure they would have gotten the better of me."

Grisha apparently hadn't noticed the wound on his head until Lydia pointed it out. As he felt the tender spot on the back of his scalp, she could see the color of his rage climbing up into his face. Then as he tried to control himself again he asked, "So Amos sent a man after you?"

"More like a woman," she replied. "But she was no real fighter. I don't know for certain, but I think that Amos is a little understaffed today."

Lydia then told him about her brief encounter, but Grisha seemed a little uncomfortable elaborating about his fight. Instead he changed the subject. "What of Sam and his crew, have you heard from them yet?"

"No, I was able to survey the building, but there's nothing ominous about it. I don't think we'll know what we're up against until we get inside," she replied.

She waited a moment for any response from Grisha, but he seemed to be thinking of something. So Lydia added, "I don't think the alarm has been raised, because aside from each of our earlier encounters, they don't seem to be aware of our presence here yet."

"Yes," Grisha agreed. "This Amos may not be as smart as we have given him credit. This should be piece of pie."

"You mean piece of cake?" Lydia corrected, hoping to lighten his mood, but with little success.

"Pie, cake—it's all piece of pastry." Grisha said, his face as hard as ever.

The conversation continued like this for about five minutes, and Lydia became frustrated. Finally she remembered that she didn't want to be standing outside like this. *Fool*, she accused herself. *Follow your own good sense.* Reaching out, she opened the door to enter the café. Once she was seated at a table with Grisha, the brooding copilot continued to simmer. She was just about to scold him and order him to get whatever was on his chest out in the open, but right as she was muscling up the confrontational strength to do so, the door opened up and Sam entered. Behind him, Labeeb and Vincent followed. The first thing she noticed was that Vincent was nursing an injured arm. The next man to enter wasn't Paul, but some other brown-skinned man. Again she got that feeling like she'd seen this man recently, but couldn't remember where.

"What happened? Where is Paul, and who is this?" Lydia asked sharply.

Sam explained. "Apparently Paul was a little suspicious of us. When we arrived at the pier, he ditched us. Maybe he was looking for his crew to help, or maybe we'll never see him again. In either case, we weren't able to find him."

"I'm guessing by the look of Vincent that you guys ran into a little trouble, also?" Lydia observed.

"More trouble than we needed. We found this guy waiting for us at the pier. I'm not sure who he is, but he has something to do with your husband. He's not a half-bad fighter, either, but he sure is strange. He wouldn't let us alone until we brought him to meet you."

Lydia studied the man for a moment. "Do I know you?"

He replied, "'To know someone here or there with whom you can feel there is understanding in spite of distances or thoughts expressed—That can make life a garden.' Johann Wolfgang von Goethe."

Lydia seemed confused for a moment, but then the realization struck her. "Monk!" she exclaimed. "What are you doing here?"

Monk smiled then replied, "'Daughter! Get you an honest man for a husband, and keep him honest. No matter whether he is rich, provided he be independent. Regard the honour and moral character of the man more than all other circumstances. Think of no other greatness but that of the soul, no other riches but those of the heart.' John Adams."

Lydia thought for a moment, and suddenly she began to understand. "If you're here about Flint . . . you're not alone, are you?"

Monk shook his head.

"I just fought a girl who claimed to be here because of me, but she was no fighter. I thought she was working with Amos. What was her name . . . Dusty? Was she with you?"

"Job 9:2. 'I know it is so of a truth,'" Monk affirmed.

Lydia sank down a little. "Now that I think of it, she was only trying to defend herself from me—oh, I feel horrible. Is Flint here, too?"

Monk nodded.

"So if I wasn't attacked by Amos's men, and you saw no sign of them, either," she ventured to Sam, "Grisha would be the only one who had an encounter with one of them, right?"

Grisha gave a puzzled look. At first he wasn't

sure how to answer, but then admitted, "It must be so. But I believe we still have advantage. He may know we are coming, but he may not know we are here yet."

"In that case we must act quickly," Lydia announced. "There are two entrances to the building. Vincent, how is your arm?"

"Totally messed up, but I can still fight," he replied.

"Okay," she hesitated. "well maybe you and Labeeb better take the back entrance. Hopefully you won't find as much resistance there. Even if you do, the hallways coming off that door should be smaller and easier to fend off an enemy in. Sam, I want you with Grisha and me. We'll storm the front doors. Find Amos, but don't kill him if you can help it. Also, if you get a chance to find this woman Kore that Paul referred to, I'd like her captured as well. Monk, can you wait until this is over? These terrorists are about to do something very terrible, and we need to stop them. When we are finished, we'll discuss Flint and why you all are looking for me."

Monk refused. "Samuel 17:10. 'Give me a man, that we may fight together.'"

Lydia had hoped that Paul would return with help, but since he hadn't, she decided that Monk would do. "Sam, you and Monk partner up. From what Flint used to tell me of him, he is very good at hand-to-hand combat, maybe even better than any of us."

Sam looked disappointed at his assignment, but accepted it without any verbal defiance. Lydia could tell, however, that he disapproved of the order. Then, pulling a compact assault rifle out of a duffel bag, he handed it to Monk. "You may need this."

Monk, however, refused the gun. Instead he approached Labeeb and took two of his throwing rings. Sam looked back at Lydia with an expression that cried, *Are you really going to partner me with this lunatic?*

Lydia ignored the protest and got up. "No sense in wasting any more time here. Let's do this."

Chapter 45

"Are you going to be okay?" Labeeb asked Vincent, who was still nursing his hurt arm.

The half open mouth and accusing eyes seemed to say, *Are you stupid? Do I look fine to you?* "Don't worry about me," the Italian replied, his voice full of ice, as he raised up his pistol. "I'm still as deadly with one arm as with two."

"Let me go first, anyway," Labeeb offered. "You can cover our rear."

Vincent made no objection. Whatever Vincent said, Labeeb was certain that his companion was only acting tough. The injury Vincent had received earlier at the hands of Monk would slow him down. With any luck, the Italian wouldn't get in Labeeb's way. Even if Vincent should be sitting this one out, he might still prove to be useful. *Just don't get yourself killed in there.*

Upon reaching the back door, Labeeb found that

it was unguarded and unlocked. Labeeb and Vincent easily but cautiously made their way inside. Just as Labeeb had assumed, there before him was a long narrow hallway. The two men began to silently move down the hallway. Each door they checked along the way was locked, and had no windows to offer any hint of what lay on the other side. The doors were marked with only a stenciled number, indicating the rooms in series.

"Try to find some stairs," Vincent remarked. But Labeeb had already found what he was looking for. Some twenty feet in front was a door with a window, and no number on it. This could only be a staircase.

Without a word, they slowly inched their way toward it. They were almost to the door when the familiar echo of a gunshot reverberated in the distance through the walls. Labeeb knew that it would soon be followed by more. Lydia and the others had begun the battle on their end. No sooner had the assault on the front entrance began than two doors ahead of him opened. There were now four men directly facing them, drawing their weapons. Vincent also cried out his own alarm. "Four men behind us!"

Eight armed men; Labeeb wasted no time. Pulling the trigger of his rifle, he spat several bullets carelessly down the hallway, while at the same time pulling Vincent through the door that led to the staircase. A few return shots pinged off of the doorjamb as they made their way inside. "That was a little too close," Labeeb stated. "It's as if they knew exactly what we're doing."

"It was a trap," Vincent confirmed, with a small cough.

Labeeb looked back at Vincent, who was sinking to the floor. The cough had alerted Labeeb, and he knew without looking that his companion had been shot. At this same instant, he heard a door slam shut somewhere above him. They were trapped on all sides, and it wouldn't be long before they were gunned down from above or through the door they had just come from.

"Forget about me," Vincent heroically stated. "I'll hold them off here, you go on ahead."

Labeeb knew that he had no choice but to obey. To stay by his friend's side would mean death for both of them. The only way to escape was to leave the Italian behind. Even then, the way forward offered no guarantee of survival. He hated to do it, but agreed.

"Good luck, my friend," Labeeb bid his companion, as he watched Vincent unstrap a Velcro pouch. Labeeb knew exactly what Vincent was retrieving. When he turned to race up the staircase to meet the men up there, he heard a grunt from Vincent as the Italian stabbed a syringe into his own chest. It was something that a few of them chose to carry into battle. Inspired by historical references to combatants being drugged up and charging, the suicide fighters would often race to the enemy front, sustaining multiple gunshot wounds without even noticing. Their enemies, often paralyzed by fear, would join their deaths.

Vincent, knowing that his own death was imminent, had just injected himself with a powerful mixture of narcotics, the effect of which would cause him to forget his pain and make him to fight in a most irregular and aggressive manner before his body inevitably failed. Knowing this was not only extremely dangerous for the enemy but also dangerous for Labeeb himself, Labeeb didn't waste any time putting distance between himself and his friend. The results could be unpredictable for a man who injected himself with this type of drug without ever having taken something like it before.

As Labeeb reached the first turn in the staircase, he pulled out two grenades. One he threw up, bouncing it off a bend in the stairway so it would land near the door on the next floor. He barely had time to shield his ears before the concussion shook the whole staircase. Continuing up, he charged the door, firing at any dazed men he came in contact with. He quickly threw the next grenade up to the third floor and prepared for another assault. He doubted this next floor would fall as quickly, since they might expect a similar tactic. But Labeeb knew that the higher he climbed, the less likely they were to expect him to have made it that far. He would at least have a better chance than if he stayed on the lower floors.

On the fourth floor, the staircase led into an open room. One quick look, and he wondered if he had gone to the wrong floor. Not only was there no resistance on this level, but there seemed to be nobody at all. The emptiness seemed to be punctuated by the dull silence. Sure there was the battle, but nothing in this room, and nothing in his earpiece. Whispering into his mic, he waited, but no reply came. Either their radios were out, or the whole rest of the team had been taken out. He doubted that his whole team was dead, sounds of battle from somewhere else in the building still reverberated. Assuming that he had gone too high, he proceeded back down a level. There was still a lot of fighting going on below, including the psychotic, inhuman yell that could only be coming from Vincent.

Labeeb was about to descend to the second floor's platform when he felt a vibrating in his pocket. It was his phone, and since his earbud had recently gone dead, he assumed that Lydia or somebody else was trying to get ahold of him. Ducking into a small corner, gun raised, he checked the phone. To his astonishment, the call was coming from his secret benefactor. While this wasn't the time or place for checking in with the anonymous person, Labeeb had never actually received a live phone call from this mystery friend, either. After listening to the caller's instructions, Labeeb changed his whole plan. Instead of rejoining the battle, he searched out an air intake vent, pulled the grate off, and concealed himself inside. Before anyone could discover him, he reached for the grate and pulled it back up to cover the opening where he was hiding. Despite the struggles his friends were going through, Labeeb was now going to sit this one out.

Chapter 46

After giving Labeeb and Vincent enough time to get to the back of the building, Lydia began her approach to the front. Once her group neared the building, they immediately noticed that their earbud radios were being jammed. It was her first major red flag, but she felt too committed to turn back now. Pulling her earbud out and tucking it away, Lydia continued to lead Grisha as they skirted the side of the building, still heading toward the front door, but in a roundabout way. Sam and Monk were to be the distraction as they walked straight toward the entrance. This allowed Sam and Monk to enter about one and a half minutes before Lydia. With their weapons concealed, they were trying to appear as though they had simply entered the wrong building.

Sam was asking an annoyed guard for directions when Lydia walked through the door. The guard pushed Sam aside, but was only successful at becoming the first man shot by Grisha in the raid. Sam and Monk retreated to a side of the room to provide cover to Lydia and Grisha's flank as they assaulted the security desk.

Lydia glanced about the room after she had secured the guard's station. Hopping behind the desk, she looked at the surveillance screens long enough to notice they were blank. She tapped on the connected keyboard, but nothing came alive. "Something's wrong," she called out. "This was too easy, and this is a dead workstation."

At that moment she heard more gunshots reverberating throughout the building. She knew they must be focused on Labeeb and Vincent. She wasn't permitted any time to dwell on the fact, because as if from nowhere a torrent of men attacked from all sides. Even the front door swarmed with men coming in from outside. There was but one hallway in front of her that offered any escape. "This way!" she hollered, but only Grisha was in any position to follow her.

She and Grisha blindly fired behind themselves to cover their retreat. Only when she was turning a corner could she see that her stray bullets had actually taken a few men down. The rest of the men were scattering to cover the building. She heard an explosion behind her as she made her way to an open staircase. Racing up it, she and Grisha ignored the second floor. Paul had described the third floor to be the one most likely for containing the offices of Kore and Amos. Lydia decided to start looking there instead of clearing each floor and room individually. Otherwise, with all the men that were here, they would be overrun before they could accomplish their mission.

Upon arriving at the third floor, they split up,

but didn't wander too far away from each other, in case one or the other needed help. This floor was filled with several offices and cubicles. In less than two minutes, each of the small rooms were checked out and cleared. There were only a few guards on this floor, two of which Grisha took down with relative ease. Lydia nearly lost her head when the third guard shot and missed at point blank. Lydia's aim was more decisive. The fighting was getting closer now, and Lydia wondered how Sam and Monk were doing. They must have met up with Labeeb and Vincent, because the fighting sounded more intense. "I think most of the fighting is on the lower floor," Lydia commented. Then, making a quick decision, she was about to direct Grisha to guard the stairs while she went in search of Amos.

Before she could say anything, and as if reading her mind, Grisha offered, "Go find Amos, I'll hold them here."

"Thanks," she said as she rushed to the next floor up. Once there she found an open room with several pillars in it. This large room had only a few small offices along the sides of the spacious area. The emptiness of the floor must have been designed to accommodate later expansion for the entity that owned or rented the building. She spun around, clearing her surroundings. With so many pillars, somebody could easily be hiding here and she wouldn't know it. Her steps echoed in the room, and she debated kicking off her shoes to muffle her footsteps.

Without clear evidence of where it came from, she heard a voice echo back to her. "Lydia, I've been waiting for you."

"Amos, is that you?" she ventured.

Amos stepped out from behind a pillar, pulling a tied hostage in front of him. At first she thought it must be Labeeb or Vincent, but with her gun raised, she stepped closer—only to see she was aiming right at her husband, Flint. He was gagged and tied, but still silently struggling against his captor. Her eyes went wide with fury and guilt. "Let him go Amos," she ordered. "He's nothing to you, leave him out of this."

Amos simply laughed. "Oh, he's something to me, my dear. Without him, there is nothing to stop you from killing me."

"I don't want to kill you, Amos," Lydia replied. "I just want to stop you."

Amos shook his head, as he laughed again. "Honestly, Lydia, it's too late. We've already released everything into the pipelines and tankers. Within hours, ninety percent of the world's retrieved crude will solidify. It's already happening as we speak."

Lydia fumbled in her pocket and pulled out her cell phone, quickly going to her text messages. After a couple of well-rehearsed taps of her finger, she then addressed Amos. "With one more tap, I can at least stop you from gumming up most of the world's pipelines. Let Flint go now, or your plan is ruined."

Amos snorted. "Ha! There is nothing you can possibly do that could stop me now. Even if you could, I doubt that you would care to wager this man's life on it. I can't see how you could love him that much, anyway. You sacrificed your relationship with him a long time ago. No, I won't make a trade on a fake threat like that. Even if you had some way of stopping the pipelines from plugging up, I don't think you're really willing to trade his life for the countless others that are likely to follow once the chaos begins. No, he is merely my protection from you."

"Little do you know, Amos," Lydia struggled to convince, "but I've been globe-trotting with an antidote to your biological weapon. I send this message, and that antidote goes into the pipelines, nullifying your efforts."

"Really, Lydia," he replied. "Even if you are telling the truth, I highly doubt that you want to send that message out. You of all people know that the world needs to wake up from this oil-intoxicated dream. Imagine the world we could live in if we were to finally wake everyone up, and break our dependence on oil. I know this is what you dream about, also."

Her lower lip quivering, Lydia answered, "Not this way, though. Never would I want to put so many people at risk. I won't let you get away with this, either."

Amos cocked his head and said, "Pity," as he started moving the pistol from Flint's head to hers. Even though she could see the gun rising, Lydia's eyes locked onto Flint's. Bound as he was, his eyes were wide with concern. He struggled to throw off Amos' aim.

Lydia took the cue and dove down the stairs, tumbling to one of the lower platforms. Slightly bruised, she picked up her phone again and pressed the Send button. She then called up the stairs, "Give it up, Amos—I've already sent the message. Within minutes, over a hundred men will be pouring an agent into the pipelines that will counteract your bacteria."

She then waited for his reply. After a moment she realized that Amos was running somewhere. She struggled back up the stairs to find him sprinting alone to a single door. She raised her gun, but Flint was still between her and Amos. The shot wasn't impossible for her, and she'd pulled off similar shots before, just not with someone she loved being the middle person. *You can do this*, she told herself, and she believed it. The knowing didn't help much though, she was still too worried. Wanting to avoid hitting Flint, she aimed too far left by accident, her shot missing Amos by a good foot or more. The door behind him closed, and she ran toward Flint, almost forgetting that Amos was the reason she was here.

Amos had shoved Flint to the floor as he ran through a doorway. Flint's hands and feet were still wrapped tightly in duct tape, preventing him from controlling his fall. Luckily his broad shoulders bore the brunt of the impact instead of his head. Despite his circumstance, he was more concerned with Lydia, whom he had finally found. He never would have guessed that she would turn militant and try to save the world from maniacs like Amos and Kore; but on the other hand, she most likely couldn't imagine him saving the world from men like Marshal Steel and Shen Mao.

With Amos in retreat, Flint watched as Lydia came racing toward him. Butterflies of confusion and excitement pulsed throughout his body. The love of his life, whom only days ago he suspected to be dead, was now crouching over to help free him. But had Amos correctly surmised Lydia's feelings toward him? Had she in fact betrayed his love? She did run away from him two years ago, never to make contact again. Maybe she did foster some form of dislike toward him.

The idea depressed him. At the same time, it had a sobering effect to counter the muddle caused by his fall. Flint's head cleared enough to push aside his questions. Lydia had a purpose here, and Amos clearly needed to be stopped. The skin around his lips felt like it was being ripped off as Lydia yanked the tape from around his mouth. She was trying to say something, but he couldn't for the life of him piece it all together. Then, as she dislodged the gag, he compelled himself to not be sentimental. There would hopefully be time for that later.

Terror coursed through every vein in Lydia's body. She could handle confronting Amos, and knew that Kore would be easy, as well. But to finally come face to face with Flint again filled her with mind-numbing anxiety. In her stupor she tried to apologize and explain, but as she threw away the wet piece of cloth that had been shoved deeply into Flint's mouth, her words came out as senseless babble. Her eyes were starting to wet as he gave her a stern look, surprising her with his command, "Go after him, I'm fine. Stop him before he gets away."

Lydia didn't argue. The love of her life was lying defenseless, but she knew that Amos had to be stopped. "I'll be back in just a few minutes to untie you. Just hold on for a few more minutes." Even as her legs carried her away, she felt guilty for leaving him helpless on the floor, but she'd already wasted too much time coddling over him. She should have at least left him a knife. But it was too late for that now. She was moving with a mission to finish, and Amos already had a head start.

There was one more staircase behind the door that Amos had gone through. It clearly went to the rooftop, and she wondered where he planned to go from there. The ascent seemed to take forever. She didn't look back at Flint, because she knew his eyes would be drilling into her back. Regret and self-consciousness plagued her every step, and it seemed an eternity before she was out of his sight.

Once at the top of the staircase, she was able to refocus her attention on the task at hand. Not taking any heed of what might lie on the other side, she burst through the last door and pulled the trigger on her rifle. The sweeping spray of bullets that she unleashed across the whole rooftop found lodging in the side of a small helicopter. Unfortunately this only served to alert everyone else up there of her presence. She was driven back again as two men unleashed a barrage of return fire. She had only enough time to notice that Amos was arguing with some woman in front of the chopper.

It had to be Kore, though she didn't get a good enough look at her to see if she matched Paul's description. Lydia was acutely aware that she needed to get on that roof. But with two guards closely watching the door, she doubted her chances of even taking a peek without getting her head blown off. She was wondering if there was any other way to the roof when she heard Flint call, "Lydia, behind you."

She could hear footsteps pounding behind her. At first she thought Flint might have freed himself, but when she turned to look she saw Grisha running up the stairs to meet her.

Lydia stopped him before he could run all the way up and out. "They have guns trained on the door, you'll be killed instantly," she warned.

"We can't stay here," Grisha panted, half out of breath. "I have only a few rounds left, and they are coming up behind us. We're out of time."

Lydia appraised the situation quickly. There was nothing she could do for Flint right now, and she hoped that his condition would grant him some mercy from their pursuers. She then grabbed a canister that was tucked in one of the bulky pockets of Grisha's combat vest. "Let's move forward, then. There are two guards plus Amos and Kore. Ready?"

Grisha nodded in approval. Lydia pulled the pin

on the flash-bang and hurled it through the doorway onto the rooftop. By this time, the engines on the helicopter were firing up, and Lydia knew she only had a minute before both Amos and Kore were gone again. Then, covering her ears, she waited for the flash-bang to blow.

She trusted that the non-lethal grenade had temporarily stunned the guards as she and Grisha stormed the rooftop. The guards were somewhat dazed, but not unable to fire a few rounds. Lydia and Grisha managed to avoid getting hit, and with two shots each, they took down the guards. Lydia and Grisha could see Amos and Kore inside the cockpit as they dashed over to stop them.

The blades of the small helo had not quite gotten up to speed when Lydia opened the door and yanked the woman out. Grisha just missed getting shot by Amos as he wrenched the terrorist from his seat on the other side. Only when Lydia and Grisha had the two held at gunpoint outside the chopper did Lydia recognize the woman. "Persephone?" she uttered with a perplexed and surprised expression. "What are you doing here?"

The woman gave a maniacal smile, but it was Grisha who answered. "Lydia, Persephone and Kore are same person."

"That can't be!" Lydia rebutted. However, it seemed the only answer. She then tightened her grip on her boss and shoved the pistol deep into her neck. "Who are you, really?"

The woman's smile faded a little, but didn't disappear. She gently pushed Lydia's gun aside so that she could speak more comfortably. "My dear Lydia, Kore was the name for a Greek goddess who was queen of the underworld. She was the formidable woman who would bring condemnation to the dead, according to the curses of men. Persephone was the daughter of Zeus, worshipped by many as the goddess of the harvest. She was believed to help spring get off to a good start. It's kind of fitting, if you think about it. The one who destroys is also the one who creates. Kore was simply the nickname associated with the goddess Persephone. So, yes, we are one and the same."

Lydia began to tremble. She pondered her last several years of working under this woman, only to be working for her own enemy. Then something even more terrifying came to her mind. "And what of all that anti-coagulating bacteria that I distributed?"

Kore laughed. "Amos here had his hands full working on worldwide strategic reserves and oil tankers. We simply sent him occasionally to help give urgency to your part in it all. So as you have likely realized, when you sent your message to all those men along the various pipelines, they are the ones who have just started the chain reaction."

"I can stop this," Lydia said. "Grisha, watch her." She stepped away from Persephone—or Kore or whatever her name really was—and pulled out her cell phone to type a new text message to all of her contacts along the pipelines.

But before she could get more than one word into the message, the phone was pulled from her hand. Lydia looked up, surprised to see that it was Grisha who had robbed her of the phone. "What are you doing? There might still be time."

"It is over now," he replied as he tossed the phone up and into the rotors of the chopper, effectively shattering the phone and spreading its parts all over the roof. "Put your gun down now."

Confused, Lydia complied, surrendering her gun to the man who had just betrayed her. She knew him well enough to know that he would not hesitate to do what was necessary. The only problem was that *necessary* no longer meant what it should have. After all this time, she didn't know him well enough to understand where his true motives had really been.

"We need to go now," Kore ordered. "Good-bye, Lydia, and thank you for all your help." Kore then got back into the chopper, along with Grisha, taking the only two seats on the small aircraft.

"Hey, what about me?" Amos asked, not wanting to be left behind.

"Oh yes," Kore replied. "I almost forgot. Grisha—"

Grisha opened his door, but instead of stepping out, he quickly put a single bullet into Amos's chest before shutting the door again.

Lydia watched, stunned, as the helicopter lifted off. The next thing she was aware of was being wrestled to the ground by the Egyptian police. A few feet away, she could see Amos. He was struggling for his last breaths.

"Forgive me, Lydia," he choked. "It wasn't supposed to be like this. I have always loved y-yo-y—"

Time seemed to slow down as she listened to Amos's final words. He sank into silence as Lydia felt the pressure of some handcuffs being over-tightened on her wrists.

Chapter 47

August 4

The handcuffs bit with a sharp sting as Lydia shifted uncomfortably. She stared down at the table she was cuffed to. The Egyptians hadn't let her sleep at all during the night. Their interrogations were unrelenting. They had their story, or at least the story they wanted to believe. Lydia could only guess what it was. Then there was her story, one which she couldn't seem to convince them of. With her eyes drooping to inspect a small trickle of blood around her handcuffs, Lydia listened as the latch to her room clicked open again. She didn't look up when the person entered. Very few women worked in this station, and the steps sounded just heavy enough to confirm that this was a man, but not likely the muscle bound officer who'd questioned her last. The door shut behind him, but he didn't say a word. "I've already told you everything I know," Lydia protested, eyes still averted. "It doesn't matter how many times I tell you, or how you ask, the story is the same."

"That's not the story that I came to hear."

That voice. Finally Lydia looked up to see the face of her new interrogator. This time, however, she didn't find the face of a police officer, but the concerned face of the only man she didn't have a good answer for, her husband.

What plagued her worse than knowing she had helped a terrorist was that she had betrayed Flint to do so. "Flint," she said, nearly breaking down into tears. "I, I—" she stammered, but couldn't finish a thought.

"I think we have a little catching up to do," Flint commented.

"What's going to happen?" she sobbed, her first real cry in a long time.

"From what I gather, the police are still trying to piece everything together," Flint replied. "It sounds like there's maybe five days left before the world runs out of fuel, and they estimate that it may take years to restore the pipelines and various methods of transporting oil again. People are calling for blood, while others are rioting. The only thing you have going for you right now is this guy Paul, who sent the police to that building where Amos and Kore were. They arrived shortly after you engaged the terrorists."

"I'm relieved that they showed up, because Monk was severely outnumbered. Your friend Sam was wounded, but will live. The one you call Labeeb hasn't been found. The police also had a run-in with a crazed, drugged-up man. They shot him a few times, unable to pacify him till a bullet found its way into his head. Apparently he was going to die anyway from gunshot wounds received in his fight with

Amos's men. They're telling me he was a part of your group, a man named Vincent. As for this Greek goddess of yours, she and Grisha have disappeared."

Lydia thought about this all. "So Paul sent the police?"

"Yeah, apparently he believed you were trying to do the right thing, but he didn't like secret groups. When he broke away from you, he wasn't trying to get his tanker in order; he was trying to get away from you so he could get the actual authorities involved. All this talk of you guys trying in vain to convince governments of Amos's terror plot, nobody can find any record of any such warnings."

"Of course they can't find them," Lydia said. "They were never actually warned. I was just led to believe they had been. The last two years of my life I've been trying to make up for the loss of our baby. In the end, all I did was ruin things even more. If the people want blood, they can have mine."

The door opened again, and the jailer entered with one other man. "Lydia," he said hesitantly. "You must know some people in some pretty high places, because I've received orders to release you."

Lydia looked at Flint questioningly.

"Don't look at me," he replied. "I had nothing to do with it."

The jailer unlocked her cuffs, and she was escorted out of the building. A car was waiting for her. She along with Flint and Monk got inside, and the driver took them without a word to the pier. Once there he pointed to an eighty-foot yacht tied to one of the docks.

They got out of the car and the driver sped away. A little scared and unsure of what was going on, Lydia walked close to Flint. Flint found her hand with his, their fingers fitting together like an old pair of gloves. The firm grip she had nearly forgotten caused a resurgence of tears to well up behind her eyes. She tried to choke them back. Her heart was a jumble of emotions from elation to unworthiness, anger to humility. All were rushing through her mind, and all at the same time. As she struggled with them, she only succeeded in causing herself to get light-headed.

She closed her eyes, and took a couple of deep breaths, allowing Flint to guide her along. It was a bad idea. At first she was aware of a little nausea, then her light-headedness progressed into unconsciousness. When she opened her eyes again, the emotional distress had subsided somewhat. She was aware that the ground below her was not entirely stable. Blinking a couple of times, she pieced together her last memories. Then, surveying her surroundings, she realized that she was on a boat.

She overheard Flint's voice in the background. "She has been though a lot lately. Look, she's coming to."

Flint was the first person she saw as she sat up. The gentle swaying of the soft sofa on the large multi-hull sailboat felt relaxing, and she almost wanted to snuggle into it, allowing it to rock her to back sleep. But she pulled herself into reality. The fact that she was on a sailboat was disconcerting enough.

She turned her head slightly to find the man that Flint had been talking to. "Labeeb?" She noticed with surprise.

"Lydia, it is nice to see that you are all right. I need to introduce you to someone," he said. He then took Lydia by the hand and helped her to her feet. "This way."

The main room on the yacht was luxuriously furnished, and toward the front of the boat, there was a pilothouse, larger than that of most boats. Walking inside, Lydia was surprised to go from stained mahogany and leather to a sterile-looking room covered with monitors and computers. Several of the screens had various news stations streaming the riots and other effects in response to the oil shock around the world. Others were displaying financial information and press releases from governing bodies. In the center of the room, just to the side of the ship's helm, was a stocky but fit man, whom Lydia guessed to be in his late fifties. He was dressed in casual clothing, but with a cheesy skipper's hat, which was clearly meant more for fun than for any practical reason.

"I have a confession, Lydia," Labeeb began. "When I was recruited to your team, I was doing so under the direction of this man. Like you, I had been interested in a plant that had the ability to create electricity. He suggested that you might be my best chance of finding such a thing. He helped me get into your organization, on the condition that I sent him detailed updates on our activities. In a sense I was spying on you for him. If it wasn't for his warning, I might have been caught by the police as you were. But after I had made it to the third floor of the building we were attacking, I received a message from him.

"The message concerned two vials of that bacteria we carried on our jet. One of them was the oil-solidifying compound, while the other was the anti-coagulating formula. Well, I smuggled both vials off, and gave them to him. He ran some tests of his own on them, only to realize that both vials were identical. There never was an anti-coagulation bacterial agent.

"Understand, I wasn't trying to betray you in any way. I had complete trust in this man, and I owed him the favor for getting me into your organization. While I was with you, he and I only communicated via e-mail and text messages. So during the raid, when he actually called me for the first time, I fortified myself and took his call. He informed me that the police had stormed the building, and that I would soon be arrested or killed if found."

Labeeb continued to fill Lydia in on the details for a minute, then the man who had engaged Labeeb stepped forward to introduce himself. "My name is Fran, though it is of little importance. Had your friend Labeeb not failed to inform me until it was too late, I might have been able to send a warning that could have limited the impact of the terror act. After all, I know many powerful people in governments around the world."

Looking down, ashamed of his failure, Labeeb continued. "That is in the past, and you all need to look toward the future now. Within a couple of days, the world will be irreversibly crippled. The stock markets are crashing as we speak, and all international travel has basically been stopped to conserve the remaining fuel. Martial law has been declared on a global level. Millions of people could very well die."

"That doesn't sound like the kind of future I want to look forward to," Flint said solemnly.

Lydia added, "I can't believe I helped those monsters."

"We are not personally accustomed to shocks of this nature," Fran continued. "And though we are not individually accustomed to it, our race as human beings are. Our earlier ancestors had to deal with severe blows such as Noah's great flood, the Black Plague, or the Great Depression and the Holocaust, just to name a few of the more recent disasters."

"Noah's flood?" Flint asked. "You mean that isn't just a fabled Bible story?"

"Let's not get into that right now." Fran seemed to both confirm and divert at the same time. "The main point is that we as a people adapt, and overcome these major shocks. We will get through this in one of two ways."

Lydia began to say something but Fran put up a hand to silence her.

"The first and most likely option that will occur if you do nothing is the governments of the world will start to collapse. Then that organization which used you and Amos, the one you know as GRIP, will try to rise in power and exert its control over the major populations. We don't know a whole lot about them yet, but without intervention, nothing will stop them."

"What about these friends of yours in high places?" Flint asked.

"They have already informed me that they are using all their resources to keep order in their respective areas. Since we can't turn the oil back on in time to save the world, the world must find a new source of hope. This will come in either of two ways. One is to find someone to blame, which is GRIP. But if we can't bring them to justice, then people will find other scapegoats. The other source of hope must also come from a new form of energy, an energy that will inspire people to rebuild and move forward again."

Slowly forming the words, Lydia ventured, "You're talking about—"

Fran finished her thought, "*Sliehacal-dohulub*, as the Arabs used to call it. Or, in English, lightning moss."

"I'm confused." Flint raised a hand. "What does a little pond scum have to do with saving the world, and why are we suddenly the only ones who can help?"

An accusing scowl shot from Lydia's face, as if he should already know the answer, but even as Fran elaborated, her face reddened with shame. "I wouldn't expect you to know about it, Flint. Lydia and Labeeb have been tracking down this plant for some time, and she is the one who knows most about it. If there is any hope of locating a remnant of it someplace, she along with Labeeb are our best hope of finding it. Since it is a plant, it would require very little effort and expense to propagate and distribute across the world. In a matter of years, it could revolutionize energy as we know it. Until then, if we are able to manage the political side of everything, using the governments of the world to spread the knowledge of it, we could inspire enough hope and help to resist falling into complete anarchy. It would save modern government, effectively killing two birds with one stone. This terror group that you have already faced, and helped—they want anarchy. Without a system of government in place, they will take control.

"I don't know how long you have, but I wouldn't waste time here. Remember, they started this, and they are ready to act. Though Egypt has better access to oil via smaller pumps that weren't affected, the price of oil and the strict internal controls that are to follow will still make it difficult to travel about freely. You must go now, before it is too late."

Lydia opened her mouth to argue, but stopped short as Monk cut her off and quoted, "*Arjuna uvaca mad-anugrahaya paramam guhyam adhyatma-samjnitam yat tvayoktam vacas tena moho 'yam vigato mama.'*"

"You quote the Bhagavad Gita," Fran noticed with interest. Then, translating, he repeated, "'Arjuna said: By my hearing the instructions you have

kindly given me about these most confidential spir-
itual subjects, my illusion has now been dispelled.'"
Then with a short laugh he asked, "How did you
know I was familiar with that scripture?"

Monk simply pointed to the other room.

"Ah, you saw my book." Fran smiled. "It's nice
to meet somebody with an appreciation for ancient
writings. But with that I must bid you good-bye. I
have much to do, and so do you."

The mysterious Fran escorted Lydia, Flint, Monk,
and Labeeb off the boat. Then, without another
word, he untied the lines that held it to the dock
and walked back aboard. As the four stood on the
pier, they watched his sails unfurl as a gentle breeze
coaxed him away from the docks.

"What do you make of all this?" Flint asked, looking at Lydia, then at Labeeb.

"Well, whether we can or can't do anything to
help, I think I need to try," Lydia said. "After all, I'm
in part responsible for it."

"Well, I'll do what I can to help, then, though I
doubt it will do any good. I still don't understand it,"
Flint said, shrugging his shoulders. "It sounds like
an adventure, but just surviving the changing world
will be an adventure of sorts, also. At least this way
we'll get some time together to catch up. It sounds
like you've had a very interesting life these last couple years. I can't wait to get to know you again."

"Flint," Lydia confessed, "there hasn't been one
day that I haven't thought about you. I hope you can
forgive me."

Labeeb chimed in, "Can you two save the dra-
ma for when you're alone? I may have been raised a
Frenchman, but I'd much rather focus on the task
at hand."

Flint turned to Monk. "Well, Monk, that Fran guy

thinks we can do some good, what do you think?"

Monk replied, "Proverbs 21:8. 'The way of man is froward and strange: but as for the pure, his work is right.'"

Labeeb raised an eyebrow. "And Monk is calling Fran strange?"

Suddenly Flint jerked his head up and exclaimed, "Dusty!"

Lydia squinted at him, and cautiously, with a hint of accusation and recollection, mentioned, "Yes, about her . . ."

Chapter 48

After leaving his four guests, Fran set a southward course. He wanted to get away from shore just enough to avoid any uprisings that might occur. After all, a sailboat in a world without fuel would be highly valued among a number of ambitious men.

Once he felt that he was a safe distance from shore, he lowered his sails and took to his computer. Within a few minutes he had an uplink with a private satellite. After a minute of typing, he proofed his message before clicking send:

Lydia and Labeeb have been sent in search of the plant. They are accompanied by two others, who referred to themselves as Flint and Monk. It is my suspicion that they were among those who were instrumental in stopping Shen Mao earlier this week. I feel confident in this new team's ability to cope with the task ahead of them.

There is no telling if they will find it, or if it will be soon enough to provide the hope and stability which will be needed. It is my recommendation that in the meantime we need to find GRIP and slow them down; if necessary, by any means at our disposal, including those that might expose everything. But I am worried that if GRIP has enough of the ancient Martian technology already, then it will be of little consequence. I will stay and monitor Labeeb and Lydia's progress from here. Please advise me on any plan of action that the council deems prudent.

Fran went to work maneuvering the sailboat. When he came back to his computer, new messages were waiting for him. The first was a short reply from someone associated with the council. The second was from the Chinese woman who had been stationed in the Philippines. She mentioned that she'd had to return to Shen Mao's compound, and her message gave Fran some cause for concern. In it, she mentioned a suspicion that somebody had recovered the broken pieces of the old propulsion device that had been used in Shen Mao's machine.

Epilog

Time and events were racing by faster than Lydia could get a grasp on. As the sailboat drifted away, she found herself in the only company she'd ever wanted, but now it was completely awkward. Nothing could have prepared her for this. Labeeb was the same, though even he hadn't been who she thought he was. Monk was never easy to be around. Flint was the worst of them all, even if he was the best of them all. She could see the longing in his eyes for her, but that didn't make anything at all easier. Besides, Lydia had seen with her own eyes the way that Flint had doted on this Dusty girl.

Who was she? Will she take Flint from me? Heaven knows I deserve as much. In idle times, Lydia had imagined a reunion with Flint in some miraculous way. This wasn't according to one of her daydreams, but it just as easily could have been. But now that they were back together, she knew it wouldn't be an easy road.

Lydia studied Flint for a moment. He looked refreshed and ready to tackle GRIP. He obviously got a better sleep at the police station than she had. One thing was similar though, she was certain that she had a similar and determined resolve that mirrored his. He really did look good. So why was it that when she looked at him, she could only see him as she had when they met at Amos' headquarters? Bound and gagged, he'd been a helpless tool to get to her, and she'd saved him. Her knight in shining armor had unwittingly played a part in manipulating her to plunge the world into disorder.

On the other hand, they were together again. Scars heal with time, and they wouldn't be separated so easily again. At least they wouldn't if she had anything to do with it. *But what to do about this Dusty?* She would worry about that if they managed to find the wench. For now, Lydia smiled, her hopes rekindled. *Easy isn't his way, and neither is it mine. We might both have our flaws, but this might still work out.* She looked at him again. The more she gazed at his determined face, the more confidence she found.

Don't miss
The Nephilim Conspiracy
Book 3 in the Nephilim series

Words from the Author

WOW! You made it through my second book! Not that I'm surprised at all. But it still makes me feel good that you have gotten to this point. So what inspiring words can I impart for you here?

Okay, I'm not the inspirational type. Instead I'll just continue telling you about my writing journey. When I first started writing this series, and it turned into a three part series, this second book was probably my hardest to write.

You've all heard about the second book syndrome, and I'm sure it goes by many other names too, I was really afraid that I would write a second book that didn't measure up. Luckily my wife told me that this was her favorite. Whether that means anything or not, I'm not sure. She obviously likes books where a female is the main character. But when it comes down to it, I lost and gained interest in this book more times than in the first and last book of the series combined. I don't even know why.

Maybe I'm wrong, but it's hard for the author to see his books in other people's perspectives. I invented the story, and I read it several times trying to improve it, never fully satisfied. Some say that the definition of a true writer is one that is never fully satisfied with his or her work. Every good author is always trying to improve their skill.

So while I hope that this book entertains, I'm also following after the true spirit of the professional writer. All I can really do is keep writing, keep improving. All, if any fans I get will be from word of mouth. Since I'm only a part time writer with a very limited budget, you the reader are really my only source of marketing. If you like my books, share them with your friends, and they continue the chain. Then and only then will I know that I'm on the right track.

If you are also a budding author, all I can say is keep at it. Only time will tell if we find favor in readers' eyes.

If you've been following my blog or visiting my website, you may know that I'm not really in this for the money. Sure the motivation to start writing started with a desire to make a good side income. But the more I write, the more I enjoy writing. If I'm lucky enough to just break even, then I'll be fine with that.

My goals since I started writing have obviously evolved over the last couple years. First I wanted money. Now I want to become a great storyteller. Along the way, I've started promoting other local authors with ties to Utah, my home state. With any luck, my next goal/

dream, even if I don't make money on these books, is that I'd like to become an independent film maker sometime around 2025. If I can manage a story per year, I think I should have a good ten books that could possibly be turned into screenplays.

And why not? Life is meant to be enjoyed. If you have a dream, then by all means go for it. I have a dream, and if I can make some progress towards fulfilling it, then great. I hope you can find a dream that motivates you, and makes you giddy with excitement.

Enjoy my third book, then don't forget me. Try looking me up every year or so for a new novel. Hey, maybe in ten or fifteen years, you'll even see one of my books up on the silver screen.

-B.C. Crow

Blue House Publishing
Is a Utah company

We are very proud of our heritage and where we live.

But B.C. Crow is not the only author we know who calls Utah home.

We've been collecting names of other authors who've also called Utah home. The list is long and growing.

Come visit our website at:
www.BlueHPublishing.com

Even though we don't represent them all, we want to help you discover them.

You'll find many authors you recognize, and you'll find several you've never heard of before.

Come check us out today!

Blue House Publishing would like to share a piece of Utah with you. Check out all the Utah author's we've been finding at: www.BlueHPublishing.com

Why does Utah produce so many great authors?
Perhaps you can decide for yourself, but let us offer a few ideas:

Utah is more than just another state in the Union. We have a highly diverse set of cultures. Since somewhere around 40% of the population are members of the Church of Jesus Christ of Latter-Day Saints (Mormons), and since many of them choose to go around the world, serving as unpaid missionaries, we have lots of world culture and languages at our fingertips. Combine that with a very industrious population, of course we're going to have some good writers. Not saying that all of Utah is Mormon, because while many of the popular writers from Utah are, remember, close to 60% of our population share different beliefs, with many of them having extraordinary talents and experiences to bring to the publishing table.

Utah has something for everyone. You can drive just one or two hours, and in most cases you'll find a whole new landscape. Whether you want to visit the slick-rock of Utah's treasured southern end, see amazing arches, visit rolling sand dunes, go hiking in the Uinta mountains, hopping from one fishing pond to the next with only a compass or GPS to keep from getting lost, or you can try some really daunting hikes, rock climbing, floating the many rivers, boating, biking, caving, skiing, racing, sailing, hang-gliding, you name it!

With all that Utah has to offer, it should come as no surprise that Hollywood calls Utah it's second home. We are a people who love adventure, who enjoy living active lifestyles, and who relish in reading and sharing stories.

No wonder we have so many great authors here. Check them out at www.BlueHPublishing.com.